DEATH BY SOCIETY

DEATH BY SOCIETY

SIERRA ELMORE

ELM STREET PUBLISHING

Death by Society by Sierra Elmore

Published by Elm Street Publishing/Sierra Elmore

sierraelmore.com

Paperback ISBN: 979-8-218-01947-1

Hardcover ISBN: 978-1-0880-4343-1

To me, for making it through.

CONTENT WARNINGS

Suicidal ideation, depression, self-harm, bullying, domestic violence, anxiety (social and generalized), racism, and rape trauma syndrome (no rape depiction) are discussed and depicted throughout this manuscript. Please take care of yourself while reading.

AUTHOR'S NOTE

The creation of *Death by Society* began with a "simple" question: what would have happened if I attempted suicide?

As an eighth-grade student, despondent and hopeless after a series of personal tragedies, I wanted to explore death through fiction. This began with a short story about a teenage girl saved after a suicide attempt and blossomed into where *Death by Society* is today.

This novel was written for teenagers who were in that hopeless place. Suicidal ideations and depression can create black holes out of vibrant girls—take it from me, and from the main character in this novel, Carter Harper. What I've found, though, is that social support systems, proper medical care, a sense of purpose, and removal from toxic environments really do make a world of difference.

My mental health isn't perfect, and never will be. I

still face days of hopelessness, wondering why I bother being alive. But those factors have made my life so, so much better than when I was that bullied middle schooler, wondering if/when I'd die.

At the core, that's what *Death by Society* is about. There's always hope, even if that hope is buried so deep and stubborn you think it no longer exists. It does exist. My hope is, that as you read about Carter, Abby, and the POPS, that you find that hope for yourself. If you can't, that's okay, too: the fact that you're still here, breathing and trying, means far more than you may realize.

CHAPTER 1
CARTER HARPER

MOST STUDENTS AREN'T afraid of winning the prestigious Future Leaders Essay Contest. But most eleventh-graders don't have an enemy like Abby Wallace.

Mr. Atkinson calls Abby and me to the front of the cramped classroom. Abby's irritatingly popular best friends, clustered in the second row, whisper and giggle with each another.

The three girls are likely laughing at me. And if they're laughing at me, that means Abby has a plan up her sleeve. I pray to whatever religious deities exist that Abby doesn't trip me—again.

Abby doesn't bully me around authority figures, though. She waits for opportunities in unsupervised locker rooms, the chronically understaffed cafeteria, and bustling hallways between classes. Places that combine easy viewing for her audience of scared students with a lack of adult supervision.

Abby may be cruel and a little vain, but you can't say the girl isn't smart.

My limbs shake as I head to the front. Abby's don't. Her long legs are covered by leggings and a skirt so short that my mother would slap me for daring to leave the house in it. Her gait is fluid and confident as she throws me a smirk, wordlessly saying, "I am better than you. I am the one who people chose to care about. Not you. It'll never be you."

I stand next to Atkinson, hoping his supervision provides me with a minuscule amount of protection.

"These ladies analyzed *Hamlet* and *The Scarlet Letter* in innovative ways," our AP English teacher says. "However, the subcommittee and I could select only one student to represent Harlow High School for the South-central Pennsylvania region's Future Leaders Essay Contest entry. As you may know, the state's ultimate winner will attend this summer's Future Leaders Conference in Washington, D.C. and receive a college scholarship."

He fails to mention the prestige that comes with writing "Future Leaders Essay Contest Finalist" on college applications. If I live long enough to apply to colleges, MIT, Drexel, Howard, the University of Rochester, Temple, and Millersville (safety) will be interested to see it listed on my apps next year.

Abby beams like she's already won. If she did, at least I'd know that she won from merit rather than popularity: from analytical essays I've read thanks to peer edits, she's a brilliant writer. I would never admit it to her, but as the (former) vice president of the Creative Writing Club, she may be better at the craft of language than I am.

Abby Wallace is one of four reasons I stay far away from extracurricular activities. I can't run the risk of running into the POPS (aka Petty, Oppressive, and Popular Shitbags) who ruin lives for sport. Queen Bee Kelsey Maxwell oversees the daily announcements and stars in every school play we have. Mei Xiang, the National Honor Society president, enjoys journalism, parties, and circulating petty gossip in equal measure. Slater García-Svensson, the only one who isn't a complete asshole, is the president of the Gender & Sexuality Alliance and a national award-winning photographer.

If they weren't so cruel, I'd admire their ambition. It reminds me of my own, before depression hit and I stopped most of my extracurriculars out of mental preservation. Now, my only activity is the mobile app I built by myself. My work for BRAIN/ZAPP is done in the privacy of my own home rather than this court of assholes.

"Harlow High's representative for this year's FLEC conference is...." Atkinson bangs out a quick drumroll on his desk. His choppy brown hair shakes as he does. "Carter Harper!"

I nearly stumble back, super shook as a swell of pride rolls through my chest. I wrote this essay during a major depressive episode and still beat the girl who would bully me into a grave if she could get away with it.

For one second, I'm filled with such joy that I forget the consequences of winning.

"Congratulations, C," Abby says. Her voice is syrupy, like honey designed to trap you. "I'm not surprised you won. After all, it's not like you have anything to do other than sit alone and write papers."

With a snap of her tongue, my high comes crashing down.

"Abby," Atkinson warns. But it's not enough to stop the class from snickering.

At least not having friends keeps me ranked third in the class, Miss Four. The only place I can bite back at Abby is inside my own head, a world more colorful than my bleak reality. Abby and I are constantly competing for the third spot in the class, and sometimes switch between third and fourth. However, neither of us is good enough to beat Anjali Mehta, the most determined and intelligent girl I know, and Aimee Hollenbeck, who's gunning for Harvard because she's a legacy but wants to get in on her own merits. My depression holds me back from the coveted top spots, and I'm sure

4

that Abby's favored hobby of mocking people distracts her from homework. Third place should be good enough, and yet I'm consistently underestimated because I'm not loud like Abby, in every club like Mei, beautiful and dramatic like Kelsey, or artistic like Slater.

Proving people wrong is always fun, until Abby mocks me for it.

"Carter, could you tell the class about your essay?" Atkinson beckons me back into the present. Abby's gunmetal blue eyes bore into me, as if she dares me to one-up her *Hamlet* essay. Even though, whoops, I already have.

"Social media," I stutter.

Atkinson sighs. He's used to my reluctance to talk due to social anxiety. "Carter connected Hester Prynne's scarlet 'A' to modern-day social media callout culture and cyberbullying. One of her main points was the inherent hypocrisy of claiming morality while crucifying others."

"Oh, please," Kelsey mutters from her seat. "The scarlet A is clearly an allegory to Hester Prynne's sluttiness."

"It's more of Hester being an *immoral* slut. Either way, that book has nothing to do with social media. Looks like somebody's wrong." Mei smirks at me.

My skin prickles at their belittling interpretation. I return to my place in the front row, though nobody told me to.

If I were braver, I would punch Abby in the throat. If I were wittier, I could craft the perfect comeback and spit it in Mei's face. If I were a different girl, they'd know not to cross me.

But I'm not a different girl. I'm me. I have to live with my inability to defend myself every day.

Abby sidles up next to me after gym class, confirming that I did not get away with "stealing her prize."

I scan the dozen-ish girls still lingering in the locker room, wondering if anybody will intervene this time. (Plot twist: they will not.) Abby's terrifying, and each social group at Harlow High School has a good reason to not challenge to the POPS.

Like the rest of the world, my school is a broken system that rewards popularity, shuns mediocrity, and pays too much attention to disruptive behavior. Harlow High is divided into five primary social groups, with various cliques interspersed within every group. We aren't like the irrational, traditionally constructed cliques seen in the movies. Preps mix with punks, theater and band kids talk to the POPS (my secret nickname for the girls who rule the school), and athletes can be best friends with National Honor Society kids.

My categorization of the Harlow High School social

groups is as follows, and is validated by years of careful field observation:

OVERACHIEVERS (MY GROUP)

- *Who they are:* College-bound nerds who love academics, extracurricular activities, and winning awards. Some are in it for the fun of it, some due to parental pressure, and some of us ENJOY being nerds.
- *Example:* Anjali Mehta, the top-ranked girl in the class.
- *Why they don't mess with the POPS:* Half are POPS or POPS-adjacent. The other half can't fight.

THE POPS & THE POPS WANNABES

- *Who they are:* A subgroup of the Overachievers. Keep their power by squashing the egos of competitors, thus ensuring that the general population fears their wrath.
- *Example:* Abby Wallace. Need I say more?
- *Why they don't mess with the POPS:* Cannibalism is frowned upon in most societies.

THE UNFATHOMABLY TALENTED

- *Who they are:* Artists, athletes, drama students, band geeks, et al. Students with a quantifiable talent.
- *Example:* Melly Cole, a pianist rumored to be courted by the top music schools on the East Coast.
- *Why they don't mess with the POPS:* Because getting your fingers broken from Abby slamming your locker door shut on your hand is pretty bad for your violin career.

THE FLOATERS

- *Who they are:* Fairly chill students who aren't at the bottom or top.
- *Example:* I couldn't name one if I tried.
- *Why they don't mess with the POPS:* Goes against their rule of doing the least amount of work possible.

ACTIVELY DISINTERESTED

- *Who they are:* Annoying "students" who reject Harlow High's culture of excellence.

Hobbies: interrupting classes and landing themselves in detention/in-school suspension.

- *Example:* Tommy Randolph, infamous for placing his ex-girlfriend's thong around the school's Hawk statue last year.
- *Why they don't mess with the POPS:* They respect the POPS's penchant for disrupting authority.

"Congrats on winning," Abby says. She takes her hair out of her ponytail and tosses her mane around. Ink black waves cloak her shoulders like a villain's cape. "You've always been Atkinson's favorite nerd."

Say something in your own defense, dammit, I tell myself. Yeah, right. I can barely form a string of sentences in my head without my heartbeat quickening and my lips gluing themselves shut.

"Atkinson must be so proud to have a suck-up like you in his class!" Abby follows me as I push past the other girls. I shield my combination with my shaking hand. Abby leans against the metal locker next to mine. Bet it's as cold as her heart. "I mean, I would've loved to spend more time on my essay, but I have things to do, you know? Friends to hang out with, a father to talk to. You wouldn't relate."

My muscles clench when she mentions our fathers.

When will the ghost of Darryl Harper stop following me around? Thanks to an ill-conceived genealogy project and Mei's loud mouth, my deadbeat father is a known entity at this school.

Somebody do something, I silently beg. The Overachievers and Unfathomably Talented deliberately ignore the escalating conflict, POPS snicker along with Abby, and the Floaters and Actively Disinterested have already cleared out.

I'm all alone here. What else is new? My hand grabs the ends of my blue and black weave so I can find the will to *calm down, calm down.*

"Leave me alone," I whimper.

The locker room falls silent, and then—

For my insubordination, I earn a hard shove into my locker. An acute ache spreads through my forearm and wrist, soon replaced by a dull throb. Blood pulses through my veins as curse words run through my mind. Despite the persistent rumor that Black people don't bruise, that's gonna leave a mark.

The assault hurts less than her snide comment about my father: the first person to ever leave me.

A roar of laughter engulfs me. I slide onto the floor and tuck my head onto my thighs, desperate to escape the noise. I look pathetic. I'm used to it.

Today will be over soon enough.

Then Abby will begin the next round of abuse.

Then I will talk myself out of my suicidal thoughts.

Pretend I'm fine.

Then those lies will shatter the next time Abby harasses me.

She's right, and that's why the words she implanted into my brain hurt so bad. I don't have a father. I don't have a social life outside of my mom. I spend most of my time buried in textbooks. I can take slight comfort in knowing Abby can't possibly know about the monsters running through my mind, chanting *you aren't worth the trouble you're not worth keeping around just* die already!

"Harper? Why are you lying around?"

I jerk my head up. My eyes bore into the bored face of Mrs. Huxley, the gym teacher. Crap. Sometime during my pity party, the locker room cleared out for the next round of torture/gym class.

"I fell," I croak out. It's a refrain she's swallowed too many times.

"You should get that checked out," Huxley says. She extends her hand. I shake my head, choosing to lift myself up. She didn't help when Abby shoved me against the locker, though her windowed office offers a pretty frickin' clear view of the girls' locker room. She didn't help when I told her about Abby "accidentally" hitting me with a basketball during free throw practice last semester. What can she do now?

What can anybody do to stop the reign of the POPS?

CHAPTER 2
ABBY WALLACE

"CARTER ONLY WON because that stuck-up fatass doesn't have a life." Kelsey Maxwell, my best friend with benefits, stabs her Caesar salad before taking an aggressive bite.

Melly Cole's jaw unhinges as she passes by our table. Her face looks like it was rubbed raw and is cracking open, so I huff at her, "Salicylic acid, Melly! It's available at any drug store!"

Melly scratches a pimple and stumbles away. The cheap shot at her looks was worth it if it gets the mouth-breather to leave us alone for the rest of the day. Hell, if she takes my advice, she'll be grateful I called her out.

"Here we go again," Slater García-Svensson mutters. Though my second-closest friend complains, she won't bother stopping Kelsey's and my conversation. Anybody who does faces instant social evisceration. Slater, with her 3.5 GPA and photographic talent, is smart enough to know that being in our vicious little friend group is a hell of a lot better than being excluded.

Mei Xiang, 3.75 GPA journalist and gossiper extraordinaire, blinks her eyes faux-innocently. "She didn't mean *your* fat ass, Slater. That one's fine." Slater's booty is the source of jokes amongst us, complaints during clothing shopping, and male objectification. I want to fight every guy who's smacked it, whistled at it, and told her what they'd like to do with it over the years. Joke's on them: Slater's as gay as they come.

Slater throws a potato chip at Mei's cardigan in retaliation. We're both dressed in cashmere thanks to the cold snap that's iced out Pennsylvania, our home and kingdom.

I smile at my friends until a familiar figure enters my line of sight. Carter Harper, stealer of awards, certified nerd, and my favorite person at this school to mess around with. Carter walks past our table, shoulders hunched, ready to run from us. Or hobble, since her annual fitness test results are always a disaster.

"She pisses me off." I shove my container of salad away. Seeing Carter sends me into a quiet rage that's only tempered by knocking her down a peg. Why can't she be annoying some other girl at some other school?

Mei stares after Carter. She shifts her bangs to the side. "Seriously. Who pairs a greyscale flannel with a brown cami?"

"Right, but not my point," I say.

"I like her flannel," Slater offers.

"You would," Kelsey mutters.

"Oh, a lesbian joke. How original." Slater rolls her eyes, a gorgeous dark green with deep brown bleeding out from their centers. I stare at them a tiny bit before moving on.

Slater's not the only queer one in our friend group, of course. How lonely would that be? Kelsey's our established queen bee, a white girl who likes boys and girls in equal-ish measure. I'm the second-in-command who doesn't give a shit about who I date, as long as they're hot. Slater is the Cuban-Swedish daughter of a model and would sooner sell her prized camera than kiss a boy. Mei is Chinese and the group's token heterosexual (not that she would know, since Kelsey isn't out of the closet).

The four of us met in a staggered timeline, but it feels like we've known each other forever. Kelsey and Mei grew up with one another, though they didn't start being friends until sixth grade. Over that summer, the two former outcasts made a pact to never be ugly losers again. Kelsey's mother's image consultant gave them makeovers, and the rest is history.

Meanwhile, my family moved from the suburbs of New York City to the area where my mother grew up (and across the street from Carter, though I try to forget about that fact). I was instantly drawn to Kelsey, whose charisma and beauty led to her being my first girl crush.

Slater's mother moved to Harrisburg the same year as I did, and we became fast friends.

These girls are the only real security I have in my life. I would die for them—in the metaphorical sense.

"You guys get off topic so easily," I grumble.

"It's not like Carter's interesting," Kelsey says. "I'd rather talk about the UTI I had last month."

Kelsey almost has a point. But Carter stole my award this morning in front of the whole class. Does she have to be such a good writer when writing is my only recognized talent? Does she have to pretend to be humble, even though she knows good and damn well how smug she was about winning? And can somebody do us all a favor and teach her how to dress?

Slater says I'm jealous of Carter. She's wrong, just like she's wrong about not plucking her *Where the Wild Things Are* eyebrows. Annoyance doesn't automatically translate to jealousy.

"However," Kelsey says in her usual authoritative voice. Mei puts her phone down and Slater leans in a bit closer. "Since you refuse to shut up about Carter, let's figure out how to get rid of her." As if I haven't tried. Hello, I'm the one who shoved Carter against a locker today!

"You mean, temporarily get rid of her." I wonder if Mei's grown a heart until she says, "I can't risk getting grounded and missing Troy's party next weekend."

"God forbid ya miss the party of the boy you've

turned down a dozen times since middle school," Slater mutters. Is she jealous? No way she's jealous.

"He's a fuckboy!" Mei argues.

"So was your last boyfriend!" Slater says.

I sigh a bit in relief. Okay, Slater's annoyed, not jealous. Not that I care or anything.

Only...Kelsey was my first girl crush, but she wasn't exactly my second. My second that I've never quite gotten over.

"Enough," says Kelsey. "Slater, go grab a candy bar or something. My treat." She hands Slater a one-dollar bill despite Slater having more money than all three of us combined.

"Whatever, assholes." Slater rushes away from our lunch table—strategically located in the center of the cafeteria and under the best lighting—and over to her friends in the Gender & Sexuality Alliance.

I scoff. Why bother having other friends, when we're all you could really ask for? Kelsey, Mei, Slater, and I clawed our way to the top by ensuring the rest of the student body fears us as much as they want to be us. As long we have each other and the rest of the school falls in line behind us, people who hate me can suck my metaphorical dick.

"And duh, Mei," Kelsey barks. She puts her feathery blond hair into a ponytail. "We aren't piling up dead bodies in my backyard."

"Okay, just making sure," Mei mumbles, biting her

lip. She goes back to reading *The Wall Street Journal* on her phone. Her goal is to be a financial reporter who exposes corruption rather than normalizing it.

"Now. Let's teach her a lesson." Kelsey smirks, and it's hot. Ugh, no, not the point right now. There will be enough time to think about Kelsey in uncouth ways later.

As we swap ideas of what revenge to take, and how far to go, my excitement mounts. Kelsey was right. Carter needs to learn not to steal things from me.

I offer a charming smile right before Slater returns without a candy bar. Power is sweeter than sugar, anyway.

CHAPTER 3
CARTER

"PROZAC?" my mother asks as we have brunch.

Ugh. I'd almost forgotten to take my daily dose of Fake Happy. "On it." I walk to the drawer where we keep our meds and pluck out the latest prescription in a medication history littered with empty promises of balancing me out.

I sip some orange juice, swallow my pill, grimace, drink more orange juice. It's supposed to make my brain feel something other than deep, constant sadness, but I've found zero relief.

Mom stares me down as I take the pill. She learned the hard way that I've lied about taking my meds after I stopped Lexapro cold turkey. It wasn't working well enough, so why bother? My "experiment" led to awful electric-like zaps coursing through my brain and body, a pronounced lack of concentration, and a hint of madness detected by anyone who bothered to pay attention. Prozac is a slight improvement, but this script isn't good enough to *work* work, y'know? Psychiatrist #3 says I haven't found the right medication mix. I'm young, and my body may not react to the antidepressants as it should.

Fuck off, Psychiatrist #3.

"Now, was that so hard?" Mom asks.

"No," I lie. I sprint off to the living room to avoid further questioning about my failing mental health. I open my self-optimized MacBook Pro, settling in for my Saturday ritual of working on BRAIN/ZAPP.

The BRAIN/ZAPP application for iPhone, iPod, and, most recently, Android, is simultaneously my greatest invention and secret. A secret, because I can't reveal my identity and risk being ridiculed by the POPS and their minions for yet another hobby deviating from their established norm. They've already significantly dampened my interests in gaming (when I was playing Nintendo at lunch, Mei told me it was the most useless hobby ever), reading (Abby placed a slice of bologna between the pages of my copy of *I Kissed Shara Wheeler*), and my fleeting interest in birdwatching (which, yes, is dorky, but did Kelsey have to write DORK on my birding journal?).

In ninth grade, I wanted to implement my knowledge in HTML5/CSS3, C#, and JavaScript. I've been into computers since I was four and played chess with Mom, and later against the computer on her bubble iMac.

BRAIN/ZAPP was conceived when iPhone apps were experiencing unprecedented growth. I taught myself Swift, then used my knowledge of psychology and neuroscience to craft an app to distract users from their problems through brainteasers designed to release dopamine. The app quickly became a constant in my life. From solving user problems to creating new marketing techniques to developing new features, the many tasks to be completed keep my hyperactive brain engaged.

Despite putting it on the App Store, I never expected the BRAIN/ZAPP to go anywhere. Let alone raking in healthy earnings thanks to ZAP/PACKS, my in-app purchases designed to expand on the already-expansive free library of content. I've even won an App Store award, and I keep getting invited for interviews about being the founder of a popular application.

Mom pauses before sitting next to me on the couch. Her hesitation means nothing to me until she says, "Where the hell did that come from?" She points at the bruise Abby gave me.

My fingers still immediately. Crap!

"Oh, this?" I glance at the dark brown bruise with feigned surprise.

"No, the tail growing out of your ass," Mom says. "Yes, your bruise. Is Abby bullying you again?"

How do moms know everything? What special detection powers was she given at my birth?

I vigorously shake my head no. "I fell in gym class. And for the record, a tail could come out of my butt. That's called a furry."

"I know what they are. I wish I didn't, but I do. You get injured in gym class, what, once a month?" Mom asks.

"I mean, sure, but I'll...live." I lower my eyes to the couch. Mom knows that I've lied about being okay before. What if she knows I'm lying again?

"Hmm. Okay," Mom says with a sigh. She opens her laptop, optimized by yours truly for the heavy amount of graphics rendering she has to complete.

"What're you working on?" I lay my head on her shoulder to peek. A one-bedroom apartment floor plan comes into view. The proposed 3D model appears small, yet has a well-organized and functional layout.

"You're just trying to distract me." Momdar strikes again, this time punctuated with a small smile. "My firm was commissioned to design a new apartment complex near the downtown bus transfer center. A bunch of studios and one-bedrooms. We're hoping for an affordable and luxury experience for state workers who're on the come up."

"You don't have to give me the sales pitch," I tease. "Isn't this your second complex in three years?"

Mom's one of the top architects at her firm. She's planning to run the place once the current CEO dies, retires, or gets caught by the IRS for his unreported income.

Mom has plenty to be proud of, starting with the Ivy League education she juggled along with having a kid at seventeen with the asshole who left town when he found out he'd gotten his girlfriend pregnant. I'm a smiling five-year-old in her University of Pennsylvania graduation picture, perched on her hip with braids cascading down my back.

She has every reason to be happy, and she's a queen who deserves it all. If only I weren't such a failure. After my ex-boyfriend, Hudson Lewis, dumped me last year, she's the only person left on this earth who cares about me. How's that for unlovable?

"Yeah, and apparently I'm the only one who can manage these projects because I 'understand urban spaces so well.'" Mom throws up her hands, exasperated.

I don't answer. We've had plenty of discussion about the racism and sexism as she experiences as she climbs the corporate ladder.

We work in silence for a while, each harnessing our talents to create something beautiful. My home is the only place in this world where I'm truly safe. The bland, gray exterior contains Mom's and my personalities, from the African-American art in the living room to the wall of alternative rock and grunge vinyls in our shared home office. It's where I've been encouraged to grow and thrive, uninhibited by the POPS, my trauma, and the father who never lived with us.

Notice I said this house, not our neighborhood. Mom and I moved into this bougie development in eighth grade, in the thick of Abby's most vicious bullying that happened before I stopped telling my mother every single detail of my life. Abby came over with a tray of cookies for the new neighbors and we learned we already knew each other far too well. (She stormed away, cookies in hand.) Sometimes when I come home in warmer months, I see her outside, hanging out with Kelsey, Slater, Mei, and the occasional wannabe POPS. I hate myself for wondering what it's like to have friends, but I do. So much time has passed since I've had companions that the memories grow fainter and fainter.

After a few hours of productive work, my stomach grumbles. Though Mom is the only other person here, heat rushes to my face. Being fat and hungry is something people love to make fun of.

"Lunch?" Mom suggests. "We can check out the new soul food place by the river."

"Sure," I agree. "Let me throw on some actual clothes."

My legs feel leaden as I head upstairs, thanks to the barrage of weight-related taunts I remember absorbing since middle school. I shouldn't be flashing back, right? I'm going to lunch with my mom, not headed back to

Abby and her pals mocking me for my weight and various other problems in the gym locker room.

Alas, this is the way depression works, coming and going at any moment. Even when things are fine, they don't stay fine for long. I have no choice but to pretend to be happy. Mom can't suspect how desperate I am to die; I can't hurt her like that.

My life is a string of distractions from my wretched thoughts. The darkness within me skulks around, a poisonous snake ready to strike. I've been depressed for so long that I don't know what's me and what's this fake personality who believes she is happy and gets good grades with zero effort and is no longer a victim.

If only she existed. If she did, I could be okay.

CHAPTER 4
ABBY

MUSIC PULSES through my Bluetooth speaker as Kelsey and I lounge around my bedroom. She sits cross-legged on the floor, pretending to study math while obsessively checking her phone. I'm reorganizing my book collection, since I'm ahead on this week's lesson—try keeping *your* GPA aligned with Carter Harper's.

Sorting through the towering bookshelf near my bed calms me. The ivory shelves contain classic (Dickinson, Plath, Angelou) and contemporary (*Float*, *Water Runs Red*, *The Chaos of Longing*) poetry volumes. I stow notebooks full of my own poetry and failed attempts at fiction in a locked trunk near my bed.

Kelsey raps her nails on her crystalline phone case. "Her flight landed two hours ago. Why hasn't she called yet?" Kelsey's mom, Ainsley Maxwell, is on yet another trip to yet another tourist trap paid for with her CEO husband's earnings. This time, Ainsley's visiting (the super white parts of) Cape Town, South Africa.

"I'm sure she's stuck in customs," I try to assure her.

She's so not. The truth? Ainsley doesn't care enough to update her daughter on her whereabouts.

Our mutual mommy issues are part of why Kelsey and I bonded. Not that I want to explain to Kelsey the specific reasons why my mother left the second my parents officially separated.

"Hmm," Kelsey says. Her chartreuse green eyes glimmer, meaning I'm either in trouble or about to be seduced.

"Trigonometry is useless," Kelsey declares before hopping onto my bed. The queen-size mattress is adorned with a faux fur blanket as soft as I could be, if I was a different kind of person. There's no room for softness in popular girls. Only hard angles and sharp glances in the Hall of Mirrors that comprises our school, our parties, and our social media.

Sometimes, when I'm alone with Kelsey, I almost become myself again. She almost extracts me from the hard shell I built post-divorce, post-assault, post-all the bad things that happened in my life. But those walls will never fully come down, much as I beg them to.

"Obviously." I stretch to switch my copy of *Citizen* with *Depression and Other Magic Tricks.*

"I'm so not in the mood for practice problems

anymore." Kelsey innocently blinks. Her pupils dilate, her unconscious signal that she wants me.

Seduction it is, then.

I inch slightly closer to her, and she follows suit. "Hmm. What'd you rather do? Stream a movie?"

"Guess." Kelsey laughs. She reaches her silky hand toward my cheek. I close the final gap between us, grasp onto her hair, and pull our lips together. I smile; it feels good to be wanted.

Our hookups began freshman year, when Kelsey randomly asked if she could kiss me as we pored over a Sephora haul. "I'm not sure if...if I'm gay," she explained. I didn't think I was pansexual at the time, but boy, I know now. I, being a wonderful best friend, leaned in and the rest is history. Now, whenever we don't have other partners, it's only us. Which isn't often, leading me to savor these moments.

She runs her fingers through my hair as the kisses intensify. She pulls back a bit. "You know you're my favorite person, right?"

"Yeah." I slide my hand up her tank top as my breath quickens.

"No, I mean—"

"Shh." I continue kissing her, not in the mood for conversation. There's time for whatever Kelsey wants to tell me later. Besides, I already know I'm the favorite. Who else would be?

You weren't even enough to make your mother stay, my

brain taunts me. God, I am *sick* of intrusive thoughts barging in whenever I have a peaceful moment. What's my mind's problem?

"What's wrong?" Kelsey coos in my ear.

"Math homework," I lie. I play with Kelsey's flaxen hair, draped around me.

She smirks. "Learn to chill out, silly. The world won't end if you blow off one assignment."

"Well, do you know how I can relax? Aside from Xanax?"

Kelsey moves her mouth down my body. Kelsey, pillow princess that she is, so seldom eats me out that I'm officially distracted by her tongue and her hands and her *everything*.

We have sex for what feels like forever. It's an allegory for the rest of our antics: mine are quick and dirty, while Kelsey likes to draw out the pain.

We work so well together.

We'll destroy people's worlds together.

CHAPTER 5
CARTER

LIKE ALL THE loners in teen movies, I eat my lunch alone.

Sometimes I sit in my car to escape the madness that is the junior class lunch period, but it makes me even sadder, so I don't do it often. At least in the cafeteria, laughter envelopes me rather than the silence that permeates most of my waking hours.

The laughter is still a problem. Laughter = friendship and happiness and a shred of possibility. Silence = me and this depression and the absence of hope.

Could I have friends? Sure. There's some folks in my AP courses who I deign to speak to sometimes, and I'm acquaintances, if not friends, with a fair amount of people in my programming courses. I choose to remain alone, though, because friends are a liability.

Slater and I used to be friends, back in middle

school before social division tore us apart. In elementary school, Mei and I were tight. And you can see how they turned out. Popular, plasticine, and devoid of caring. Slater can be the GSA President and say hi to me when she's alone all she wants. It's all a well-managed act. No one with a soul could stand to be one of the POPS.

I scan my well-worn copy of *The History of White People*. I tend to select this and other racial theory books to read when another wave of extreme police brutality floods the news and white people pretend to get a clue for ten seconds before finding comfort in their skin color all over again.

The story remains the same, and all I feel I can do is educate myself, continue to be a source of Black excellence, and use my allowance to donate to bail funds and racial justice organizations.

It's more than enough, yet it never feels like enough. As Chadwick Boseman (may he rest in power) said in *Black Panther*, "Wakanda will no longer watch from the shadows."

Sometimes I feel like I'm buried, hidden to protect myself when instead I could help others. Mom always brings up the idea, to take on one or two of the interview requests I get regarding BRAIN/ZAPP. "It would look good on your college applications. Not to mention you're a prime example of Black Girl Magic," she says to try to entice me.

The thing is, I know that the app could be even bigger if I didn't hide my identity. The only thing people know about the BRAIN/ZAPP app is that the creator is a young woman who wants to increase mental health access. I've declined a lot of interviews, the opportunity to be on the *Forbes* 30 Under 30 list, and even survived a DDoS attack thanks to my anonymity. Giving that up would be hard but could be a good choice. A Black, bisexual teenage girl creating a mobile application that helps people? That's a headline to remember.

The college apps possibility is a good hook; not so much of the concept that I'm any level of magical, that I could be a role model when I can barely pull myself out of bed some days. Not to mention that I'm the most unpopular girl in school, so it's not like I have influence. How can I give other Black girls a feeling of power when I don't have any?

Sometimes I think about what it'd be like to have popularity, or at least the benefits of it. I allow my gaze to drift over to the center table, where the POPS sit for lunch. I deliberately stay on the other side of the cafeteria, only passing it when I have to throw my trash away thanks to our janky cafeteria layout. I keep my head down as I pass, ensuring that I don't trip or get food thrown on me or whatnot.

I can never breathe again until I'm back at my table toward the front of the room. It's close to the exit and the cafeteria registers. In theory, the adult supervision should protect me. But, as I learned at a young age, there's no point in depending on authority figures when authority is so corrupt.

Unwittingly, I look at the POPS again. The rest of the school loathes and admires them, and even I can admit there's something magnetic, nearly hypnotizing, about the four girls. Kelsey, Abby, Slater, and Mei may be four of the biggest bitches on the East Coast, but at least they have each other, their band of loyal followers, their ability to make even more friends, and their ability to hold conversations with people their own age.

Whereas, until six PM when my mom returns from work, I have no one.

I try not to think about that.

I sigh, tuck my bookmark between the pages, and gather up my trash. I could do this at the end of lunch, but I try to get ahead of the crush of teenagers scrambling to get to class. Being amongst so many peers spikes my anxiety and even now, when most people are seated, I wade to the trash cans with my hands shaking. I throw away my lunch, counting every breath as I do.

Okay. *We're okay,* I try to convince myself. The reassuring thought doesn't help, as I know I will not be truly safe until I reach my table again. The POPS are typically too absorbed with one another to bother harming me at lu—

I don't realize I'm falling until my head smacks the

linoleum. I lie sprawled on the floor, wishing I could get struck by lightning or have a massive brain aneurysm at this exact moment so I can, you know, *die*. My messenger bag, which I keep on me at all times, falls with me and there's a loud CLACK against the floor. I hope my laptop isn't cracked—it's one of the only things I own that it would actually hurt to lose.

I don't know who did it; I messed up, and didn't look at the ground as I typically do. I ceased to protect myself for the slightest of moments, and, well, here we are.

It feels like five excruciating minutes have passed, but surely I've only laid here for several seconds. I know, because a few seconds is all it takes at this school for laughter to ring out.

I scramble upright, quickly putting my earbuds in to muffle the laughs. *Everybody saw*, I think. There's no music playing. *Everybody knew.* The laughs expand, ripple across social circles, break established silos and cliques. Most of the cafeteria joins in to witness my spectacle.

The thing is, Abby and the POPS aren't the only people who bully me. Their presence is most salient, but plenty of other people join in on the fun.

I should be used to this. Somewhere along the way, it became cool to hurt Carter Ashley Harper, like I am a pawn in the popularity game rather than a person with feelings.

Except I never. Get. Used. To. This.

I'm standing around awkwardly, my fight-or-flight instinct switching over to the third possibility: freeze. I can't move, my limbs locked in place despite me silently pleading with my legs to *work, dammit, leave. You have to leave!*

"Can you walk?" says a snarky voice next to me.

Somehow, I'm able to turn my head. When I look into those steely eyes, I know who did this.

Abby Wallace.

"You should probably get out of here," Abby suggests. "Knowing you, you'll steal something else from me." There's a warning I her voice that I'm confused about. Why would she think I stole from her? We live across the street from one another, so clearly our parents make around the same amount of money. Is it because I'm Black? Possibly, but I've never seen Abby do anything particularly racist; that's Kelsey's purview. Abby was actually one of the people who organized the school's Black Lives Matter Day last year, a twist that I did not see coming.

I'm considering that she's maybe mixed me up with someone else when I realize what she means. The Future Leaders Essay Contest. Is that what her vitriol is about? I won last week, and I figured she'd stopped caring. I certainly would have by now. Sometimes people are better than you, Abby. Get over it.

"Is everything okay here? Carter, did you hurt your-self?" Mr. Lenker, my sophomore year social studies teacher and a pain in my ass, approaches me and Abby. He can detect that something's wrong; I see it in his dashing eyes and rushed speech.

Still, he will not do anything. He's one of the "cool" teachers, the one who lets students get away with things we shouldn't in order to score popular points with the kind of girls he never had a chance with in high school (and, FYI, still doesn't have a chance with. If there's something the well-bred POPS girls won't stoop to, it's falling for a fool and a creep like Mr. Lenker).

And me? I haven't stood up for myself since freshman year. We all know how that worked out: a light punishment for the POPS, ramped up bullying for me.

I'm all alone here. I can't even muster the strength to protect myself. I have to keep quiet.

Leave, I order myself. *Leave.* And it's remarkably easy to do so once my body follows my commands. I leave the cafeteria, wishing I could just go to my car. If I go now, though, I'll end up being late to health class. Which, boo hoo. I already know all about condoms.

The door to the health classroom is locked, so I stand around while I wait for the teacher, an open target. No one's here yet, so that's something. I feel my heart aching again.

Anger rises within me. *No.* I'm tired of being broken. I need to find a way to break them back without becoming the kind of girl I loathe.

Only, how?

How do you stop the girls loved and feared by all?

CHAPTER 6
ABBY

SOMETHING'S WRONG. My father is cooking breakfast.

I come downstairs at five in the morning wearing pajamas, since I don't bother putting on real clothes until after I complete my six o'clock daily run. I love the morning, how everything feels possible while the sun peeks from behind the clouds. People (namely, known night owls Kelsey and Mei) don't get why I've stopped waking up late and begun to find the light comforting. By the time the night comes, the day is done, your mistakes are made, and there's nothing you can do about it.

Meanwhile, Slater and I understand in the importance of getting ahead of the day's challenges by waking up early. She wakes up early to do Pilates with her mom —that is, when her mom isn't traveling or interviewing or visiting Slater's older brother at college.

besides, i am used to shunning
　　　the dark
because when shadows play
our true natures are revealed.

"Daddy, you're not supposed to burn the eggs," I tease when I see them all stuck at the bottom of the allegedly non-stick pan.

My father offers me a sheepish grin as he flips the eggs to hide the evidence. He would know all about that, considering that he's a healthcare lawyer who oversees the legal (and illegal) practices of Pennsylvania's largest hospitals. "I know that. I just don't cook often."

Yeah, neither of my parents will audition for *Hell's Kitchen* anytime soon. I learned quick and early that if I wanted to be fed more than Chinese takeout and pizza night after night, I needed to pick up cooking and baking as hobbies.

Which is why I'm the one who's made breakfast since Mother left. When she lived here, the atmosphere crackled with tension and nearly two decades of unresolved issues between my parents. I don't blame her for that, though. Daddy and Mother share equal blame for not divorcing sooner, for allowing their Catholic upbringings to trap them (and me!) in the convent of a marriage that hadn't worked since it began.

So, yeah. No family breakfasts happened then. Now

that it's just me and Daddy, the mornings relax me rather than place adds weight to already overburdened shoulders.

"What brings this on?" I ask, gesturing to the now-finished eggs, two bagels that Daddy managed to not burn, coffee (his), green tea (mine), and the spread of watermelon cubes and papaya that make up our breakfast. I've seldom skipped a day, so there's no reason for Daddy to make breakfast unless he's going to ask me something that'll upset me.

He taught me that technique: disarm people early, and they just might believe you when you claim you're doing something for their own good. Explains why he and Mother bought me an iPad mini before telling me about their divorce. Not that I needed a bribe to hop on *that* train.

I grip my tea, bracing myself for whatever Daddy's about to say. My knuckles grow white as my skin stretches over my bones. *It won't be that bad*, I assure myself. What's he going to do? Get another divorce? Unless, *God*—what if he's dating again? What if he's become the cliched middle-aged businessman who starts screwing his far-too-young secretary? What if—

I'm jumping to conclusions *way* too hard. *Daddy's not a predator*, I reassure myself again. This, at least, I'm sure of. I've seen how he treats creepy men. Daddy gives the term "cold shoulder" new meaning.

I am safe with him.

Daddy sits across from me at our six-person dining table. Until Kelsey, Mei, and Slater fill the kitchen after school and on the weekends, it feels cavernous. "Well, I did want to speak to you about something."

I nod. "Okay. What?"

Daddy scratches his head, causing a few flakes of skin to drift downward. I wince. I keep telling him to lotion his massive bald spot, but he keeps forgetting to. His lack of care in that area says all I need to know about his non-existent love life.

"You know the Berwick case?" Daddy asks.

I nod. Daddy tends to tell me about his cases over breakfast. This one involves a chronically ill man with a history of suing Northeastern hospitals for medical malpractice; his newest conquest is a regional hospital that doesn't have enough money for Daddy, but Daddy took the case because he thinks that if the hospital wins the countersuit, they'll recover some of the man's previous awards in damages.

Personally, I think the guy's had some bad luck. Of course, I won't know the entire story unless I look at the case files. Fat chance of that happening. Daddy may have loose lips at mealtimes, but he guards his files even more than he guards me.

"I don't care where you go," he explained when he installed the app. "I remember what being a teenager was like. Barely. Anyway, I need to know where you are in case you need me." Daddy installed the same app on his own phone in order to prove it really was just a safety precaution. I can also see when he checks my location; he's only done so once, when I forgot to tell him I was sleeping at Kelsey's house and he spent half the night sick with worry.

"Since the patient is still sick and has residency in California, they want us to conduct the discovery and trial—or settlement—over there," Daddy continues.

I perk up. "Cool! We're going there?" I would love to work on my tan, since Northeast winters turn me pale as a vampire. Suck on that, Edward Cullen.

"Abby, this case could drag out for weeks. Maybe even months, depending on the show the plaintiff puts on. They're trying to make this into some social justice case, getting *The Marshall Project* and some other criminal justice publications to look into me and my firm."

I don't mention that I'm subscribed to *The Marshall Project*'s weekly newsletter.

"This battle will be long and ugly, and you have school. If you didn't, or if you were online like last year, you know I'd love to bring you along and show you what healthcare law is all about."

NO THANKS, I think but don't say. I'm only interested in the glossy details of law cases, not the mountains of paperwork and hours of phone calls involved with litigation. "So...you're leaving me alone for a while?" That'd be a little scary, but I think I could manage it. I can see why Daddy would be so nervous about telling me, though.

Daddy looks askance. "No, Abs. I asked your mother to come stay with you. She would still have to take the train up to Manhattan for weekend showings, but she says she can make it work. I leave Saturday, and she'll be here Saturday or Sunday."

Just like that, the plans I've constructed for myself fall to pieces. Mother's coming back? How could she bear it, especially after leaving in such a spectacular fashion?

Look, it's not that I don't love her. Well, maybe I don't. I do respect her—as a woman who gets whatever she wants, at least. I can't respect her as a parent. I've never known how.

"Daddy. Is that really necessary?" I ask. "Surely there can be another way, or I could stay with one of my friends. Like Slater. Or Mei." I couldn't stand living with Kelsey 24/7 (she snores), so I don't even bother mentioning her. I have friends other than Slater and Mei who I could stay with as well, including the Yang family from across the street (Mrs. Yang bakes *cookies* and *hugs* people. Since when do mothers do that?). But I'm not close enough to any of them to want to stay with them. If there's one thing I look for in a place, even if I'm staying there only overnight, it's security. I learned early on that I can't entrust my safety to just anybody.

"Slater has an older brother. And I've never even met Mei's parents."

Yeah, because you and Mother are racist-ass Republicans, I think to myself. Daddy was homophobic, too, until I came out to him and he realized he would lose his only daughter if he didn't get his ass in gear.

"Santiago is *gay!*" I lie. Unlike his sister, Santiago's as straight as they come.

"Abby," Daddy says gently. "She's the only person I trust to take care of you. With everything that's happened in the past few years...you know I've always trusted you, kid. You have a good head on your shoulders and you fix your mistakes. It's not you I don't trust. It's those *bastards*," he spits.

Great. Daddy's scared that someone else will take advantage of me. Again.

It's not like his fears are unfounded. His former best friend betrayed his family in ways that may never heal.

"*He's* gone now," I whisper. No need to mention that *he's* still there in my nightmares, when I examine myself in the mirror, even when I'm with Kelsey.

Maybe Mother being here won't be as hellish as I'm imagining.

> she is the one person who hates
>   *him* just as much as i do,
>   if not more.

even daddy's anger couldn't
    match
this particularly feminine type
    of rage
passed from daughter to daughter
    to daughter
to ~~victim~~.

"I have to do this, don't I?" I say. I stare glumly at my breakfast. The fruit looked good five minutes ago. Not anymore.

"I'm sorry," Daddy says gently. "I wouldn't have asked her to come if I thought there was another option. You know how hard the firm's worked on the case."

"No, I get it, Daddy." I shove aside the plate of eggs. "I'm surprised she even agreed to come babysit me."

"It's not babysitting, Abs. It's parenting. And of course she would say yes. She's your mother."

My eyes burn. "That's exactly why I thought she'd say no." I shove aside my plate and get up from the table.

"You done with breakfast?" Daddy asks, surprised. I always, *always* finish breakfast. If I don't, I won't have the energy to survive math class.

"Not hungry!" I say before stomping up the stairs to put on my running clothes. My body will pay for the decision to train without eating, but I can't stomach the thought of eating right now.

Not when Mommy Dearest is about to arrive and flip my life upside down all over again.

CHAPTER 7
CARTER

BIWEEKLY THERAPY IS EXACTLY as useless as it sounds.

By the time it rolls around, half the issues I would've brought up in the session are either solved or not at the forefront of my mind anymore. Therapist #6 suggested journaling more, but I'd rather not. What if I brought it to school, and one of the POPS found it and plastered my diary excerpts around the school or online? Sounds implausible, but it's happened in enough young adult novels that surely someone, somewhere's dealt with it before. Or what if I'm careless and leave it around the house, and my mother reads it? I don't think she'd stoop so low, but what if I started presenting as way too depressed again and—

"What are you thinking about?"

I lie on the therapist's couch, feeling fleshy and vulnerable and exposed. Therapist #6 said that I don't have to be in this position—which, duh, I know that. If I lie on my back instead of sitting up, I don't have to look at her *face* and her *concern* and her *really bad dye job*.

"School," I lie. No point in telling her I was thinking about her ineffective methods for treating my depression.

"I see. Did anything in particular happen recently?"

I roll my eyes. "Something's always happening. That's why I'm here, right?"

"Well, I wouldn't know. You're not very forthcoming."

I'm shocked. That's the closest to a "fuck you" from a therapist that I've ever gotten. This therapist might be as sick as me as I am of her.

I wonder if I can use that.

"It's just...hard, you know? Sometimes, it feels like I'm better, and there's nothing to talk about. Then, today, well, was harder."

"Could you explain to me what happened today?"

I gently clutch my jacket before recapping Abby tripping me, the laughter, me escaping. I leave out, of course, the suicidal ideations that I had (and am still having). Quite frankly, my messed-up headspace is none of her business.

"Are you positive that Abby meant to trip you? It could be a coincidence."

Ah, this is one reason why I don't bother to tell her anything. At least Therapists #1, 2, 4, and 5 tried to listen to me, as much as I would let them. Therapist #6 doesn't even bother to pretend.

I bark out a sardonic laugh. "Do you know anything about Abby and I's history?"

Therapist #6 blinks her narrow green eyes. Someone else would call her pretty, but I just see another social work graduate who had grand dreams of changing the world and who's now reduced to counseling bratty teenagers and neurotic adults.

"Yes, I do know about you two, as much as you'll let me know. I don't believe that everyone is out to get you, the way you think. Accidents happen."

Yeah, like me. My parents didn't mean to have me, though my mom claims that I was the happiest accident that could have happened. More like the grumpiest.

"Not at that school. Not with her."

Therapist #6 nods. "Let's say that Abby did mean to trip you. Did you tell a teacher? Did you talk to anybody about this, like your mother?"

"No."

"Carter, you have to do *something* to push those girls out of your mind."

"What, like meditate?"

"Well, it couldn't hurt—"

Alright, that's the last straw. The second someone acts like sitting in stillness will solve my problems, I'm done.

"—Carter? Where are you going?"

48

I'm out the office door before she can finish reciting another cookie-cutter, empty platitude about hope and recovery. I'll tell Mom to stop scheduling appointments with this clown, that I can't deal with another one. For God's sake, there's no way there are this many therapists in the Harrisburg area. One day, Mom will have to stop trying. Or by then I'll be in college ~~or dead~~, hopefully at MIT ~~or in the graveyard~~, and there will be a fresh crop of ineffective therapists she can foist upon me.

If I know one thing about my mother, it's that she won't give up on me, no matter how much I wish she would try.

It's raining outside, the torrential kind of Northeast downpour that slithers into every part of your clothing. I have no umbrella because this storm's arrived sudden and quick, with no warning before it decided to ruin people's afternoons.

Me, I like the rain. The roar around me has a way of filling empty spaces without making me feel lonely.

Therapist #6 is quick to follow me, though I refuse to turn around. "Are you okay? What happened?"

Nobody really wants to know the answer to "are you okay." They want a lie so they can pat themselves on the back and say they cared enough to ask.

"What happened is that I'm quitting therapy," I say. "You'll hear from my mom soon."

"Don't give up on yourself. You have a bright—"

Oh, come *on*. "I'm not giving up on myself," I inform

her. I'm pelted by rain, causing my hair and clothes to stick to me like flypaper. *I'm trapped,* my anxiety sings to me. *I'm trapped and she'll keep me here and she'll tell Mom but she* can't, *she just* can't.

"You say that, but you wouldn't be leaving if you weren't." Therapist #6 looks desperate now, as if she can't live without me, or she thinks I can't live without her.

My heart pangs. *Maybe she cares. Maybe I shouldn't leave—*

No. Nobody but Mom has cared about me since last year, when I had Hudson. He abandoned me like everyone else in my life.

"I'm not giving up on myself," I repeat, as if saying the words twice will make them true. "I'm giving up on *you.*"

***

Therapist #6 was right about one thing, though. I need to figure out a solution to the POPS problem.

I'm in my bed, huddled under the weighted blanket that feels like the hugs I used to get from Hudson. I've stripped off my rain-soaked clothes, wrapped my wet, limpid weave in a towel, and put on a pair of raggedy sweatpants that Kelsey and the POPS wouldn't be caught dead in.

I switch on my phone, typically off even though Mom has told me a million times to keep it on at all times in case of an emergency (since, you know, I'm a walking crisis case). I don't have social media, so I mostly use my phone to check my grades and assignments on Canvas, test new features for BRAIN/ZAPP, monitor my bank account, and browse the BRAIN/ZAPP email account.

The usual mesh of notifications greets me: receiving a 4 on my AP Psychology practice exam, my Singapore developer finding an (EXTREMELY RARE) fault in my code, Spotify charging me for premium again, and an email from a *Teen Vogue* editor.

I do a double-take when I see the email. Why the hell would *Teen Vogue* be interested in me?

Hi Carter!

I'm Sally with *Teen Vogue*. Our next major digital feature is a Girls in STEM roundup, and we would love to have you participate....

How do they even know that I'm a girl in STEM? I flash back to my scanty website bio, which explains how they found me:

CARTER H. (she/her) created the award-winning BRAIN/ZAPP application during her freshman year of high school. After being diagnosed with a life-changing mental illness, she decided to create a way to help others in her position. Now seventeen and a high school junior, she hopes to study computer science in college while continuing to improve the BRAIN/ZAPP application to benefit herself and others.

Right. Smart thinking, Carter. Especially because the part about me using the app myself is a total lie. As far as I'm concerned, my role is to plug and play.

Really, I should erase the bio from my website. Mom's the one who convinced me to put it up, because not including some information about myself would sabotage my college applications.

"Literally anybody could have created BRAIN/ZAPP," Mom argued when I was still totally anonymous. "At least now if colleges want to cross-check, they see that a Carter H. applied to their school, and a Carter H. created BRAIN/ZAPP. If they can't put two and two together, they don't deserve their title."

Well, she wasn't wrong.

I'm about to delete the email before remembering what Therapist #6 said. *You have to find ways to push those girls out of your mind.*

Okay, but...what if it there was an *external* way that I could get the POPS off my back? Me meditating won't stop Abby from sneering at me in gym class. A stress ball won't stop Mei from getting into my head. And I know from personal experience that distractions like books and homework won't stop Kelsey from approaching me to berate me some more.

They don't care. I've given every hint in the world that I want to be left alone and they do not listen to me.

If I want the POPS to hop off my ass, I have to get better tactics. I have to think like them. Which is a scary prospect, because all they think about is how to destroy girls who aren't good enough for them, girls who haven't succumbed to society's rules and don't even want to try.

This article could work. The POPS have to read *Teen Vogue*, right? It's fairly popular, popular enough that even I browse their website sometimes. If there's one thing those sycophants cling to, it's *popular*.

Finally, I have something none of them have: a highly-grossing product that actually helps people, and attention from a national publication. I know they haven't had that. (Kelsey was in a *Seventeen* magazine digital fashion feature one time, but that's it. They only included one photo of her.)

"Okay, *Teen Vogue*," I say to myself. "You've got your girl."

CHAPTER 8
CARTER

NOW THAT I have done it, I simply do not understand how some people (Kelsey) can mull around and talk about themselves all day.

"Wow, that's a great question," I lie. "My interest in STEM was clear at a young age. For my third birthday, my mother bought me my first Lego set. She left the living room to help my grandmother with the cake, and when she came back, I'd built a miniature of our hometown out of, y'know. The Legos." I tuck my hair behind my right ear, hoping my nervousness doesn't come across on video. "When I was four, she taught me how to play chess, which she'd learned from my grandfather. We learned from an early age that I had logical-mathematical intelligence. I also enjoy literature and social sciences, but my passion lies with science and technology."

Our interview is taking place over Zoom since Sally,

the *Teen Vogue* editor who contacted me, is recovering from surgery. Under normal circumstances, Sally explained, she'd bring the girls of the feature to the New York City office to mingle, have a photoshoot, network, and, of course, raid the fashion closet (which even I would want to do, if only to find a pair or two of limited-edition Doc Martens).

Fine by me. I don't want to pretend to like other people, and I've seen what happens when you bring together a bunch of hypercompetetive adolescents. Things get nasty, fast.

"Wow, that's impressive," Sally says. She scribbles more notes in her spiral-bound notebook. Actually, no, the Legos story isn't that interesting, at least not to me. It's a party trick, something Mom and I pull out at opportune times to showcase my brilliance. *See, we always knew she was gifted!* As if gifted isn't an arbitrary label put on kids who happen to have high IQs. It's not your IQ that matters; it's what the hell you do with your talents.

Also, all the kids in my school's gifted program are either depressed, anxious, or stoned all the time. We may be successful on the outside, but there's clearly some inner turmoil going on there that should be addressed.

Sally and I run though more questions about my mother, what classes I'm taking, and what inspired the app. That's where I stumble, giving an answer about how I *used* to be bullied and how I wished to *help other people like me*. There's no way that I'm admitting that I'm mentally ill. Not that the POPS haven't already guessed.

"Carter, I get more and more impressed by you the more we talk!" Sally gushes. I offer her a small smile, feeling like I've passed some kind of test. I'm good at this. Talking with adults, anyway.

It's people my own age that I've got a problem with.

Which brings me to one of the four people I hate the most. One who I've brought to my house today.

Slater.

Yeah. I don't get it either.

"Can you lift your chin up a bit more? No, to the left. *My* left." Slater's growing impatience with me is understandable. I, Carter Harper, am a very bad model.

I've never done a professional photoshoot before, unless you count Mom's awkward holiday photos and my annual school portraits. I don't know how to make myself look good, how to utilize my best angles. Likely because it often feels like I don't have any.

Yet here I am, in my bedroom that Slater has turned into a bona fide photo studio, pretending to care. We also took some photos outdoors when it was a bit lighter outside. I'm exhausted after what feels like hours of makeup by Mom and color coordination and panic seeping in the second we let Slater into my bedroom.

I hate that I care so much. I'd hate myself more if I didn't care. This is my debut onto the world stage, my first real attempt to garner attention. After the article runs, my life will change. People will know who I am. I'll have to suffer the mortifying ordeal of being known.

I hate that I care so much.

"Carter, you're doing great," Mom says as a show of encouragement. She's sitting on my bed, while Slater and I are taking the *Carter in her natural environment, coding and smiling* series of photos at my desk. I filled the screen with dummy code, lest some corporate yuppie zoom in on my screen and try to steal the code I've worked my ass off to build. Not today, Zuckerburg.

Slater puts her camera down for a second and smiles at me. "She's right, Carter. You're getting more natural. More comfortable."

The fake smile slips from my face. I don't want to grow comfortable in front of any of the POPS. When I let my guard down, bad things happen and I'm reminded why I fortressed myself in the first place.

Oh, crap, what if this is when she posts photos of my bedroom to Instagram or finds my raggedy childhood blanket and why did you let her in?

I inhale deeply. No. Slater isn't heinous enough to try something in front of my parent. Abby, Kelsey, Mei? Maybe. Not Slater, though. She has a moral compass, even if said compass spins around like it's hapless, broken.

"...anks," I say. It was supposed to come out as a full word, but that'll do. I've never been very good with speech, not unless I've rehearsed what on Earth I'd like to say. I can construct words in my head, but once they exit my mouth, things fall apart.

After two more shot sequences, Slater finally declares that we're done. Mom heads to her home office, leaving the door open so she can ~~hear me if I scream~~ make sure we're not doing anything untoward. She remembers all too well that I once had a fleeting crush on Slater, because moms are programmed to remember all your embarrassing moments.

I stretch my limbs, stiff from sitting in the same position for so long. For once, my body is tired but my brain isn't. In a parallel universe, I could see how physical exertion could be fulfilling. Even...fun.

"I'll send you at least fifteen photos to choose from as soon as I can," Slater says. "Probably this weekend, actually. Then I'll edit those."

I pause, not wanting to offend her. "Actua—actually, could you, show me the photos before you edit them?"

Slater scrunches her eyebrows. "What?"

"I...I wanted to see the pictures. All of them."

"I'm an excellent photographer."

"No, I know that. I—I know. I just wanted to check them out."

"Trust me, Carter—"

"I can't." Trust her, I mean. The hurt in her eyes shows me that she's caught my meaning.

"Here. It's just easier if you do it." Slater hands me her camera, a bit forcefully in my opinion.

With shaking hands, I accept the camera and brace myself for what I'm about to see. I've never been much of a looker, despite my mother and ex-boyfriend's assertions that I'm *beautiful* and have *unique bone structure.*

Yet, somehow, Slater's made me breathtaking. Almost...pretty, really. Soft shadows play across my face, highlighting my full lips and illuminating my mahogany-colored eyes. And my body, often slapped with the detrimental labels of *chubby* and *chunky* looks full, balanced. Curvy. I don't cringe looking at myself.

She really is brilliant. I want to tell her so, only the words won't leave my mouth.

Going through the photos and deleting the unsavory ones is a painstaking process, and I can see why Slater's annoyed at having to take the time to do this. She'll likely have to do this *again* to select the photos she thinks are best. But I can't take the risk that she sells out to her friends or posts some weird outtake of me to social media. I wouldn't even know about it, because I haven't had a social media account since my disastrous brush with Facebook in middle school.

"I'm done," I whisper after what feels like a million years. I look up and blink. While I looked at my pictures, Slater packed away the rest of her equipment. Even the white backdrop.

"If you don't trust me," Slater asks me when she's packing her camera away, "then why did you ask me to help you? There's plenty of other student photographers 'round here."

"You're the best," I say simply. "And I...I n-need the best."

Slater smiles as she leaves my room. "You're right," she says. "I am."

CHAPTER 9
ABBY

I JUMP when the doorbell rings, the way I've done since it's been confirmed that Mother is coming to essentially babysit me.

The idea of it makes me want to laugh, but the joke's not funny at all. I don't want her here—what if something bad happens, again, and she overreacts?

If I were a mother, perhaps I could understand why she did this. As a broken daughter, I can't. I won't.

At least I've gotten a small reprieve. My mother was supposed to be here two hours ago, but her train was delayed.

Instead of waiting this out alone, I've invited Kelsey, Mei, and Slater over for a *Twilight* movie marathon. (Only, Slater's late. Which she never is.) I don't bother to check my phone for her cold, clinical texts updating me on her arrival. I know her ETA and can usher my girls out before they have to meet my mother.

We're halfway through *Eclipse* when Slater finally arrives. I skipped *New Moon*, hating how haunted and broken and pathetic Bella looked when Edward left her. I've looked that way over a guy, too. Except he wasn't the love of my life. *He* was my hell.

"Hey," I say. I toss Slater a box of Junior Mints, her favorite, from the snack corner. I joked once that she eats them so much because she must always want to kiss someone. Slater blushed, stammered, and immediately changed the subject. I semi-regret saying that. It was a joke, and my jokes are certainly funny.

I wonder, sometimes, what it'd be like to kiss her. But that'd be one best friend too many. Who's next? Mei?

"Where were you?" Kelsey demands. She snuggles a bit more into my side. Protecting her territory.

Slater looks at us and cringes. What's that about? "I was...busy."

"Doing what?" Mei perks up. She's on the other side of the couch, since she's not the most affectionate. Meanwhile, Kelsey and I are practically dry humping in the living room.

Not that we've, um, done that before. (Okay, we have.)

"Jesus *Christ*," Slater groans. "Can I hang out with my friends without facing the Spanish Inquisition?" She drops her small backpack on the floor and gently places her camera bag next to it. Oh, she must've been at a photoshoot. Probably for some nerd at the school newspaper. Mystery solved: now we can get back to if Bella's going to risk it all for Jacob.

"We were just curious," Kelsey mutters as Slater plops down next to me. She puts her legs up on me and Kelsey's laps, leaning against Mei. She takes up a lot of space that way, but that's what she does, in her ebullient way.

"Missed you," I say to Slater since Kelsey and Mei are being asshole-ish right now. Mei has straight up said to me that she doesn't know why Kelsey let her into the circle, and Kelsey seems to have her regrets about it as well. In the meantime, Slater's the one I feel most emotionally safe with, plus she's funny, popular, and her mom is famous, so she stays. I would put up a hell of a fight if Kelsey and Mei tried to cast her out.

I think they know me better than that to let that happen.

There's a knock on the door. Instinctually, I get up to answer. Also instinctually, I hesitate before opening the door. You never know if the person you allow into your home one day will hurt you the next.

"Surprise," Mother says when I open the door. Her words ring flat. It's like looking in the twisted mirror of a fractured fairytale. Mother and I share dark hair, stormy eyes, slim figures, and a penchant for cruelty. Other than that, I'm nothing like the woman who semi-raised me.

"M-Mother?" I'm so shocked to see her that I nearly drop the mug of tea in my hands. I take a sip instead, allowing the warmth to flood my face now that my cold mother is back. "You're here early."

"Yes, well, you would know that if you checked your phone. Aren't you typically glued to that thing?" Mother sniffs.

"Mrs. Wallace? I didn't know you were coming!" Kelsey bounds up next to me. My already-pale face feels like it's been blanched of all color. My friends. Now my friends have to witness my mother's and my painful awkwardness around each other, an awkwardness that could kindle into full-blown hatred with any set of wrong words.

My mother's face brightens. Incredible, that she likes Kelsey more than me. It wasn't always like that. Though she's been unreachable since my breech birth, Mother and I got along when I was younger and unable to really think for myself. Her and Daddy pretended to be a happy family, for me and for their friends, until poison wrapped around them and they remembered that they hated each other, right around our move to Pennsylvania.

"Kelsey," Mother says with a hint of warmth in her tone. "It's lovely to see you again. How are your parents?"

Kelsey doesn't betray any sign of worry about her still-MIA mother when she says, "Fine."

I never used to lie about consequential things. Not until third grade, when a teacher asked me if I threw dirt in Ariana Martinelli's face and I said no. And now the lies and lies have built up so high that nobody knows if Kelsey, Mei, Slater, and I are telling the truth. In our trade, lying is essential.

When did we little girls grow up to become such perfect liars?

Speaking of Mei and Slater, I turn around to see what they make of this situation. They're sitting on the couch, gawking at Mother and me like the freak show we are.

"Since when is she back in town?" Mei whispers to Slater.

"I don't know. I've never even met her," Slater whispers back. Which, true. By the time Slater and I became friends, the divorce was filed and Mother had left.

"Abby, help me bring in my suitcases," Mother barks at me. She points a long, bony finger at the four Louis Vuitton suitcases nesting in our driveway. The cab driver must've taken off once he realized she doesn't tip for "subpar" service.

Smart person. I would escape her if I could, too. (And I almost did.)

"Can't you do it yourself?" I say to Mother so she knows she isn't the boss around here anymore. I'm harder, badder, cooler than I have ever been.

"I'll help," Kelsey pipes up before Mother can (metaphorically) bite me back.

I look at her quizzically—Kelsey isn't into physical labor. I haven't seen her lift a finger since she quit the volleyball team freshman year, claiming it was "eating into her social life." Truth was, she was pissed that another freshman got varsity over her. I followed her lead, though volleyball was fun. It got me out of the house, at least. But the upside was spending more time with Kelsey, leading to us becoming whatever we are, because we aren't in love enough to be in a relationship and we're too much like lovers to be friends.

"Uh, okay," I say. I'm too shocked to make any smartass comments.

Mother offers her version of a smile. "*Thank* you, Kelsey," she says.

Ugh. Spare me.

I set my teacup down on our console table before stomping out of the house, Kelsey following close behind. Our house is large enough for going to the driveway to be an annoying trek.

"Why didn't you tell me that your mom was coming?" Kelsey whispers to me. She, of course, selects the two carry-on suitcases to carry, leaving me with the two oversized ones.

I shrug. "It's not that big of a deal."

"You didn't even mention it in passing," Kelsey muses as we head back to my house.

"It didn't need to be mentioned," I snap. It feels like there's wires wrapping inside of me, holding tight to my organs and constricting my breathing. I can't handle these questions about my mother, her life now, why she's back, and *why she left*.

> hating her
> and hating what she did
> are two different feelings.

> only at this point, i have forgotten
> the difference.

"You don't have to be such a bitch," says Kelsey, the queen of bitches. "I just don't get why you would keep this a secret."

"I've kept a lot of things secret," I say. Darkness creeps into my tone.

Kelsey pauses. "I didn't know that," she says quietly.

Kelsey, Mei, and Slater leave without Mother even asking them to. Say what you want about her, but she can clear a room.

I send them off with a batch of brownies I stress-baked before my girls came over. I don't want to eat them, and God knows my mother won't. She's been dieting since I was born, a scary prospect once you realize she's a size 4. Slater looks concerned about the brownies, but then again, she looks concerned about half the things I do. I would call her the mom friend, only I don't know how a mom is supposed to act. Someday soon, she'll have to realize I'm okay most of the time. Really.

Mother elegantly drapes herself on the sofa. "You've created a fine mess in here," she notes. She's referring to the way I go all out for my monthly-ish movie days, from the popcorn maker I bought on Amazon to the boxes of movie theater candy littered around the living room.

"I always clean up," I say. I sit on the opposite end of the couch from her.

"Hmm. Your dad should re-hire our cleaner."

I shake my head. "I can clean the house myself." I don't even mind it, and it hasn't been forced on me. Cooking, gardening, and cleaning are all therapeutic for me. I'd make a great homemaker, if I thought I'd ever want to be married.

"Do you have the time to, considering your course load and extracurricular activities?" Mother asks. For a second, I think she's concerned about me.

"I can handle it," I say. "Besides, I'm not in any extracurriculars at the moment." I don't realize how bad that sounds until the words leave my mouth. I should probably join another club, though it's pretty late in the school year to do so. Not because I want to—I like having my afternoons free to do whatever I want.

"Why not?"

I shrug. Why the barrage of questions about my life? "Well, Kelsey wanted to quit volleyball, so we did. Then I didn't really want to be in Creative Writing Club anymore. I'm still in National Honor Society, though."

Mother sighs. "One girl shouldn't determine the course of your life and career."

"She's not just some...she's my best friend," I say. "And I thought you liked her."

"I do. But I don't always like what she does to you."

Whatever that means. Unless, oh God, what if she knows that we're hooking up?

I quickly change the subject. "I have my SATs in two weeks."

"This your first time taking the test?"

"Yeah."

"Well," Mother says. "Be sure to bring more pencils than you think you need."

"Thanks for the motherly advice," I say. "It's not like that tip is in every prep book known to humankind." I've studied my ass off, even taking a weekend math prep course to help with my weakest subject. I won't let this test, and my chances at college, slip through my fingers.

Instead of being snarky, Mother's voice softens. "Look, Abigail, I don't want to be here, and you clearly do not want me here. But for better or worse, we're thrown together again. Could we at least attempt to be civil with one another?"

"You've never been good at that, and neither have I." I cross my legs. "Why did you even agree to come back? I could've stayed with Slater or Mei."

My mother pauses. "I don't know why," she admits.

My heart cracks a bit. "There's some meals in the fridge if you need anything. I made up the guest bedroom," I mutter. I go upstairs, wishing my mother could follow me and tell me that she's sorry, that things are okay. But I've driven her too far away for us to reconcile now.

    even though, sometimes
    i wish we could be the mother
       and daughter pair
    that i secretly ache for.

CHAPTER 10
ABBY

JUST WHEN IT seems like nothing interesting will happen in this town again, it does.

If you could call Carter Harper being in *Teen Vogue* interesting. I wouldn't bother reading the interview if I didn't know her.

"Did you know that she plays *Animal Crossing* to wind down?" Kelsey asks with a mouth full of kale chips. We're at lunch, simultaneously scrolling through the article. Thanks to Mr. Atkinson announcing Carter's accomplishment in AP English, we all know about Carter's precious *Teen Vogue* interview. Word spread fast amongst the junior class, and now the result is us glued to our phones, reading about Harlow High School's own little superstar. The cafeteria supervisors have been playing whack-a-mole with each table, trying to get us to put our phones away. Even I'm intrigued enough to read the interview, which includes other girls in STEM who sound much cooler than Carter.

"Are we supposed to care about *Animal Crossing*?" I say, not mentioning that I played the game for hours in a row all last summer, quitting when school began and I had actual work to do again.

"It's fun," Kelsey says. Wow, who knew that a mega-bottom like her would own a Nintendo Switch? Maybe we don't know everything about each other. That sounds like it shouldn't be a big deal. But when I think it, I flinch. No, I'm all Kelsey's and she's all mine. We're bonded as closely as two people not romantically involved can be.

I peek over at Carter's lunch table. It's typically empty, but people have been coming up to talk to her throughout lunch. I can only imagine how poorly *those* conversations are going—the girl has no social skills.

Fame, no matter how fleeting, is like a magnet to the grasping social climbers of HHS. This is worse than when Kelsey was in *Seventeen* one time. At least then, despite her charging people a hundred bucks for "modeling lessons," I could be proud of my friend. This is... brutal rather than entertaining. Not to mention painfully embarrassing, considering that these people didn't give her the time of day before she was in *Teen Vogue*.

"The article itself is boring, but you have to admit it's at least a little interesting that she's in *Teen Vogue*,"

Mei says. "Not that I'm up her ass about it. Watching people fawn over Carter is laughable."

It's like Mei's read my mind. I take a sip from my bottle of iced tea.

"Where's Slater?" Kelsey asks. She says it loudly, as if to prove some kind of point.

I shrug. "She said she's going to the darkroom today." Slater does that sometimes, needing to steal some time away for herself. I get that. I've done that more and more since living with my mother again. Interesting, considering how it hasn't been as bad as I thought it would be.

Kelsey frowns. "Hmm," she says, as if she can't place her finger on why Slater, a known visual artist, wants to be surrounded by photography rather than people. She goes back to her phone. "She's more interesting than I thought. Abby, why don't you like her again?"

I set down my sandwich. "Kelsey, *you* didn't like her *first*. You knew her way before me."

"Can you just answer the question?"

"Can you stop deflecting?" I take another bite of my sandwich before answering. "She's annoying, she doesn't take care of herself, she's boring...." I could go on.

"Also, all she cares about is making sure she's better than everyone else," Mei says.

"Those are barely reasons," Kelsey argues. "I'm gonna go talk to her for a bit."

I cackle loudly enough that the tables near us stop and sneer. "*You?* What do you and *Carter Harper* have in common?" The idea is so ludicrous that I start laughing again, Mei joining in. I mean, *really*. Mei and Carter may have been friends once upon a time because they're both hypercompetitive dorks, but I can't see Kelsey and Carter even being able to hold a normal conversation. What do they have in common? The weather? Being in AP English class?

Kelsey gives me an ice-cold glare. "Can't I do something nice?"

"No," Mei and I say immediately. We're not used to Kelsey caring for anybody but herself and, sometimes, her friends. Not charity cases like Carter Harper, unless you include the one or two social bottom feeders she invites to her annual spring blowout party, only to rub her wealth and popularity in their faces. It also makes her seem kind, which isn't the same as actually *being* kind.

"Wow! Thanks, everyone." Kelsey stands up. "To prove it, I'm going to go *talk* to her."

"Holy shit, she's actually doing it," I say as Kelsey sashays over to Carter's table. Her boots clamp on the floor and her ponytail swings gently between her shoulder blades, drawing attention to her (and her ass).

I turn away when Kelsey and Carter first start to talk, cringing too hard to want to look at this train-wreck. Curiosity wins, though, and I look back over at

Carter's homework-covered table. Now, Kelsey sits down with Carter. Carter fidgets with her pen. I can tell she's stumbling over her words as she always does.

"How embarrassing for her," I mutter. I mean Kelsey, not Carter, for once. Kelsey's sudden warming to Carter after years of swinging from indifference to bitchiness is wild to watch.

"Eh, it'll pass. Kelsey only has a fleeting interest in people."

"Except for us."

"Except for us," Mei agrees.

Carter's fidgeting leads to her hitting herself in the eye. Mei and I start another round of laughter. As if she can hear us, Kelsey shoots a death glare toward us. I blow her a kiss in return. Carter's eyes skitter back in forth between Kelsey and me, as if she's the butt of some joke. Perhaps she is—if so, I wish Kelsey would let me in on it.

"Look who got bored," Mei singsongs as Kelsey leaves Carter's table. Rather than coming back to us, Kelsey sits suspiciously close to Ethan, a recent transfer student she keeps flirting with. Five bucks says they'll hook up and she'll be bored of him within the week. Nevertheless, Kelsey remains practically in his lap for the rest of lunch, knowing that if she comes back to Mei and me, we'll just roast her. Because that's what best friends do.

Mei and I continue to talk until the end of the lunch

period, shifting topics from Carter to Ariana Grande's surprise album drop. Ironically, Carter, Mei, and I quite literally bump into one another while throwing our trash away. Carter's eyes widen in terror, and she takes a quick step back. She looks like a frightened rabbit, about to be mauled by a fox.

"Just...watch it," I mutter before clearing my tray. Normally, Carter's clumsiness would be cause for anything from a sharp retort to shoving her back. Harder. Hardest.

I don't care enough to bother. She's had enough people caring about her for one day.

CHAPTER 11
CARTER

I HAVEN'T BEEN in trouble since that time Mei and I ate dirt in elementary school on a dare (don't ask). So when I was summoned to the principal's office, I was unsure of what was coming, but I wasn't at all afraid.

I should have been. Even if this insipid meeting gets me out of gym class. Things have largely stayed the same there, with Abby and the gym teacher both commenting about how slow my legs, my arms, my lungs are. Yes, I know I won't be an Olympian anytime soon. No, we don't need to make snide comments about that fact.

"Hello, Carter," Principal Adams greets me. "We haven't spoken in a long time." He sounds like a TV show villain, luring me into a trap. *Not everyone is out to get you*, I remind myself.

I cautiously sit in the pleather chair across from him. "Yes," I agree.

"I suppose you're wondering why you're here."

"...Yes."

Adams tilts his computer toward me. My own smiling face is on the screen. I notice, for the first time, that Slater's photo credit isn't on the photo, despite it being the main one on the article. I'll talk to Sally about adding her in. "As you know, you were featured in *Vogue* recently."

Close enough.

"Mr. Atkinson informed me about the article, as well as directed my attention to allegations made within it."

Not Atkinson *again*. I think Atkinson thought he was doing me a favor when he told the class about the article. I just sunk into my seat and prayed for the moment to pass. Oddly, the POPS didn't snicker this time. Some people in the class looked annoyed, but that's about it. Score one for Carter.

I furrow my brow. Wait a second. What allegations did I make in the article? I talked about the app and—

"What I mean is, you mentioning that you were bullied while attending this school."

Ah, crap.

When I said that, it was to make myself seem like I'd overcome a struggle without delving too deeply into my mental health issues. I also lied to the interviewer by stating the bullying was in the past and I now have solid support systems and friendships.

Now my words are coming back to haunt me. Not just because of this silly meeting, no, I also manifested the *bullying being in the past*. The latter is comforting, at least, if it lasts. The former, not so much.

"Yes," I say yet again.

Adams looks annoyed, which, fair. "Don't you have any other words?" Before I can answer with another *yes*, he plows on. "Never mind that. I wanted to meet with you personally to apologize for any bullying you have experienced at Harlow High School. We strive to create an educational experience that is inclusive for all, and strive to report and eliminate all bullying that we know about."

I tighten my lips. He's only talking to me to prevent a lawsuit—God knows when the Frog Incident and Toilet Trouble happened, my mom threatened the school with all the strength she could muster. The only reason she didn't go through with it is because I begged her not to.

Embarrassing. Though the school sure as hell didn't do anything to stop them, the school board didn't raise the POPS. Society and the pursuit of popularity morphed them from mere girls to sadistic wenches who don't care who they hurt.

"I know," I finally say.

Adams smiles at me. It looks more like a grimace. "I'm glad we can understand one another."

We don't. What I *want* to understand is how so

many people, adults and students alike, can look the other way when someone's in pain. Riddle me that, Adams. Let's talk about that.

Only, I can't.

Principal Adams studies me. "I do admit that we've dropped the ball on our anti-bullying programming. We believed that by high school, you would all understand the consequences."

No, they don't. The POPS don't know (or don't care) that they carve broken girls with every twist of the serrated knife that is their words.

"To remedy this, we will be holding an anti-bullying presentation in the next week or so. Since you've had such a...visceral experience that you're open about, we want you to speak at it. If you don't mind, of course."

"No!" I nearly shout, forgetting where I am. *Public speaking?* About *my bullying experience?* I've smoked weed a total of one (1) time in my life, so I know what I'm talking about when I say Adams has to be smoking something strong to even consider this.

Adams frowns, and I remember myself. "I mean... not really, no. It's not in my area of interest, but I support your efforts." Lies, lies, lies.

"Well, then, alright. I suppose we're done here; I really just wanted to check in with you about how things are going. You can head back to class." Adams pauses. "Unless, of course, you have anything else you would like to tell me?"

I look down.

Abby making fun of me in class.

Mei tearing my paper apart.

Abby bruising me in gym class.

Kelsey whispering that Abby is better than me in every possible way.

Slater standing by, uncomfortable yet amused, as Mei asks me about my dad yet again.

Abby tripping me at lunch.

Abby, Abby, Abby.

"No," I lie. "I have nothing else to tell you."

CHAPTER 12
ABBY

THE SMELLS of sweat mingled with perfume and unwashed floor in this testing center are atrocious.

Yet another reason to hate test day. First of all, I had to go to a high school out of the way because Harlow High School didn't offer testing on this date, so none of my friends are here. Only a few people who either want to be my friend, who I used to be friends with before battle lines were drawn, or who I've seen in the hallways but don't know the names of. Second of all, I barely slept last night, thanks to my mother's snores from across the hall. I'd gotten used to the sound when she lived with us, only to have that progress stripped away once she decided to come back. I admit, though, living with Mother once again hasn't been the hell I'd thought it would be.

I focus in on the boring, easy-to-parse passage I have to analyze for the critical reading section. I'm acing this part, and I've completed two sections of the test. I'm so close to the finish line that I can almost taste the Five Guys I'm going to get after this to celebrate.

I'm wrapping up a vocabulary question when I catch sight of the next paragraph. My pencil drops to the floor when I read the author's name, one that I know all too well.

tom *tom* tom *him* tom tom tom *HIM* tom *tom!* tom *tom* tom *him* tom tom tom *HIM* tom *tom!* tom *tom* tom *him* tom tom tom *HIM* tom *tom!* tom *tom* tom *him* tom tom tom *HIM* tom *tom!* tom *tom* tom *him* tom tom tom *HIM* tom *tom!* tom *tom* tom *him* tom tom tom *HIM* tom *tom!* tom *tom* tom *him* tom tom tom *HIM* tom *tom!* tom *tom* tom *him* tom tom tom *HIM* tom *tom!* tom *tom* tom *him* tom tom tom *HIM* tom *tom!* tom *tom* tom *him* tom tom tom *HIM* tom *tom!* tom *tom* tom *him* tom tom tom *HIM* tom *tom!* tom *tom* tom *him* tom tom tom *HIM* tom *tom!* tom *tom* tom *him* tom tom

They have the the exact same name, same first, same last. Maybe the author and *him* share the same sick tendency for little girls.

> "you weren't innocent, you never
> have been"
> "i caught you kissing liam a few
> times"
> "you knew you wanted me"

"~~i wanted you~~. I couldn't help
myself"

He's here, in this testing room, reminding me that I can't escape him. Most of my life is fine, pleasant even, until these memories crawl up and *ihavetopuke* I want my mother I want my father I want somebody.

I remain frozen until the allotted break, until most of the students pour out of the classroom. Even as I slip away from myself, I remember to stay calm as I slide my test packet to the proctor and tell her to cancel my score. Even as she runs through the consequences and I get curious looks from the Harlow High students.

I'm not going to show them how much I ache on the inside. I am the goddamn queen, and a queen never trembles, even when her insides feel like jelly and she's low-key hyperventilating.

They cannot see you fall. They cannot see you break. They cannot see you struggle.

A crown is a heavy thing to possess, something everybody wants but only few would truly kill to have. And I have killed to get it. Parts of myself, mostly. There's no way this SAT passage is going to steal my shine.

Except...it does.

Once out of the testing center, I vomit into a shrub. "Sorry," I croak to it, like it can hear me. Great, now I'm talking to plants.

I drive home on autopilot, wading through streets with perfect accuracy even as my mind falls to pieces. In the back of my mind I realize that maybe I should, I don't know, call somebody and have them bring me home. But no.

I can't tell my friends that I froze while taking my SAT; they'd laugh at me. Well, Slater wouldn't, but she'd give me that clear-eyed gaze of concern that makes me melt and want to tell her what happened.

I can't tell Daddy because he isn't here to hold me, make things better.

I can't tell Mother because, knowing her, she'll hire a hitman to off somebody on the testing committee.

I can't tell. I can't tell, because the last time I told, my life blew up, so I learned to stay quiet.

I think I would stay quiet even if my mother hadn't done what she did to *him*.

> i flip between gratitude and anger
>   for what she did.
> gratitude, because she stood up
>   for me.
> anger, because she did not give
>   me a choice in how she did so.

"I thought you had your SATs today," Mother says the second I come in the door. "Wouldn't you be done later than this?" She's in the living room watching TV.

"They had the same name," I say to her.

I didn't mean to talk to my mother. I'm haunted now. This doesn't happen often, me being so slammed with memories that I can't think straight.

"What?" Mother sounds concerned. No, she's not. That's my delusions, deciding to taunt me a little more.

"They had the same name," I whisper. I lie down on the couch, not caring that Mom's sitting in the living room with me. I can't be alone right now, even if that means I have to lie down next to her.

I wake up after a restless sleep haunted by visions of men, women, monsters, blood, me running in a labyrinth that I can't escape.

Something weighs on me, but not in a bad way. The heaviness comforts me, snuggling me when I wake up in the near-nightly terror caused by nightmares I can't escape.

Blinking awake and breathing slowly to calm myself, I realize I wasn't hallucinating: there really *is* a weight on me. It's my weighted blanket that I use sometimes to help me in this exact situation. Hmm, weird. I don't remember grabbing it before I conked out in the living room, and it's not like Daddy is here. He knows about the nightmares and the screaming and thrashing they can bring, and he'll sometimes come in and put a glass of cold water on my nightstand or put the blanket on for when I wake up.

I'm unsettled rather than comforted when I realize that just because neither Daddy nor I put the blanket on, doesn't mean someone else couldn't have done so for me.

CHAPTER 13
CARTER

I FEEL terrible for unleashing this wreck of a bullying assembly onto the student body. Due to me shutting Adams down when he asked me to consult on the school's presentation, a low-quality PowerPoint will guide us through the all-too-familiar world of bullying and relational aggression.

They're wasting their time. One-on-one counseling to solve Kelsey and Abby's issues would help more than this nonsense.

Normally I'd cower in the front row of the auditorium, as far away from the POPS as possible, but *no*. Kelsey and Slater corralled me to sit in the back with them, with Abby and Mei to their other side. I wanted to say no, but Kelsey straight up grabbed my arm and steered me to their row.

What was I supposed to do? ~~Run.~~ Tell her to fuck off? ~~Yes.~~

Notably, Abby sits as far away from me as possible. Or not so notably. Despite her friends trying to milk my "popularity," Abby's wanted nothing to do with me.

Yet I was correct in my hypothesis that the POPS would garner some kind of respect for me once I gained national recognition. Aside from Abby and Mei, who are as cold as ever, the rest of the school has fallen in line and *left me the hell alone.* Of course, sitting with the POPS during an anti-bullying assembly isn't what I had in mind when I decided to fight back. But it's better than being their chew toy, a role I have played for so very long.

My mental health has never been better. I'm still depressed, of course; not much can change my biology, especially when my antidepressants refuse to work. But not enduring daily abuses from Abby and her friends makes school feel a whole lot safer.

I wish this would last. Maybe it could; maybe I can maintain peace with the POPS and, since the majority of the school follows their lead, have the protection of popularity without bowing down to Kelsey.

Or they could push me down the stairs right after this assembly ends. Anyone's guess.

Mei sighs. "When are they going to start? I want to get out of here." We're on an assembly day schedule, meaning shortened classes to make room for the presentation, and, if we're lucky, an early dismissal.

I rub my eyes, and dark brown eyeliner smears onto

my hand. "Dammit." I forgot that I decided to wear makeup today, my eyeliner pen a relic from my shoot with Slater.

Mei fumbles in her bag and hands me a makeup removal wipe. "Here."

I'm surprised she's helping me, though I'm sure it's just so I don't drag the whole group's image down. She'd hate for Kelsey's pet project to look like, well, a pet. "Uh...thanks."

Adams starts the assembly as I scrub my eyelid. "Hello students, thank you for coming today." We didn't have a choice, dude. "Due to recent...revelations, we decided it was time to talk to the student body about bullying."

I shrink in my chair. We all know what those recent revelations were. I shut my eyes, knowing that all eyes are on me.

She's a snitch.

I heard she banged an editor at the magazine. That's why they put her online.

Have you seen her new hair color? It's red. She looks like a literal clown.

I hear their shrill cries in my head, despite not hearing any of it out loud. I know it's what they're thinking. I'm the enemy again.

"Carter?"

Slater's voice nudges me out of my avoidant stupor. I

tentatively open my eyes and, to my surprise, only a few people have glanced my way.

This is weird. I'm so used to being laughed at that being treated like a normal human being feels wrong, somehow.

Wrong, yet so, so good.

Adams drones on. Yes, I know that physical, verbal, emotional, and social bullying, and cyberbullying all exist. I've dealt with every kind and your staff did nothing to stop it.

Most people are as bored as me. Some are on their phones. I'd whip out a book to read, but ironically, teachers are more apt to notice unauthorized books than unauthorized cell phones.

Wow. I did not realize a presentation on such an important topic could be so boring. This basic bullying program spouting facts and statistics is not going to help. The reason people sob when seeing teenagers who attempted or committed suicide because of bullying is because of the visual. Those documentaries and video clips show selfies, taken in rare joyful moments. Tearful parents, wishing somebody would have stopped their child's death. Meanwhile, we're fed useless numbers no one will remember after we leave the auditorium.

Say something, my kind-of-confident side says. *Adams would let you.*

I would rather choke on my own vomit, Rational Carter informs. *So, there.*

"In the worst cases, students who are bullied may attempt or complete suicide," Adams says.

My eyes latch themselves to the ceiling rather than to him. I knew they'd talk about suicide, but it looks like this is a full part two of the assembly, since there's twenty minutes left.

"Carter, you okay?" Kelsey asks.

"Huh? Oh, yeah." I'm gripping the armrest a little too hard. I relax my grip. I hate this. I don't have many physical reactions to bullying, but the whole family of anxiety, depression, and fear comes out when I so much as hear "suicide."

"You don't look good," Mei informs me. "You never do, but you look extra not good."

Mei is always like this, even with her friends, even when we were friends, I rationalize. *This doesn't mean she's going to harm you again.*

"I'm fine," I lie. I sit through the rest of the assembly, rigid, doing what I can to calm myself down and not bring any more attention to myself.

After the assembly, I dart out of the auditorium like my limbs are on fire. I don't want to spend any more time than needed with the POPS. I'm stuck in that strange place between loving the POPS for finally realizing I'm a human being and hating them for all they've done to me. How they think trying to make me *popular* is going to erase years of history.

That's what you wanted, right?

Well, it's sort of what I *wanted*, but not what I *expected*. I seldom get what I want.

The hallway encounter I'm about to have is a prime example of how even when I'm up, things go down. Abby is hurtling toward me, anger flashing in those gunmetal blue eyes.

I shut my locker right before she gets all up in my face. At least she can't destroy the books, lotion, and USB-light plant I have in there.

"How's Cory Denning doing?" Abby says loudly. "Did your boyfriend read your *interview?*"

I barely stop myself from rolling my eyes. Even *I'm* over the Cory Denning rumor, the whispers that I dated a perfectly nice boy in our class who was even dorkier than me.

After Science Olympiad practice freshman year, Cory showed me his butterfly collection, a bunch of dead things trapped by pins. I lied and told him it was cool. We kissed under a tree, an awkward peck out of pity for one another rather than any romantic interest. I don't think the rumor began because anyone saw us. I think Abby and the POPS zeroed in on the least popular girl and boy in the class before doing their dirty work.

I wonder how he is. He transferred last year.

I don't answer Abby, so she tries something else. She moves closer to me, so close I smell the sickly sweet violet notes in her perfume and we're almost kissing.

I dare her to do it. I'm not attracted to her, per se, but there's a cruel beauty about her that, in this moment, makes me want the crush of her body against mine. Either that, or I'm desperate for human touch after not being kissed for months. I'll go with the latter. I could never be attracted to Abby. We're too different.

"It won't last," Abby whispers to me. "These assholes who think you're hot shit now will drop you in an *instant*. They will drop you for *nothing*. Because you are nothing."

You know the old rhyme about how *sticks and stones may break my bones, but words will never hurt me*? Yeah, that's all lies. Abby's words hurt me because they're *true*. I know the POPS will drop me soon. And every day, every aching second, I feel the weight of not being enough. The weight of being nothing.

I can't breathe. Ican'tIcan'tIcan'tIcan't—

"Abby, what are you doing?"

Abby and I look at each other, then at our interrupter. For once, we wear the same incredulous expression. We know that voice. We know whose best friend that is.

She sure as hell isn't mine.

Kelsey strolls up to us, angelic and crisp in a white

lace dress that belongs on a runway, not a public school on a tight budget. "Leave Carter alone."

Abby's shock is plain. "Huh? Why?"

I share her confusion. Kelsey, the worst of the worst, asking Abby to back off of *me*? This situation is too bizarre for words.

Kelsey ignores her and turns to me. "Hey, are you okay?"

"No?" I say.

Kelsey returns her attention back to Abby. "God, why do you always have to screw with her?" Her, as if I'm not even here. I guess she only spoke to me to prove a point, to make herself look better. Again.

Abby cocks her head to the side. "You mean...like you do? Like you've never participated in hurting her. In hurting *anyone* here."

She's got a point.

Kelsey's voice projects. "You're the one obsessed with her. Obsessed with bullying her. I really should report you."

"You're joking." Abby laughs. A giggle almost escapes me too. What kind of twisted fantasy land am I in now where *Kelsey* snitches on *Abby* for bullying *me*?

Kelsey's face remains hard. "No. I'm not. You should know that by now."

"How could I?"

Abby and Kelsey volley back and forth, a dance of

words that have everything to with each other and their catalogue of issues.

Okay. This is no longer about me.

And people are staring.

I slowly back away, despite not being given leave by either girl. I breathe in, breathe out. Head to my car like I am at all sure of myself, rather than a mess of coiled intestines, my stomach flipping over itself so hard that I feel like I'll throw up.

But I'll try not to show that I'm upset, shaking. I don't like all of this turmoil, though some of the turmoil has worked in my favor.

No one likes a crazy girl.

You are nothing.

By the time I come home from school, my nerves are a little less frayed. Not by much, but it's a start. The bullying wasn't so bad this time. Almost tolerable, even before Kelsey interrupted Abby.

This won't last.

It has to.

I distract myself with homework until my mother returns home from work. Miss Parker assigned an arduous problem set in AP Physics, so I settle in at my desk and plow through it. A quarter of the way through, I realize that the problem set, and the concept itself, isn't as difficult as I'd made it out to be. This happens often; sometimes my brain can't keep up with the speed of my pen. I finish the problem set, jamming to Hozier's *Wasteland, Baby!* as I work. "As It Was" was my song with my ex-boyfriend Hudson, so I skip that track.

Hudson emailed me today, congratulating me on the article. I replied with a perfunctory "thanks!" and "how are you!" We talk occasionally, and more than I'd really like. It's hard to speak to the boy who broke your heart, and, for him, it's hard to speak to the girl who never let you in.

Maybe that's why he picked that Hozier song as the one that defines our relationship. Great. Thanks, tall, brooding, mythically talented Irishman.

Mom's car pulls in as I wrap up my AP Spanish reading. I glance at my watch; it's now almost six PM. Time flies when you're having fun; I've spent nearly five hours on today's homework and some future assignments. I like to get ahead, just in case my depression pulls me under. It happens sometimes, yet I always manage to get back on track. No way am I ceding my class rank because of mental illness.

Despite her demanding job, Mom tries to arrive home around six or seven PM so we can cook and eat dinner together. She believes in some family time, no matter how busy we might be. Either that, or she's making sure I'm still alive. Which, fair. I would, too. Whatever her motivation, it's become a savored part of both of our days. (Of course, sometimes we simply get takeout or throw something in the Instant Pot.)

"How was school today?" Mom asks. She cuts into her flank of steak, which we made with a side of carrots, broccoli, and other vegetables stashed in the freezer.

"It was weird." I give her a rundown of my day, excluding Abby's bullying in the hallway. I do, however, tell her about the POPS trying to befriend me.

"That's strange," Mom agrees. "I thought they thought you were a loser and left you alone after all that business with the principal."

Yes, when Abby, Kelsey, Slater, and Mei got suspended in ninth grade for throwing my textbooks into the toilet. All of our parents were called and the POPS had to write an apology letter to me, buy new textbooks, and suffer through two days of in-school suspension. I don't think the punishment was really about me. It was about the destruction of school property, which will almost always be held above the destruction of human beings.

I shrug. "Maybe they're trying to make a fresh start. Since the article and everything."

Mom glows with pride when I mention the feature. "Someone at my job saw that, by the way. You were in *The Patriot News* today, did I tell you that?"

I nearly gag on a chunk of steak. "Um, wow. No, you didn't." Well. That explains Hudson's email. God knows he's as bad with social media as I am, only logging onto

Twitch, Discord, and Reddit. I doubt my story made it onto any of those platforms.

"I'm glad that your talent's being recognized, baby," Mom says. "You've always worked so hard with school and your app. You deserve to get your due."

I smile, small and proud. "Thanks, Ma."

"And personally, I think it's a good thing if those girls want to do better by you. You've suffered enough at their hands. This could be a new start for you."

I pause. "You know," I say. "I think you're right."

Things have been getting better. Perhaps, for once in my life, they can stay that way.

CHAPTER 14
ABBY

"KELSEY. *KELSEY!*" I half-run after her after she interrupts my tete-a-tete with Carter. The school is quickly clearing out, and Kelsey's headed out the front door. "What the hell was that?"

Kelsey continues to walk out of school, as if my words don't matter to her. "Could you stop making a scene, Abby? You're embarrassing yourself."

"I'm making a—" I shake my head, incredulous. "You're the one who handed my ass to me for Carter! You don't even like her! You called her My Chemical Hoe-mance when she had that emo phase, *remember?*"

Still walking. It's easy for me to follow her, thanks to my rigorous running schedule with Mei. Only, Mei's on the cross-country team and I'm not in any organized sports. "Yes, I remember, and maybe I regret it," Kelsey says. "Haven't you ever done something you wish you hadn't?"

"Not really."

She rolls her eyes. "Typical you. You only do what you want and you don't care about anyone else."

"So do you! That's why we work!" I'm aware that I'm yelling and my heart is pounding and I'm so angry I can barely see. Kelsey's a blur in front of me, a blur of white and gold and pink.

Kelsey pulls me into a corner. My heart thrills, in anger or anticipation, I don't know. Does she want to kiss me or slap me? I don't always know with her. I bet she doesn't always know with me, either. We're both more puzzle than girl, giving each other only enough information to forge silently forward in our tangled situationship.

Once we're a little more alone, she looks me in the eye and says, "Maybe we're not working anymore."

I laugh out of shock rather than actual humor. "Last I checked, April Fools' Day isn't any time soon."

Kelsey looks down and plays with her rose quartz bracelet. Her mother gave it to her to "ward off bad vibes," not realizing that her daughter has the worst vibes known to humanity. "You keep going around hurting whoever you want. I mean, *God,* Abby, what's the point of screwing around with Carter?"

Carter? We're having this conversation over that hot mess of a human being? "Because it's fun?" I say. "Last I checked, you like doing the *exact same things* as me."

"I can change, Abby. I can get better."

"Sure, if you have a reason to. Which you don't—"

The truth hits me like a ton of bricks. No, no, Kelsey does have a reason. It's just not a good one.

"She's popular now," I say. "She's popular, and you want to see how far she can go." I hate this. I hate that she's setting me aside for Carter, even if she's being dramatic and this fight is only temporary.

Yeah, she's told me that we're done before. And a week later, voila! We were friends again. Funny how that works.

Kelsey shrugs. "Is there something wrong with that?"

"Yes!" I scream.

The thing is...I'm a lying, manipulating, wanting bitch, too. But there's this moral center that tells me that a lot of what I do to claw my way to the top is *wrong,* that I could be a better girl.

I just, um, tend to ignore that intuition a lot of the time.

Something tells me that making Carter think she's popular and then dumping her is crueler than anything I've ever done. Knowing your enemy is safe. Not knowing who you can trust is dangerous as all hell. Carter may be the most socially awkward teenager of all time, but she should know that. She has to know that.

Right?

"Shut up, you cu—ugh!" Kelsey snaps, not being able to bring herself to say the word.

"Oh, my! Not the *c word*." I pretend it's a joke despite it being a legit trigger for me. It's what *he* called me the last time he ever saw me, when he approached me in the school parking lot before he ran off like a dog with his tail between his legs. *You ruined my life over a lie, you c—*

That was the day I shoved Carter down the stairs. I couldn't kill, choke, or maim him, but I could do that to her with little to no consequences.

I do regret hurting her like that, though she only ended up with a few bruises and likely psychological damage. I try not to regret much, but that was pretty awful of me.

"Whatever," I say, dismissing Kelsey. "The point is you're leaving me for someone you don't even like. You think Mei and Slater will do the same? That they'll stand by you?"

Secretly, I'm scared they will, that I don't have the power here. I don't know who's going to win this game, because Kelsey and I have always been on the same team with all our ruthlessness.

Now she wants to stand divided.

I still want her.

Kelsey looks at me like I'm the biggest clown in the universe, like she wants to come over and give my clown nose a little honk.

Then she laughs. So loud, so uproarious, that it draws more attention to us than I'd like. Some people dare to inch closer to us. My heart jumpstarts in my cage of a chest.

Yeah. Me, Abby Wallace, not wanting attention. Imagine that, while my heart is being shredded into pieces.

"Slater? *Slater?* She already *did it!*" Kelsey smirks like she knows a big secret that I don't. God, I wish she'd get on with it instead of dragging out my misery. Is that how everyone else, how Carter, feels? Because, fine, it feels like ass.

"What are you talking about?" I ask in a low, raspy tone.

Kelsey pulls out her phone and heads to Carter's link. She zooms in and—

Wait.

You have *got* to be kidding me.

"Your precious Slater was on Carter's side before even I was, Abby. She took the photos for the article."

And that's when I have to leave before I vomit.

I make my way to Mei's car—she's been hiding out because of period cramps, and I've got to know if she knew about all of this too.

Carter Harper, of all people, is stealing my friends away. She found a way to make herself look like the golden girl of Harlow High School and stole Kelsey and Slater away from me in the process. What's next? Her becoming truly popular, rather than the passing fad we all know she is? I have to laugh!

"What's up?" Mei asks. "You look even more pissed off than usual."

I slam her car door shut, even though that makes her mad. I explain what just happened with Carter and Kelsey, leaving out the worst of the breakup. That's too raw a wound to discuss with Mei. Or Slater, if she's even my friend anymore.

"They're both so *annoying*," Mei says.

"Tell me about it," I grumble. I take a hit off her vape and cough slightly. I seldom do drugs but I have to escape this. "She probably only got that interview because she threatened to kill the editor."

This feels good, or at least better than the rotten sweetness that Kelsey's showing. We aren't nice girls. I don't know why she would pretend to suddenly be one unless it's for a delicious prank. We're mean, bad, the ones early 2000s movies warned everyone about and caused a moral panic over. People think girls like me, Kelsey, Mei, and Slater went away, but we only increased our power thanks to social media and the rise of influencers. We are your daughter's biggest nightmare.

"I saw her Prozac once," Mei said. "It's possible."

I pout. More secrets. "You didn't tell me?"

"I didn't tell anyone because I don't *care* about this girl the way you all do," Mei says. Fair point. She'll join in on our antics, but she seldom directs attention at any particular person.

I pause. "We can use that," I whisper. "The Prozac."

"What can we do, though?" Mei says. "If Kelsey says we should leave her alone, I guess we leave her alone."

How can one girl have so much power? No, I won't succumb to Kelsey, especially since she decided to break off our friendship. If she wants to fuck around, so. Will. I.

"We'll leave her alone," I say. "For a little bit."

"And then?"

"Then we destroy her."

CHAPTER 15
CARTER

"IS it true that you wanted to kill Anne Howard, and that's why she transferred schools?"

Standing outside of my locker, I nearly drop my AP Physics and AP English textbooks out of pure shock. "N-no?"

Mei squints her light brown eyes. "Hmm. Your denial sounds fake." She types something on her phone. "Are you sure you didn't do it?"

"Uh...." If I knew what the hell what was going on, maybe I would know what to say. "I have class." I stare slightly past Mei, focusing on two Unfathomably Talented basketball team members punching each other's arms.

"Guess you did want to. Nice, Carter. Real nice," Mei snarls. I focus on the cut of her crisp jeans, perfectly tailored plaid vest, and white, puffy button-down shirt as she flounces away.

I contemplate Mei's ambush on my way to AP Physics class. Why does Mei believe I'm homicidal? Why did she approach me so early in the day? And who is Anne Howard?

I'll shrug this off as the result of Mei drinking whisky before class or something. Day drinking is more plausible than me being a murderess.

Slater's already in AP Physics when I arrive, an empty gaze turned toward the SMARTboard. Weird. The POPS always get to school late, which is why I'm always one of the first to arrive. The less we have to interact, the better. I settle into my normal seat and pull out my copy of *The Coming Plague*. I've become more interested in epidemiology and biostatistics lately.

I'm wrapping up the chapter on drug-resistant bacteria when a shadow hovers above me.

"Carter," Slater whispers.

I peek my head up and offer the smallest of smiles. I wouldn't say we're friends or anything, but I've been able to tolerate her since she helped me with the photos that got me school-famous. So, yes, I can smile at her. Anything else is impossible.

My smile drops when I notice, really notice, Slater's expression. Her hazel eyes are rimmed with red, maybe from crying. Her shoulders shake from rage or sadness. I don't know which since I'm not very good at...people. But even I can tell that something out of the ordinary has happened. Something that clearly has to do with me, because it's not like Slater would come speak to me in homeroom of her own accord.

I squeeze my eyes shut and brace myself.

"I tried to stop them. I'm sorry."

"Stop what?" I ask.

Slater inhales. "I'm dead if you find out." Wow, how ironic, considering I should be the one doing the killing according to Mei. Wait, does this have anything to do with what she said this morning? "Well, uh. Mei found out you're on antidepressants. Abby and Mei are goin' around telling people you're off your meds. And you, um, want to kill Abby because you hate her. *And,* that you drove one of our friends to switch schools." Somewhere in the back of my mind, I wonder why Kelsey and Slater are removing themselves from the narrative. Surely they have something to do with the ruination of Carter Harper.

A wash of ice coats my veins as I absorb Slater's words. A rumor about potential homicide, no matter how ridiculous, is grounds for a psychological evaluation, which could reveal mental health issues I pretend are milder than they are. Not to mention the extremely obvious social implications.

Who would celebrate someone with murder attempts? (Aside from the Dahmer and serial killer stans I've stumbled upon. I try not to think about them.) "Crap," I whisper.

"I'm sorry," Slater says as if she couldn't do anything to stop them. *Too late, too fake, too useless.*

I lay my head on the lab table, the surface hard and cold. My brain fogs with suicidal thoughts, slamming through me at warp speed now that they've been brewing under the surface since the article hit. I can't do this. I can't do this. I. Can't. Do. This.

God, why can't I broadcast this torrent of dark thoughts as proof to the student body that the only person I want to kill is *myself?*

Footsteps echo as students trickle into class before the bell rings. I remain glued to the table. Miss Parker's sneakers squeak in my direction. I internally groan.

"Carter? Are you alright?"

I twist my head and stare into her kind eyes. She's someone who can be trusted. I could tell her what's happening.

Never mind. What good does telling do? I've told several gym teachers about the POPS. They didn't care. I told my mother when the bullying first started happening. She reported it to the school, but the POPS only redoubled their efforts. I told my ex-boyfriend that there were girls who violently hated me. He told me to meditate.

They urge me to *tell, tell, tell,* and I'm still the same broken shell of a girl. It's not like telling elevated my social status or healed my depression. The right people have not listened to me when they could have stopped everything.

I try to blink back my tears. "No," I say. For once, I'm tired of lying about being fine. "But I'll get through this."

Miss Parker sits in the empty seat next to me. "What hurts, honey?"

I almost lose it right then and there. Black women calling me *honey* always makes me feel loved, no matter how wretched my current state is. Yet I go with telling her it's my stomach that hurts, rather than my head, my heart, my resolve to live.

Miss Parker doesn't ask more questions, and excuses me for the rest of class. I hide out in the nurse's office, hoping he doesn't hear my quiet sobs.

You'll be okay. You'll be okay. You'll be okay.

No, I don't think I will. It was bad enough when the POPS bullied me simply for being myself. Now that I've had hope, have seen what bullying looks like? Taking that away from me is plain cruel.

They won. If the plan percolating in my mind is any indication, Abby's gotten what she wants: me out of her life forever, crawling like a dog to some better ending.

No one likes a crazy girl.

This is how a rumor feels.

It's leaving the nurse's station after AP Physics ends and you're finally feeling a bit better, only to hear people in the hall discussing your latest "secret." It's seeing "concerned" notes placed in your locker with the numbers of local psychologists, one of whom writes your prescriptions. It's knowing that even if you had the courage to tell the truth, people prefer believing the lies bored people craft. It's a vicious cycle that lasts for days that drag like weeks that end once a juicier rumor wipes away your false sins.

Unless you're me. A girl people love to hate. A girl no one stands up for. Then the rumors follow you for life. You lose your identity, you lose everything—thanks to people who don't care to separate reality from falsehoods.

I should know. I've been here before, but this the worst it's ever been.

"Try to not kill everybody in AP English, 'kay?" Abby smiles as if she's doing me a favor rather than furthering a rumor.

I'm catching my breath outside the door before my third class begins, hoping for a moment of calm as the rumors swirl around me. *This isn't true, this isn't true, you know these are mostly lies. But they strike too close to the truth,* I scream inside my mind.

"Abby!" Mei says in fake indignation. "Be careful! She's on antipsychotics. Or off? Which one is it, Carter?"

Since when is Prozac an antipsychotic?

"Oh, shut up, Abby," Kelsey snaps. "We know she didn't kill anyone. You're just being a clown."

Huh? Since when does *Kelsey* stand up for me? There was that one time, but still...she must have something else up her sleeve.

"She'll still snap harder than a headband at any moment," Abby cackles.

Mei nods her head, agreeing. "A psycho is a psycho is a psycho."

"Jesus," Slater mutters. But she doesn't stop them. She never does and she never will. Same with the other social sycophants surrounding us, gawking at the scene. No one ever stands up for me. No one cares.

You're not psychotic you're not psychotic—

To them, a mental illness means I might as well be psychotic. There's no nuance or understanding of the differences between depression, anxiety, personality disorders, and every other listing in the Diagnostic and Statistical Manual of Mental Disorders. These plebeians only understand Good and Evil. Suicidal or Homicidal. A Tragedy Worth Saving or An Example of How Our Education System Has Failed Us.

I imagine going into class. Hearing the amplified whispers, thanks to Atkinson's absolute obliviousness. I consider the POPS stalking me after class, making sure I hear the rumors about my "failing mental health" and how I'm "psychotic."

No thanks. I'd rather not deal with any more emotional pain. I'll blame my absence on stomach cramps, an excuse that will hold thanks to my earlier trip to the school nurse. I've done it before, when the bullying grew too vicious for me to bear. I'll do it again and again and again until they stop.

What if they never stop—

I shove open the bathroom door, trying to ignore the catastrophic thoughts hitting a little too close to the surface. Though it smells like literal shit, the room is empty. I switch to mouth-breathing as I fumble through my backpack. There's one thing I can do to calm my torrent of thoughts. That will make me feel something, anything other than the pain the rumors bring.

The final bell rings as I pull out the blade. After cutting and then cleaning up my mess, I exit into the hallway, feeling no better than I did before. The blood-bath in the bathroom was only a momentary distraction. (Don't worry. Nobody was harmed, aside from me. And after all the ways they've hurt me over the years, the POPS should be grateful for that.)

The POPS.

The rumor.

A squeeze in my chest, extra thumps that beg the question: *What have you done? What will you do? What have they done to me? What more can they do?*

That squeeze is what does it.

I slump onto the floor like I did in gym class, only

this time it's different. Hope whooshes out of me. In its place is an acute sense of panic I don't feel often.

When I do, that overwhelming panic takes over my thoughts.

That panic guides me to *su*—

I squeeze my eyes shut, allowing an agonizing flood of memories. Pain licks through my body, as grave as the day I had each traumatic experience.

Mei arrives to middle school with her braces removed and her attitude cold, attached to Kelsey's newly slim hip. Over the summer, she decided to become cool rather than the spelling bee finalist I'd bonded with in fourth grade. Like the dorky headbands she's ditched, she no longer has use for me. She mocks me when I whine about her leaving me, saying "we were never friends." I've been to her house before, so that's a lie. I don't want to make other friends if it means they'll leave, too. I start to shut myself out. I create a Facebook account. The POPS send me friend requests. I accept, which leads to them calling me a wannabe for months on end. I delete my account. After I do, Abby calls me a coward and puts mayonnaise in my soda at lunch. It's disgusting.

More hurt. More awful.

More thoughts of *suici*—

Hudson's mismatched, plush lips twist into a frown as I refuse, yet again, to let him into my head. It's too dark in there, I argue; you'll leave me if you know how depressed I am. In the end, Hudson leaves anyway thanks to my inability to open up more than my legs to him. Now, I'm adrift and alone.

I can't even bring myself to think of the rest of what the POPS and wannabe POPS have done to me. So many instances of harm. So many seemingly tiny things that built me into a shell of a girl with nothing else to give, other than her body to science and whoever's next on organ waiting lists.

Too much. I can't do this anymore. I no longer want to live like this. Death has always been my last resort, hasn't it? I can do it. I *should* do it.

Should I go to my locker? Nah. It only has textbooks the school will take back.

I do want to visit Abby's locker, though. She needs to know this has been the last straw. Everyone should know that though she's not to blame for all of it, she's to blame for my final push toward death.

I rip a sheet of college-lined paper out of my binder. Sitting on the dirty hallway floor, I scrawl out a note to Abby. Thanks to a personalized "ABBY" sign, it's easy to find her locker. I stuff the note between the slots, hoping it floats to the bottom. I doubt she'll find my missive until I'm dead.

To avoid detection by the administrative offices right by the school's front doors, I exit out of a side entrance near the parking lot. I check at the March cold, wishing I'd had the foresight to grab my jacket.

No time now. I hustle to my car, which was my

mom's until I turned sixteen and *oh no Mom, she'll be devastated I can't hurt her and—*

I turn my key in the ignition. No. I'm not going to hesitate. I refuse to back down.

It's time to fix the problem created seventeen years ago.

CHAPTER 16
ABBY

"CAN Carter Harper come to the office? Again, can Carter Harper come to the front office immediately. Thank you."

Carter didn't bother showing up to English, gym, or lunch: what makes them think she'll come to the office? I muse as I walk to the bathroom for a quick make-up/hair/clothing check during lunch.

When I consider Carter today, there's a raw gnawing in the pit of my stomach I'm attempting to ignore. The same feeling of dread I had when *he* entered the guest room. The same feeling I had when my parents told me they were divorcing. The same feeling I had when Caleb, my cheating ex-boyfriend, started dodging my calls and texts.

Something's coming for me, and I may not have the power to stop it.

I distract myself from my coiled insides by reapplying my silky, deep red lipstick. I normally go for a dusty rose color that plays up my blue eyes. Not today. On days I ruin people, I need the security of the color that's both saved and condemned me.

red for power
red for the hunt.
red for rage,
red for the kill.

I check the bathroom mirror to see if the rest of my outfit is intact. Of course it is. Four-inch, strappy black heels that make me taller than Carter by a few inches. Burgundy skinny jeans and a matching crushed-velvet jacket make the outfit school appropriate, while my corset laces like armor around my heart.

I stare at myself some more. My wide eyes, high eyebrows, and ruddy cheeks belong on someone far less in control than me. I'm always in control, except... except for when I'm not.

God, why do I get so weird and worried sometimes? You'd think I'd be less jittery in everyday situations. No, my weird brain likes to be, uh, weird.

I finger-comb my flattened waves, apply a spritz of hairspray and perfume, and straighten my back. "My name is Abby Wallace, and I'm the most extraordinary girl I know." It's my mantra, a tiny influx of strength.

I march to the cafeteria. Wait, I forgot my Biology II

book for this afternoon's class. Resigned, I walk two flights of stairs to my locker. My feet are aching by the time I reach it—today was apparently the wrong day to wear heels.

As I reach for my textbook, I notice a scrap of college-ruled paper on the floor of my locker. Weird. I crouch down to pick it up.

Meanwhile, my biology textbook, halfway off the shelf, falls victim to gravity and bumps me on the shoulder. Thanks to my shock and stilettos, I'm knocked on my ass.

"*Damn it!*" I exclaim.

I slam my locker shut and sit cross-legged on the floor. I open the wrinkled page, smooth it out on my thigh, and read.

Wait. What?

I drop the note to the floor like it's a burning baking pan. I reread the note until the words blur on the page.

This has to be a joke.

I know it isn't.

Suicide notes aren't jokes.

Until they are.

But they're not. They're not.

For a second, I consider leaving it alone. Who am I to decide whether Carter lives or dies? She means nothing to me.

I shake my head. I may be a bitch, but I'm not heartless.

I pull out my AP English notebook and write out the pieces of the puzzle. In my science classes, we learn to apply the scientific method: ask a question, gather facts and conduct research, then create a hypothesis.

Wow, who knew something I learned in school would be applicable to a real-life situation?

WHAT HAPPENED HERE?

- Carter left school at some point between AP English and lunch. It's also possible she left before gym class. Or after?
- Carter didn't mention a method in her note. Considering how sloppily written it is, speed was on her mind. ~~She may have selected a method that's killed her already.~~
- One of the school secretaries made a school-wide announcement asking her to come to the front office. The first announcement was 20-ish minutes ago, the second just several minutes ago.
- She hasn't been located. This means that she's either still alive and safe, still alive and doesn't want to be found, or ~~dead/dying and doesn't want to be found.~~

I reread the note once more. Is there an accidental clue hidden within? No, nothing but weird, chaotic scrawls.

"Where would she go?" I mutter to myself. I tap the pen against my chin and try to use my deductive reasoning skills. If I were irreparably traumatized, where would I escape to?

Well, I can answer that one. After the—*everything*— all I wanted to do was go home. Maybe that's what Carter's doing, too.

It's the best lead I've got.

I call Slater. "Where'd you go?" she asks. Her voice is muffled, like she's eating chips. "Hey, I know y'all aren't friends, but have you seen Ca—?"

I cut her off as I run out of school. A teacher shouts after me. I wouldn't care about leaving in the middle of the school day even if this weren't a life or death situation. "If I'm not back or call you in an hour, activate Find My Friends and call the police. I know I sound loopy, but trust me on this one." I hang up. My phone continues to vibrate as Slater incessantly calls back. I've set off the fire alarm, knowing she would be looking for a good reason for me to have pulled it.

There's too much for me to do to ease her concerns. I have to figure out where Carter is, de-escalate if I can find her, call the school so they can call her mom if I can't find her, explain the whole situation to my parents, warn my friends about what's going down....

At least Slater knowing something is wrong is a tiny

bit of insurance that, if something bad happens or if Carter attacks me, somebody will know to call the cops.

Though maybe I shouldn't call the cops on Carter. They don't have the best track record with Black people under duress.

But, this is an actual emergency, and I know she could be dead. I need all the help I can get.

I drive home as fast as possible, ready to hunt for Carter and *oh man she could be dead this is my fault.*

Of course, it's up to the girl who helped destroy Carter to save her. Of. Course. I'd laugh at the irony if the joke, for once, wasn't on me.

Carter's car is parked in front of her house. Hope surges through me.

Time to ruin Carter's life one last time. Only this wasn't what I'd envisioned when I told Mei I'd do that.

You got your wish, didn't you, Abby?

CHAPTER 17
ABBY

SPOTS OF BLOOD remain on my corset, on my jeans, on my hands and forearms. I stare at them, trying not to freak out. I already gave up on my velvet jacket, which I took off once I realized how fast my heart was racing, how constricted I felt.

Despite the tightness in my muscles, I never thought about taking the corset off, so now I look like a zombie stripper. Not to mention the blood bringing back memories of my worst nightmare coming to life. I want it all off of me. I fear that if I pull a Lady Macbeth and scream about *blood, blood, BLOOD ON MY HANDS,* I'll end up in the psych ward, so I'm keeping quiet.

I'm lucky enough to be able to go home. I've been deemed a neutral party in Carter's suicide, though I still had to suffer through a long interrogation about the events leading up to it. Mother was by my side, being surprisingly helpful as she advised me what to answer and what to not say unless I had a lawyer present. Unfortunately for all involved, our family lawyer is now in California.

I haven't told Daddy, and I have no idea how he'll react. There isn't much *to* tell, since I don't even know if Carter's alive. The police cited confidentiality when I begged them to tell me.

Useless. There's a reason why I didn't tell the police about *him*. They would've asked too many questions that I didn't want to answer. And that was *if* they believed me—yet another woman with yet another tale from yet another too-powerful man.

After finding Carter, I called Slater after school ended and asked her to drive me to the hospital. It's not like I can drive myself—I'm too freaked out by what I saw—and Kelsey and Mei can't be trusted to not spread rumors. Also, I've spent too much time with my mother today and she's not the most comforting presence. Her version of soothing after the interrogation was saying, "You're not getting arrested, that's good. And Carter sounds like a little bitch—she can't even handle a little talk, a little rumor. You didn't see me slitting my wrists in college when people said I had a threesome with two boys from my ConnLaw class. As if either of them could handle me."

I booked it the second Slater's car pulled up.

"You good?" Each time Slater gets a chance, she glances over from the driver's seat. Her head twitches back-and-forth like a marionette, a little too reminiscent of the scene I witnessed mere hours ago.

"No," I whisper. My throat is hoarse from recounting the story of Carter's overdose. In another situation, Mei and I would connect the puzzle pieces together to spread a delicious story amongst our friends. I ache in a way I haven't since—

"Figures. Still needed to ask."

I can barely move my lips enough to say, "Okay." I slump in the leather seat, more useless than my screams when—

> two years ago, it was my blood
> my hurt written on the sheets.
> today, it was hers, written on the
> walls.

She asked why the hell I was there and her body convulsed so I called 9-1-1 and she said fuck you and I said it back before regretting it and she sputtered out something about A LOT OF PROZAC and she laughed maniacally and grabbed a knife to plunge into her heart so I stopped her and the knife hit her forearm and now there's dried blood on me and she passed out and—

> now there is blood
> blood
> and more blood

because I am the leech who
sucked the life out of carter

"You did the right thing." Slater turns to me at a stoplight. Her fuzzy eyebrows are furrowed, and her obsidian hair is falling all over the place. I tuck a lock of her hair behind her ear. I need to control something. A ghost of a smile plays on her lips. This isn't the time to be homoerotic, but I'll be damned if I don't take comfort where I can get it.

"Before or after I caused all this?" I ask.

"You didn't." Slater's voice wavers, the way it does when she's lying to herself.

"Her note was pretty clear about the four girls who were to blame."

"She gave you her...suicide note?" Slater asks. She draws back her plush lip. Bites it. I stare, unsure of what else to focus my eyes on.

"Yeah." I squeeze my eyes shut until all I see is black and white and purple and blue dancing on my eyelids. I don't even know where the note is. Probably sitting in a pool of Carter's blood. "I almost killed her. *We* almost killed her." I will not shoulder this blame alone. Not this time.

Slater doesn't try to refute me again. We drive in silence until she navigates through the maze-like hospital visitors' parking lot.

"Y'know, I believe in fate," Slater says as she slams

the car door shut. "You moved from New York City to Harrisburg for whatever reason. And Carter wrote that note for another reason. You found it in time for yet another reason."

"Slater. I adore you. Which means you'll understand me when I say, shut up."

"I'm not helping?"

"No."

Slater sighs. "Alright, alright, new method. Come here." Slater opens her arms, clad in her signature honey-colored motorcycle jacket.

Dammit, the tears are coming. I suppose the Harrisburg Hospital parking garage isn't the least-dignified place I've shed tears. I accept Slater's hug, and my nose fills with notes of her citrus perfume.

Now that I've unleashed my vulnerability, I can't lock it back in, and she sops up my mess of tears and snot. Gross. But this is Slater. She's the safest person to cry in front of, a fact I should not know.

I accidentally broke down in front of her in the aftermath of *him*. She demanded to know why I'd shoved Carter down the stairs, which earned me a two-week suspension. Slater kept hounding me and hounding me until the whole story spilled out and so did the tears.

Though she could have traded in my secret for clout with Kelsey and Mei, Slater kept it. Even better, she hasn't brought it up since, though I know she'd like to. She's likely waiting for me to speak up.

> but how can i speak
> when, once again, i freeze every
> time i try?

I'm sick of crying. All my ugly weeping won't ease the burden of pain within me. I need the tool I use to evaluate life's situations and turn imperfections into magnificence.

Writing poetry.

I plop myself on the hard concrete next to Slater's car.

"Way to get an ass bruise," Slater says. She sits on the ground next to me, far more gently than I did.

I rummage through my Betsey Johnson, searching through the disorganized satchel for my Moleskine and pen. "I've had worse."

I pour my heart into the pages of my Moleskine, torn from months of use and dozens of poems spilled. After minor edits and some missteps in language, the poem is ready to go. If only I could say the same for myself.

"I'm Abigail Wallace," I mumble before nudging a half-asleep Slater with my heel. "You. Come. Now."

"Hmph? That's what she—hey!" Slater exclaims as I yank her arm.

"Come on."

"Someone's in a better mood all of a sudden," she says as we walk inside the hospital and to the elevator. "What's up with that?"

"My mood's faker than Ms. Hampshire's boobs," I say. An elderly couple trapped in the elevators with us gives us a double take. "I feel like a piece of garbage that got run over by a garbage truck."

As we weave through the labyrinth-like halls, I'm remembering the last time I went to a hospital. The day after it happened, I lied to *his* wife about having bad stomach cramps. I lost my nerve as we waited in the ER for two hours. I told Mrs. Gregory that I would suck it up and buy some ibuprofen. Instead, when she drove me to a drugstore, I bought Plan B. She learned what happened, anyway. Weeks later, Mrs. Gregory broke down crying on the porch, begging for forgiveness for an act of violence that was not her fault.

I don't know what happened to her. They moved to separate cities after their inevitable divorce. Though Daddy knows where to, I haven't bothered to ask.

"Abby?" Slater asks. I don't even realize I've stopped walking until my friend calls me back to life. "*Abby.*"

"Huh?"

"We're here."

We've reached the nurse's station. I blink, slow and muddling, as Slater explains why we're here. We're immediately shut down by a firm yet kind Korean lady, who tells us to please contact a family member if we would like to see the patient.

The patient. Clinical and detached. I know she has to be professional, but Carter's more than a *patient.* She's a human being, though she hasn't often been treated like one. By me, mostly.

God, I wish I could take it all back.

I return my attention to Slater, who's furrowing her brows. "Okay, Plan B is we find out what wing she's in and break into her room. We can find a cute nurse and—"

"Abby? Abby Wallace?"

I curse under my breath. Who knows me here? I'm used to being recognized at school, not in hospital waiting areas. I plaster on a fake smile. Despite my current distress, I'll be damned if I don't look dazzling. I spin around on my heels (yes, I'm still wearing the cursed things), prepared to greet my admirer.

My smile drops. She's not an admirer. She's a nightmare, a reminder of all I'd wish to forget.

Carter is the near-spitting image of her mother. Carter is a shade or two lighter and has ombré, midnight blue hair instead of layers of deep brown. Also, her mother is stunning, while Carter maybe could be if she put some effort into her looks.

The girl is ~~dying dead~~ something and you're roasting her? Nice.

"Yes. I'm Abby Wallace." My name in my mouth

tastes sour. It sounds all wrong. I should be saying, *Hello, I'm Abigail Carolyn Wallace, and I'm a murderer.*

"I thought so," Carter's mother says. Her voice is thick with unshed tears. Nothing like the strong, crisp tone I remember from the time Kelsey and my bullying landed us in the principal's office. "You look the same."

I shouldn't appear any different, aside from my runny makeup. It's only been two years since we threw a dead frog at Carter in Honors Biology class. Predictably, she cried. Unpredictably, our teacher intervened and sent Kelsey and me to Principal Adams.

"Thank you." I have zero clue what else to say. *Sorry I almost killed your daughter, but I love your kitten heels?* Or perhaps, *Hey, is Carter dead?*

"I suppose you're welcome," Carter's mother says. "Why are you here?" She hugs herself for comfort. Sigh. Her daughter could comfort her, if she hadn't tried to off herself.

My fault.

"We wanted to visit her. Or at least find out about her condition," Slater says. "We're...so sorry about your daughter, ma'am."

"Weren't you at the National Honor Society induction this year?" Carter's mother shakes her head. "Never mind, I don't care about any of that right now. Anyway, you can't visit Carter. Even if I wanted you to, there's no point. She's still in a coma. She had serotonin syndrome. Has. Has serotonin syndrome. The doctors said if all goes well, she'll awaken." Her voice cracks on the last word.

"We heard that if you speak to coma patients, they might wake up." My voice shakes. I'm not often intimidated, but this angry parent in a power pantsuit does the trick. "I know you and Carter hate me. You have every right to. But we wanted to—we need to try."

Carter's mother stares at Slater and me, searching for malicious intent. She won't find it, because for once I'm being sincere. She crosses her arms. "No."

My heart deflates. I understand why Carter's mom pushed back, of course. I just...

Something creeps up my throat, a feeling like I'll drown, and *I can't do this* and I—

"I'm sorry. I have to go," I blurt. I haul ass into the nearest bathroom, hoping to outrun my fears. My demons catch up to me at the most unfortunate times.

Slater doesn't follow me in. I resent and love her for that.

"I can do this," I whisper. "I can do this. *He* isn't here. *He's* gone."

"What's wrong with her?" Carter's mother says. Her voice is muffled on the other side of the bathroom door.

"She...has issues with hospitals," Slater says.

"This isn't me; this isn't me," I murmur. I scroll through my phone for the BRAIN/ZAPP app. (I had it downloaded way before I knew Carter created it, okay?) I pull up the section matching my current need, a guided breathing tool. I match my breaths to the slowly growing and shrinking circle.

I can do this. Breathe in. *I should do this.* Breathe out.

I turn my phone off Do Not Disturb, which has been on since I entered the police station. I regret the decision once I see the barrage of texts and missed calls from Kelsey and Mei.

KELSEY

what happened slater told me
you sounded weird on the phone.

KELSEY

slater's not answering either and
you're both acting super weird

KELSEY

just tell me if you're okay.

KELSEY

abby are you okay??? i need to know
that you're okay. i know we're fighting, but…
i still love you.

MEI

Can you PLEASE text Kelsey back

she's at my house, ranting to
me and my mom, and pacing back and forth

MEI
(Also, hope you're okay)

ABBY
I'm alive lol
Family emergency, long story.

I sigh. I hope Slater can create some kind of excuse because I'm so not in the mood.

Slater knocks on the door. "Abby—"

"One SECOND," I snap. I stare at myself in the mirror, drink in the wretched fear in my watering eyes. I'm not me. I'm a monster, and for once in my life, I want to be less feared. Less fearsome.

"My name is Abby Wallace," I whisper. "And I am not ruined."

Too bad I already feel myself coming undone.

CHAPTER 18
CARTER

I DON'T KNOW what day it is.

I haven't known the exact date since Abby barged into my life and ruined my death. Thanks to a rare onset of serotonin syndrome, I was close to clocking out forever. The doctors told me it's a "miracle" that I'm alive.

I don't know what day it is when my hospital roommate wakes me up with screaming due to her nightmares. I'm almost grateful that she does. My dreams center on the days that should have been a homegoing rather than a homecoming.

I don't know what day it is when I get more bloodwork taken, followed by a five-minute shower with a counselor's foot in the door, my first cleansing since I got here. It doesn't feel good. The water pressure doesn't scrape away the leftover blood, blood the nurses claim they can't see but I know is there.

I don't know what day it is when I begin my next round of bland breakfast, paired with an SNRI that my new psychiatrist thinks could work. Aside from mild nausea Psychiatrist #4 promises will go away, this new medication doesn't seem as bad as the Prozac. Apparently, nothing's as bad for my body as the Prozac was; the psych thinks it's part of why my brain was so fried at the time of my near-death. Why I made so many strange decisions, from quitting therapy to my popularity plan to, well, stabbing myself.

I can't disagree. But I do know that, Prozac or not, I did not and do not wish to live. This new medication won't matter.

"I don't know what day it is," I say during the weekly community meeting when the counselor asks how I am. I don't mean to say it. I don't mean to care about this, this small thing that could help me realize how long I have been here. How long I've been trapped in a psychiatric hospital I was involuntarily admitted to.

The group counselor taps the whiteboard where, sure enough, today's date is listed. I don't know how I didn't see. "Carter, do you feel ready to speak in group?"

I curl into a ball. *No.*

I don't know how to get better. I never have. My version of better is being dead.

I was so close.

"What do you call a can opener that doesn't work?"

I stare blankly at my mother. I did this to her, the new bags under her eyes, the frizzy weave, the worry lines that prove that Black, when under duress, can indeed crack.

"What do you call it?" My voice doesn't sound the same, either. Lifeless. But not dead, which was the goal.

I was so close.

"A can't opener!" Mom cracks herself up. "Get it? Because it can't open anything!"

I almost pretend to laugh before coming to a disturbing realization. I'm the can't opener. I can't open up, can't pretend to want to live anymore, can't do anything right.

I was so close.

"Alright, that one was corny. Are you keeping up with your classwork?"

This should create a spark. Academics make me happy. Or they did. I lower my head a bit more. "No," I say. Shame drips from my voice.

Mom rests her hand on mine.

I was so close.

"Don't worry about it, baby," she says in a voice that should be soothing. Why isn't it soothing anymore? Why can't she reach me? "You don't have to catch up just now. Or at all. Only if you want to. The school told me that since you have such a good track record, you can miss all this class and still graduate." She chuckles. "I couldn't get away with that, not with my whack high school grades."

Mom went to the University of Pennsylvania. Her grades couldn't have been bad. She's trying to make me feel better. Because I'm the broken one.

We are better than this. We are united by love, strength, and mutual appreciation. I want to tell her that I'd like to engage with her beyond one-word answers, but I can't do it.

I was so close.

"I met with the school today. Aside from me cursing them out, it went well."

I find it in me to crack a smile.

"You can come back whenever you want to and won't be punished for missing so much school. You'll be required to see the guidance counselor once a week, which I agree is a nice first step. I'm working on securing an appointment with a new psychologist and psychiatrist, since your old ones didn't do anything except land you in here."

Though they tried their best, they could not treat a silent girl.

"They switched around your classes. You won't be placed with Abby, Kelsey, and Mei. Abby told me in the hospital that it would be best." Mom grimaces. "Those girls didn't do anything to hurt you again, right?"

Mom doesn't know about the rumor?

"No," I say in my Dead Girl Voice. "Nothing happened." Aside from Abby saving my life, which comes back in flashes. I'm trying to block it out because it's not only traumatic: it's absurdist.

Mom lets out a small sigh. "Just 'cause Harlow said everything will be fine doesn't mean we can't consider switching schools. We can look into private or cyber—"

"NO!" A roar tears out of me, unprompted and unwanted.

The other patients and their loved ones stare quizzically before resuming their own conversations. I cringe, waiting for Mom's reaction to my disrespect. Normally, I would get the life snatched out of me for snapping at her. Today? I get a concerned "Carter? Honey, what happened? Tell me what's wrong."

This is our new normal, and I can't deal with being near the wreck I've created.

I can't tell Mom that letting those girls chase me out of school would make me feel like more of a failure. That at least I have my teachers, who push me to be better. That I only have one and a half years until graduation. Better yet, I'll die before graduation because this hospital stay has not changed my mind.

I can't.

I. Can't. Do. Anything.

"I'm...going to go," I whisper. I leave my mother behind, wading back to my bedroom. My roommate isn't back from visiting hours yet. I can shut the light off, hug my comforter from home, and scream into my pillow.

I was so close.

My suffering was almost over.

CHAPTER 19
ABBY

MEI SLAMS her Smartwater on our lunch table. "You need an intervention."

Through clouded eyes, I look up. "Who needs an intervention?" Vaguely, I wonder why she's over here, rather than with Kelsey. Slater and I have camped out toward the edge of the cafeteria since Carter's suicide attempt, avoiding Kelsey and Mei and the questions they'll surely have about Carter's absence. Battle lines haven't officially been drawn, but this is close enough. Our friendships can overlap for only so long now that Kelsey and I are over.

"You, Abigail Wallace." Mei sits down, smushed in the booth next to Slater. "Even Kelsey's concerned about you and she doesn't like you anymore."

My gaze drifts over to Kelsey, seated at the table where I actually belong, not this random booth toward the edge of the cafeteria.

"Kelsey's opinion...does not matter," I lie.

"Well, mine still does," Mei says. "You've been weird since Carter tried to...you know...bite the dust." Mei's voice grows so low I have trouble hearing her.

My eyes widen. I certainly didn't tell Mei about the suicide attempt. I haven't told anyone except my parents and....oh, come *on*.

"Slater." I groan. "Why did you tell her? No offense, Mei. I just know you can't keep secrets, especially from Kelsey."

Mei shrugs. "You're not wrong."

Slater's face flushes a deep scarlet that maps itself all over her face, neck, and the top of her chest. "I...it was an accident...I didn't...we were texting and...."

I frown. "Thanks for that."

"I'm sorry," Slater says.

I ignore her. No one's safe, are they? People constantly betray each other. It's embarrassing, really. And this was something really, really important, the second-most important secret I've ever kept.

"Mei," I say. "Do *not* tell Kelsey. I will literally kill you, *tell everyone about the blush brush,* if you tell Kelsey."

Mei thrusts her hands out, as if telling me to stop. "We don't have to use the blush brush threat." Mei's referring to the time we all got drunk on wine coolers and she admitted to masturbating with the rounded edge of a blush brush one time out of sheer desperation. "It was not," she said, "a satisfactory experience."

"Just promise. *Please.*" My voice cracks. *I can't hurt Carter anymore. I can't kill her again. Telling Kelsey means certain death.*

"I don't care enough to tell Kelsey," Mei says.

She's lying. I can tell by the shift of her eyes to the left, a tell I learned when we played non-nude strip poker with some of our guy friends once. Well, Mei and Kelsey played strip poker. I played poker, but insisted on my clothes staying on. Better be a rumored frigid bitch than have a panic attack in the middle of a game.

People talk a lot of shit about being popular. In reality, my social status is—or was—credit toward a better existence. The goal of high school is survival, and it's not like all of us will make it out alive. I'm doing my best with what I have, and if people don't like it, whatever. Play stupid games, win stupid prizes, and fleeting popularity might be the stupidest game out there. Once you lose it, you've lost everything.

I scratch my hair. It lays limp and greasy from not being washed since Carter's suicide attempt. When I look in the mirror, my dark blue eyes are marred by puffy lids and streaks of red.

"Mei, why are you here?" I ask. I know she said I need an "intervention" or something, but really, I'm fine. Aside from the aforementioned physical defects, of course. Oh, and—

"You're wearing sweatpants," Mei says. "Which, as we all remember, you said we don't wear in public because they're for—"

"—Basic girls who want to pretend that they're cool, but we are cool, so we don't need them," I quote myself. I wave my hand at Mei. "Yeah, yeah, I got it. So what? They're comfortable. They have pockets. They make my ass look great."

"No, they don't," Mei and Slater say in unison.

"Oh." I frown, wondering what else my mirror has lied to me about lately. More than ever, swing between thinking I'm too thin, too fat, too much, not enough. I can typically be confident, but my self-esteem dips sometimes like any other girl.

> you never grow used to
> the mirror shouting obscenities
>   at
> the body you are trying to love.

"To be fair, it is kind of concerning, Abs," Slater says. Trying to play the diplomat, as usual.

"I don't have a problem," I repeat. It's sorta true. I'm not the one at a psychiatric hospital.

"That's what someone with a problem would say," Mei singsongs. Not much fazes Mei. She and Slater's cool, rational thinking have extracted us from many unpleasant situations.

145

Kelsey and I were a smoldering fire, ready to combust at any slight.

I miss that. I miss *her*.

After school, I can't help but think of Carter again.

Keeping the secret of her suicide attempt is destroying me. I'm sure that pain goes double for her. Carter's a loser who doesn't have friends to turn to. At least, when *he* happened, I knew I could turn to my friends if I allowed them in. Carter probably has her mom, who knows half the truth.

I consider the last time I didn't tell my mother a secret.

> the secret ate me alive
> until i gathered the strength
> the strength, to tell.

I step outside. The frigid March air reaches past my skin and into my bones. I'm more of a summer girl, myself.

Carter's car is in the driveway. Her mother's is not. I sit on my porch, waiting for her to return. I know what I have to do now.

Tell the truth.

I'm not very good at that.

Visitors would never know this neighborhood is scarred with violence. The large, tastefully colored homes contain the secrets of the inhabitants within them. Every secret, that is, except for mine. And, depending on how many people saw the ambulance three weeks ago, Carter's.

Am I doing the right thing? I know Carter's mother, Ms. Ashley, doesn't know about the rumor leading to her daughter's suicide attempt. If she did, Kelsey, Mei, and I would have been punished for our role in it. Our rumor-starting wasn't under the radar this time.

Ms. Ashley's car careens into her well-paved driveway. I march over to their house.

"Abby?" Ms. Ashley is carrying groceries, some of which I grab from her. "Uh-kay, thanks. What's going on?"

"There's something I need to tell you," I say. "Something I should have said three weeks ago. It's about Carter. I know why she took those pills."

CHAPTER 20
CARTER

"GUIDE yourself into the Warrior II pose. Point your dominant foot toward the front of your mat. Bend your knees slightly. Ground your body, rooting your feet to the earth. Steady yourself in this position, taking the time to tap into your body's unique rhythm. When you're ready, sweep your arms out to your sides.

"Face your dominant foot without twisting your body, only your head. Focus on a focal point beyond you and soften your gaze. Feel this moment. Feel your body working to support you. Know that you are loved. Understand that you possess the tools you need to succeed in your journey toward recovery."

Though I'm unsteady at first, I get the hang of what the soothing voice is telling me soon enough. This is trauma-informed yoga, not Calculus III (which, despite the hype, isn't hard). I press my feet into my black yoga mat and do as the yoga podcaster, Ophelia, tells me.

I was released from Winterwood Psychiatric Hospital a few days ago into a partial hospitalization program closer to home. This program is as annoying and boring as Winterwood. Recovery isn't the place for me, Little Miss Suicidal.

The one highlight of inpatient was discovering that yoga is pretty dope. It's the one thing I've been forced to try that gets me out of my own mind and into a place of inner calm. In inpatient, we had daily ten-minute stretching sessions and tri-weekly therapeutic yoga sessions. I'll continue my newfound yoga habit until I die or get bored. I know which one I'd bet on.

Transitioning my therapeutic yoga practice to my home was easy. Rather than attend a class full of sweaty suburban moms, I subscribed to a yoga audio service, courtesy of my BRAIN/ZAPP company credit card (in Mom's name but funded with my cash). I feel kind of bad using my app earnings right now, since I haven't even patched bugs myself for weeks, leaving that to the developer in Singapore I hired to take care of urgent fixes while I'm asleep. I've given her temporary, full-time responsibility of the app as I "recover."

Mom was ecstatic that I found something else I loved. She went all out, buying me three plush yoga mats; yoga blocks; cute yoga outfits that actually fit my plus-size body; an aromatherapy diffuser with "essential oils" that her best friend sells as part of her latest MLM scam; and texting me a ton of YouTube yoga videos.

It's depressing, seeing how hard she's going to guarantee my recovery. I don't bother to tell her there's no reason to believe in me. I stopped believing in myself so long ago that I don't know what believing in myself looks like. How can I break my mother's heart by telling her?

You almost did when you tried to die by suicide, Rational Carter says. She's the "reasonable" voice that tries to drown out my depressive thoughts. She annoys me.

The living room door opens. Great, time to pretend some more. I shut off my yoga audio and the aromatherapy diffuser exuding the woodsy, slightly tangy smell of frankincense. I complete a final sun salutation and Savasana.

Calm. Peace.

Until Abby's voice reaches me.

"I know running is hard on your joints, but honestly? I prefer it to other exercise. Outrunning bad things sounds good to me," Abby says.

I skitter back from my bedroom door when it hits me that she's here. The girl I loathe, sitting around with the mother I love. Sucking up to her by talking about my mom's treadmill.

"Girl, you're too young to even think about your joints. Talk to me when you're thirty-four. Pass me the bottle of olive oil, will you?"

Olive oil? I wrack my brain for a context in which

this conversation makes sense. Olive oil. Groceries. Right. Mom was going grocery shopping. She asked for me to go with her, and I told her I would rather nap.

Big mistake. If I were with Mom, surely Abby never would have approached her. Yes, Mom told me Abby tried to visit me in the hospital. I don't think it was Abby; it had to be someone else. Mom was mad with grief in the hospital; how could she remember faces, names, conversations?

But at that time, who else knew you were dying? What other girl would have tried to make amends for crimes Abby and the POPS committed? This only scratches the surface of the questions on my mind. Did Mom see Abby on her way home? Did she give her a ride from the store? Why is Abby helping my mother? Why did Mom let her in our house?

I didn't tell Mom the reasoning behind my suicide attempt. All she and my therapists at Winterwood know is that I, not in my right mind, left Abby a note in her locker condemning her for past actions. They don't know the rest of it. The rumor, the abuse that continued longer than I said it did, the involvement of the other POPS.

It's better this way. If the school assumes the POPS have no ultimate responsibility for my suicide attempt, there won't be an investigation. Investigations mean questions I don't want to answer, parts of my mind I don't want unlocked, punishments that will lead to even greater retaliation. I'll be real: as a Black woman, I don't have much, if any, faith in the criminal justice system. Or in my school system. Not when some teachers *saw* the bullying in middle school and did nothing to save me save the occasional write-up. Not when the solution to what I said in the *Teen Vogue* article was a quick chat in the principal's office and an anti-bullying assembly full of sad-ass PowerPoint slides.

And if Mom found out the truth...I shudder at the thought before tuning back into the conversation. I tiptoe to the staircase to see Mom and Abby sitting at our kitchen island. I have a full view of Abby. Her hair is droopy, she's not wearing much (if any) makeup, and she's wearing cozy-looking leggings and a sweatshirt rather than a short skirt or a designer bag.

She looks like a normal person. Appearance doesn't matter as much as the POPS believe it does. I've never gotten their schtick. They're smart, talented, and moti- vated. Who hurt them so bad that they decided to use their talents to hurt people instead of, I don't know, improving society?

It's not like you're doing that, my Asshole Voice sneers. *You're a drain on everyone around you. You're not even updating your own app anymore!* I smile in relief at my ~~toxic~~ normal thought pattern.

"Thanks for helping out. Carter's still asleep," Mom says.

Abby spins her coffee mug, filled with tea since

nobody in our household drinks that trash. "How...is she?"

Like you care. You only saved my life because of moral obligation. Anyone who knew of it would have stopped my suicide attempt due to sheer compulsion.

Don't act like you care now when you are the reason I was dying in the hospital bed.

"A hell of a lot better. She's been receiving different treatments, and she'll be back at school next week." I roll my eyes. Black moms will forever tell all your business to people they don't even know like that. "I thought I'd lost her again in the psychiatric hospital. She was resentful at first. But she got better. I can see it. I don't know if the attempt woke her up, or if it's the meds, or new therapists. It's somethin'. I'm glad there's something there now."

I grimace, hearing the hope in her voice. There's no way I've been laying on my Happy Carter act this thick. *Unless your treatments are helping,* Rational Carter says. I dismiss that thought. There's no way that, after all these years of hopelessness, three weeks of intensive mental health treatment have helped teach me how to deal with my problems.

"I don't know why I'm telling you all this. I shouldn't," Mom says before taking a quick sip of tea. "I think it's 'cause, in a way, you were there for my baby when I couldn't be. I do wish I had let you see her in the hospital...I was so angry that it clouded my judgment."

153

Abby isn't good, Mom. You can stop treating her like she's a girl when she's a monster.

There's a measured silence. Abby looks nervous as hell. Since when does she get nervous?

Why is she in my house?

"I wasn't there for her," Abby whispers. I have to lean over the handrail to catch what she's saying. "Ms. Ashley, I don't think you know why Carter...why she did this. If you did, things would have happened that, um, haven't happened."

"What do you mean?"

Another long pause. "On the morning Carter...we started a rumor. Mei and I. A really bad one. Kelsey and Slater were being nice and..."

Mom leans back in her chair. "Another rumor? Thought y'all stopped bothering after the whole business with the frog."

Miss Parker reported the bullying once. She's the only person who had the balls to stand up to the POPS, and I love her for that. Abby got two days of detention for throwing a dead frog at me during dissections. Thankfully she hadn't sliced into the poor thing yet, so guts didn't get all over me. Only formaldehyde. *Ribbit, ribbit"* followed me in the hallway for weeks after, and the POPS redoubled their efforts to bully me as punishment for getting them in trouble.

Abby looks into the tea as if she wishes she could disappear. "We never stopped hurting her."

"Bullying." Mom's voice is no longer cordial. She hardens, ready to protect me.

"Teasing, mostly." Abby's voice isn't at her typical level of boisterous; she's smaller, cowed by my mother's inquiries.

"Bullying. The social, verbal, emotional, and/or physical harm of a socially inferior individual." With a daughter like me, Mom had to memorize that definition long ago.

Abby shrinks back in her chair a bit. "Oh. Then I guess it was bullying."

"Hmph. I'd like to know more about this little rumor of yours. What was it about?" Mom's tone is boardroom-commanding, the same method she uses when gaining respect from an adversary at work. Her voice is steady. She's controlling herself, so she doesn't lash out.

Oh, no. Abby's about to sell herself out and blow the lid on my lies. *Stop, stop, stop!* Abby opens her glossed-up mouth despite my internal protests. "Mei found out about Carter's, uh, meds and it got out of control. We told people Carter was a psycho, but she was taking pills to control it. People took it from there."

No, you *took it from there. You pushed and pushed me until I broke.*

I grip the railing, knuckles growing taut.

"And this incident almost took my daughter's life." My mother puts her head in her hands.

"I'm so sorry, I was feeling guilty and—"

Mom snaps her head up. "Oh, now you're guilty? You motherfu—"

As I lean on the railing, my foot lands wrong. I slide on my butt down the stairs for what feels like an endless period of time.

"Carter? Carter!" Mom rushes to my side. "Are you okay? Are you concussed?"

I don't believe I hit my head. Just my ass, thighs, and pride. "Nah, it's good." I try to play it off, like I didn't hear their train wreck of a conversation.

Abby reaches her hand toward me. She inches closer and closer. Would she hit me in front of Mom?

Panicking, I make my second screwup of the day. "DON'T TOUCH ME!" I scream at Abby. I should cower, knowing I'll pay for my anger toward her. But since the attempt, I care less and less about so many things that meant the world to me.

"I should go," Abby whispers.

"You should," I say. My body's twitching again, in the familiar way it did when I attempted suicide.

Drugs aren't inundating me this time. It's rage.

Abby slips out of my house. I double-lock the front door so she can't return to wreak more havoc. She's wrought enough for a lifetime.

"You sure you're okay?" Mom asks. She's still next to me on the floor.

I nod. "See? Couldn't do that if I had a concussion."

"Yes, you could. Smartass." Her face sobers. "Did you hear us?"

No point denying it now. "Yes."

Mom pauses before asking her next question, hesitant. "Is what Abby said to me true?"

I stare at the ground. Wow, our hardwood floors sure are interesting.

"Carter."

One plank, two planks, three planks counted....

"Carter Ashley Harper."

Oh, shit, she full named me. I inhale, using my belly and chest to aid the deep breath. "She didn't lie. All of that...it happened."

Mom closes her eyes and murmurs something. It sounds like a prayer. "These girls have been bullying you for years? Even after you told me it stopped?"

"Years," I confirm. "I'm so—"

"You are not the one who needs to apologize," Mom says. She grits her teeth. "Every bruise I saw. Those were from Abigail Wallace?"

"Yes." I squeeze my eyes shut.

"When you came home crying sometimes, that wasn't from school stress?"

"No."

"And the scars. Carter, your *scars*. She gave you those?"

I rub the self-harm scars marring my left forearm. "In a way."

"What you're telling me is, you lied to me for two years of your life."

I lower my lids once more. "Yes."

Mom sinks further to the floor. The local news plays as background to this conversation. I've seen my mother cry before, notably when her mother passed away five years ago, and her father the year after that. But this waterfall is a special kind of torture. I know she's crying because she cannot make me better. If she could, she would pour every resource into healing me. But she can't, even though she's my mother. And it's all my fault.

"Mom," I whisper. I hold her. She clings to me.

"Don't go, baby," she begs me. "Don't leave this Earth. You're loved. I swear you're loved. Don't leave."

"I won't," I lie. *I could fix this,* I vow as she continues crying. *I will do my best to heal.*

That's the small, growing, optimistic part of me. The rest of me is despondent.

If I end up not killing myself, I've put us both in pain for nothing.

I would have been better off not trying at all.

CHAPTER 21
CARTER

MOM and I haven't spoken much since my revelation.

The silence isn't charged with anger. It's tinged with regret. I've been inhaling frankincense, lavender, and eucalyptus oil (not at the same time, ew) like you wouldn't believe to relax myself. It's almost working to override my remorse over letting my mom down.

"Are you sure you'll be okay? I still have eight weeks of leave I can use," Mom says. Today's the final day of her family medical leave, the final transfer of my primary care from her loving hands to school and my new psychologist, who I'll be meeting this week.

"I'm good." I smooth my hair, fingers twitching through the freshly installed weave. Yet again, I chose a combination of blue and black. Perhaps I should pick colors that won't make me stand out as much, but I'm too attached to my bright hair to let it go. "School will be okay."

"It better be before I sue their asses," Mom mutters. See, this is why I don't tell her anything.

We pull up to the school. "It'll be fine." I kiss her on the cheek. "Love ya." I slam the car door shut before she can change her mind about me coming back.

Mom rolls her window down. "DON'T SLAM MY CAR DOOR. I TOLD YOU THAT."

I rub my forehead. "Mom!" A gaggle of boys nearby howl with laughter. For once, I can't blame them.

Mom smirks and waves her fingers. "Love you, baby." Mercifully, she drives off.

Students swarm, stomping through the doors and laughing with friends. I stand still, allowing the current to flow around me. It's like my first day of high school all over again. This could be a new beginning. Or another year of torture.

Only one way to find out.

I enter the portal to hell. I'm greeted by the bleached-blond attendance secretary, Maxine. She's well-aware of my existence thanks to my impressive number of yearly absences.

"Welcome back, hon," she says. Maxine hands me an excuse slip to show my teachers, as well as my brand-new schedule.

"I've been praying for you," Maxine says. Ugh. Of course she knows about me choking on pills. Mom said an all-staff meeting was held last week to "facilitate my safe return to school." I must've been a fun topic of gossip in the teacher's lounge. *Oh, poor Carter. Oh, we should have helped. Oh, I can't believe it! The inhumanity! The horrid inhumanity!*

"Uh, thanks." I suppose the promise of prayer is nice. The last time I prayed was when my now-dead grandmother forced our scattered family to thank Jesus for this meal (the meals she cooked, not Jesus) during the holidays.

Maxine's lipstick crackles as she smiles. It's the last thing I see before I rush back out into the hallway. I can't deal with any more pity.

Strange looks and a laugh or two follow me as I walk to my locker. Nothing unbearable, considering the rumors that must have swirled around my absence. Some boy looks at me with fear and I remember the rumor that got me here in the first place. Great, these social sycophants think I killed someone and *that's* why I got kicked out of school.

Wait. That means people may leave me alone. Nobody wants to piss off a murderer. I can roll with that.

I shove my textbooks in my locker before checking out my new schedule.

Homeroom/Period 1: AP Physics (Parker)
Period 2: AP Physics (Parker)

Period 3: AP Spanish Literature & Culture (de la Garza)

Period 4: AP English Language & Composition (Atkinson)

Period 5: Calculus III (Jackson)

Period 6: Lunch (Staff)

Period 7: Physical Education (Girls 10-12) (Clarke)

Period 8: AP Computer Science A (Roberts)

Period 9: AP Comparative Government and Politics (Hughes)

Perfect. Same homeroom, and only 3 of my classes were switched around. I was expecting worse.

I book it to AP Physics class. Walking into the half-classroom, half-lab calms me. I missed this. Learning about science and math through textbooks isn't the same as having a teacher who takes the time to explain difficult concepts, and it's certainly no substitute for putting into practice what I learned through rote memorization. Science, math, and technology interest me because they're something concrete to believe in when the rest of my life is twisted. They are solid, tested, and true.

Despite my detours, I'm the first student to arrive. I pull out a worn copy of *Hidden Figures*, settle in, and read. Students trickle in as the clock inches closer to the final bell. Aside from more weird stares, nobody bothers me, which is nice. Thanks to my new schedule, the POPS aren't an issue anymore, minus lunch. Keeping the same lunch period was unavoidable.

Miss Parker shouts when she enters. "You're back!"

I smile, glad to see her again. I know it's not a coincidence that the only person who's ever stood up for me at this school is a Black woman.

"Everything's better?" Miss Parker asks. Her hazel eyes are lit with concern. I turn my head away.

"Mostly. My grandfather died." My eyes bore into hers, begging her to accept the lie Mom and I settled on. If there's even a hint that I tried to kill myself, the assholes at this school would have so much ammunition against me that I'd be ruined. I already got a taste of the backlash this school has about "murderous" girls: there's no way they're sympathetic toward the suicidal. Or worse: pity, the sympathetic stares of people tricked into thinking they care about me now that I almost died.

Either way, I lose, and I have Abby to blame for all of it.

"Right, right. Sorry about that," she says. "I wish he...hadn't died."

Translation: I wish you hadn't attempted suicide.

"Yeah." I swallow a glob of spit. "Same here."

Miss Parker pauses for a moment before continuing. "I know you took your quizzes and tests online, that's good. You'll have to catch up on your labs. I'd like someone to help you." She looks at the other students before I can protest that I'm fine working alone.

"Slater?" Miss Parker calls.

Crap. I don't want to work with one of the POPS.

Slater is laughing with one of her friends. I recognize him as one of the Floaters who was in my sophomore year gym class. Guess he's not as unmotivated as I thought, if he's in this class.

When Slater hears Miss Parker's voice, she whips her head around, hitting the boy with her fresh blowout. Her eyes land on me. She offers me a large, toothy smile. I look to the side, like I don't know her. "What's up, Miss P?"

"Could you help Carter catch up on her assignments? Since you're ahead on this project."

"Sure thing," Slater says. She hops off her stool—literally hops like a bunny—and traipses over to me. I grimace. Great, forced social interaction!

"Thank you. Now, where did I put your handouts?" Miss Parker mutters to herself. She walks over to her disorganized desk.

Slater fiddles with the neckline of her striped sweater. "Okay, we're learning about friction."

Wow, it's not like I read the lessons or anything. "Yeah. I know."

Slater casts her eyes to the stars on the ceiling, smiles, and nods her head. "Right. You're always on top of things."

What's with the random compliment, one of several since the photoshoot happened? Sure, Slater's "the nice one" of the POPS, but she's still one of them. Fun fact:

actual nice girls don't sit idly by as their friends bully people. Like Mei, Slater and I were friends before she sold her soul to the POPS.

Miss Parker brings over a plastic tub full of lab materials and the experiment instructions. "You'll have to determine the coefficient of certain materials, and how they affect the friction of an object. You'll be figuring out the coefficient of the blocks here. Do you think you can finish today?"

"Of course." As if I've ever given her reason to doubt me.

"Perfect." She leaves us to it.

"Good morning, Harlow High students!" Kelsey's chipper voice comes through on the loudspeaker and interrupts my speed-reading the lab instructions. I suck in my breath and grip my throat. I cringe and look around to see if anybody's noticed my latest bullying-worthy quirk. Only Slater wears a puzzled expression. "I'm junior class president Kelsey Maxwell here with your Hawk News daily digest. We're operating on a cycle day 3 schedule. Before we bring you the latest information in sports, clubs, and special news, please rise for the Pledge of Allegiance."

Once the pledge is finished, Kelsey babbles about what sports teams are scheduled to attack each other with balls this week and which college applications-boosting clubs are meeting, and then she allows the head principal to come on to admonish us for wearing leggings.

Finally, she stops yapping and I can work in peace. I complete the experiment within a half hour without any intervention from Slater.

"Wow," Slater says when I get back from putting away the materials. "I'm impressed."

"It's playing with blocks." *Stop. You're being mean.* It's not Slater's fault I'm having a bad day—er, life. "Uh, I-I guess it was hard?" *That's better.*

"Still, the experiment took me an hour."

"I r-read the instructions." I sneak my book under the table and start reading again. Slater's attempts to connect with me are annoying, and I need a break.

"Hey, you should come to tonight's GSA meeting," Slater whispers.

One condition of me staying at Harlow is to join an extracurricular, to "connect with school life." Does Slater know that? Why else would she invite me to join the Gender & Sexuality Alliance at this critical time? Or is this part of her campaign to be nice to me?

I hate this. Why do people bother?

Before I can answer Slater, the loudspeaker comes on. Maxine's smoke-heavy voice asks, "Can Carter Harper, Kelsey Maxwell, Slater García-Svensson, Mei Xiang, and Abigail Wallace come to the main office? Thank you."

The standard *ooooooooo* student chorus sounds

after the announcement butchers half our names, especially poor Slater's. My heart races as my skin grows clammy. There can only be one reason why we're being called at the same time.

Me.

CHAPTER 22
ABBY

MY DESIRE TO do the right thing screwed over everyone in this room. How was I supposed to know Carter's mom would report us to the principal? Okay, like, I should have known, but I wanted *Ms. Ashley* to know what happened between my ex-friends and Carter, not our *parents*.

I'm the last person to arrive thanks to Meg, my Advanced Fiction & Poetry teacher. She felt like she had to explain the homework assignment to me in minute detail before letting me go. I love Meg, but she can be so extra.

Most heads turn toward me as I enter the conference room, with two notable exceptions. Carter's staring at the table, and my mother is on the phone.

At least my dad isn't here to learn about my many crimes. Neither is Slater's—he's on a trip to Milan with his boyfriend. Carter's mother, Mei's parents, Kelsey's parents, and Slater's mom are all here.

How did they all get here on such short notice?

Unless...this was planned. And Mother didn't bother telling me. Great. Score one for mother-daughter relationships!

"Thank you for showing up, Abigail," Principal Adams says.

"It's Abby," I say.

Kelsey rolls her eyes. I'm not in the mood to deal with her attitude today.

"Ms. Wallace?" Principal Adams says. Mother puts a finger up, telling him to wait a second. At least it wasn't her middle one.

We wait for my mother to finish. "I'm in the middle of closing a fifteen-million-dollar listing," she explains after putting away her phone. "There better be a damn good reason for this meeting."

"Thank you all for coming in on such short notice," Principal Adams says. "I'll cut straight to it. Your daughters have been involved in a concerning altercation."

Mei's father, Bao, rubs his eyes. "I had a twelve-hour surgery yesterday. Today is my first day off in ten days. I would like to go home and sleep." Bao is a pediatric oncologist. Meanwhile, Ting, Mei's mother, manages my favorite independent bookstore. Totally different, demanding professions, yet they're the most stable and loving couple I've met. I don't know how they let Mei get away with....everything.

Principal Adams clears his throat. "I understand your busy schedule, Mr. Xiang, and will attempt to keep this brief. It seems that—"

"Your kids started a rumor about mine," Ms. Ashley says. I'm surprised that Carter nearly dying due to that rumor hasn't been mentioned, but it makes sense that Ms. Ashley wouldn't want Mei and Kelsey to know about that. I won't bother telling her they probably already do. "First up on the agenda: where you got your bad parenting skills from."

All hell breaks loose. The parental units scream at Ms. Ashley, each other, and Principal Adams, defending their girls and their parenting skills in equal measure. They speak over one another, refusing to hear alternate viewpoints.

These adults are why we're girls who have grown claws.

Minus Carter. I don't know how she's meek with a mother like that. It's like how Slater dresses like a California skater girl even though her mother was a model.

"My daughter wouldn't do such a thing!" Ting Xiang insists.

"Yes, she would. I told you we should have sent her to Catholic school," Bao Xiang says. "Public school girls are animals. They've corrupted our daughter."

Okay he isn't *wrong,* but I want to tell Bao that Mei

was corrupted long before she met us. But this isn't the time.

Ainsley Maxwell, recovering from her recent jaunt to Bali, shrugs. Her sunglasses slide down her nose. "Even if Kelsey was involved, there must have been a good reason for it." She turns to Mariposa García. "Do you know when Christian's coming back? I need his help shopping for an anniversary gift."

Mariposa gives Ainsley a dark look. Though Ainsley is friends with Slater's father, there's no love between Ainsley and Mariposa. "I don't track his schedule."

Kelsey's dad pulls out his worn checkbook. "Could we take care of this matter financially?"

"Whitaker, are you joking?" my mother asks him. "Our girls aren't guilty. Money is an admission of guilt."

"Regardless, there's not much that money cannot solve," Whitaker says.

Kelsey, Mei, Slater, Carter, and I look at each other in bewilderment throughout the flurry of conversation, united by our confusion and annoyance.

"Enough...ENOUGH!" Principal Adams shouts. "We'll sort through this situation calmly and gather all of the facts before making a disciplinary decision."

"Disciplinary?!" Mother shrieks. "We're supposed to take the word of one clearly vindictive woman?"

"Oh, I'll show you vindictive. If your kid even *looks* at mine again—" Carter's mom starts.

"Ms. Harper. Please, calm down."

"I have to calm down, but the Stepford Wife doesn't?"

It's a fair point.

Principal Adams sighs. "The situation seems to be that Kelsey Maxwell, Abigail Wallace, and Mei Xiang created a disturbing rumor about Carter Harper's mental health. It appears as if Slater García-Svensson had prior knowledge of the rumor's creation but did not attempt to stop it from spreading."

"Uh, I didn't do anything," Kelsey lies.

I let out a snort. Sure, Kelsey didn't start the rumor, but she didn't exactly end it. Kelsey and her parents give me the patented Maxwell Family Death Stare. It doesn't work on me, as I've faced bigger monsters than two egomaniacs and their brilliant, twisted daughter.

"Surely Carly deserved it," Mother says. I shrink in my chair.

"*Carter,*" Bao corrects her.

"Does it matter?" Mother says back.

"Why?" Carter's mom interjects. "Because she's a little weird? Because she doesn't have friends? Because she dyes her hair unusual colors? What on Earth did my daughter do to deserve all of this?"

Carter looks at her mother. "Thanks," she says sarcastically.

Ms. Ashley shrugs. "Those aren't necessarily bad things."

Ting interrupts their tete-a-tete. "I doubt Mei's

involvement. She's too busy working on her studies." She rests her hand on Mei's shoulder. Mei shrugs her off. "Did you know that she's in *five* after-school study groups?"

This time, I am able to suppress my snort. Mei's in two clubs and one study group. The rest of her time is spent with us.

"You know where they have more study groups and structure? *Catholic school!*" Mei's dad says. I mean, Mei does already dress like she goes to one.

"Slater would've tried to do the right thing," Slater's mom says. "You must not have all the facts."

I stare at all our parents in turn, incredulous. Do they think we grew up to be perfect angels? That we are pure sugar, rather than spice and everything vice?

More arguing ensues between the parents. Until it's all halted by an unexpected source.

"It didn't—none of this h-happened!" Carter stammers.

The simultaneous conversations stop.

"Abby told me about everything. Then you confirmed it," Carter's mom says, selling me out.

Kelsey, Mei, and Slater turn to me. "*Abby?*"

I offer a weak wave.

"I know Abby told you about what allegedly happened. I went along with it because I was half-asleep and didn't know what was going on." Carter stares at her mother, begging her to agree.

I back her up, trying to spin a narrative that gets me and my (maybe) friends in the least amount of trouble. "I made it all up because I—I was mad at Kelsey and wanted her to get in trouble. I didn't think Carter would go along with it."

Kelsey death glares me but says nothing. She's storing her fury for later.

"I wasn't there when this all happened," Mei lies.

"Cork it, Mei," Slater mumbles.

Carter turns toward Principal Adams. "I'm sorry about the confusion here. It was a simple disagreement. This won't happen again. I think it's best that we all go back to class."

Principal Adams rubs his temples. "I don't get paid enough to deal with this," he mumbles. "Yes, Carter, you all may go back to class. I'll deal with you and Abby later."

We all stand. Carter's mother latches onto her arm. Carter doesn't wince in fear, like she should. What's up with that? "We will talk about this. Later."

Carter nods. "I know. And I'm sorry."

Once we're out of parental hearing distance, Kelsey lets out a huge, dramatic sigh. "Well, that was annoying and unnecessary."

"At least we're in the clear," Mei reassures her. Hey, that's my line. I'm the second-in-command, Kelsey's comforter and confidante.

"Yeah, he shouldn't bother us anymore," I say.

Kelsey sneers. "It's your fault he bothered us in the first place! What were you thinking, telling Carter's mother—Carter, we are *not done here!*"

Carter pauses, caught. She was about to make a break for it. "I have c-class," she mumbles.

"Get your ass back here for three seconds. Then you can go back to your precious class."

Carter looks torn between escaping her enemy and knowing there will be hell to pay if she doesn't speak to Kelsey now. She shuffles toward us.

Kelsey stares at her. "Why didn't you tell the truth? It was right there. Nobody would've blamed you." Kelsey reaches toward Carter's hair. Carter rushes backward. Kelsey lets out a loose, sexy laugh. "Relax. I just noticed you'd done something different with your hair. I like it."

What's with the compliments? Surely, she's not interested in her like *that*....

"Th-thanks?" Carter says. "And I...well, I lied for myself. Not for any of you."

"Hmm," Kelsey says. She taps her long fingernails on her thighs. "I don't buy it."

Carter shrugs. "I figured." She walks away.

Kelsey doesn't bother stopping her. But I don't think she's quite done with Carter yet.

CHAPTER 23
CARTER

I FURIOUSLY POUR out my innermost thoughts for Therapist #8 via a thick packet of intake forms. *In order to get better, you have to be willing to talk,* Rational Carter says. If only talking wasn't so hard. I had enough of that when Abby encroached on my territory at lunch the other day. Now I have to deal with this?

Mom returns to the conversation we'd been having in the car. "I almost understand why you decided to lie to the school. But honey, don't you think it would've been better if you'd told your principal about the bullying? You and I both know Abby wasn't lying."

I hug the clipboard closer to myself. Mom doesn't get it. I couldn't sit there and let the school open an investigation. I would have to relive the abuse over and over again, like that doesn't already happen in my head.

"Mom, I didn't mean to lie. I started freaking out and came up with the best solution I had at the time.

And it worked! They were nicer before the...thing, and they've been nice to me since I helped them. Well, they saw it that way," I grumble. "Even Abby and Mei are off my case." Mei's being nice too. I wonder how long that will hold.

Abby's back to treating me as if I don't exist. I *really* want to know how long that will last so I can have due warning when she snaps.

Mom seems mollified, at least for now. "It still wasn't a good thing to lie about, honey. Where's your protection if those girls begin to bully you again?"

My pen stills. She's right. This honeymoon period can't last forever.

What will the POPS do to me next? Stab me with a plastic fork at lunch? Steal my AP Gov paper and dramatically read from it, making fun of my prose? Whatever their comeback, it must be dark and vicious and hurtful because that's what girls like them do to loser girls like me.

"I have to finish these." I gesture toward my intake forms. I've got to end this conversation before I lose it. My maybe-therapist's office is the worst place in the world to break down.

"You can't avoid your issues forever," Mom chastises me.

I know. That's what I'm afraid of. I finish off the remaining questions, which I'd been avoiding.

What is your current level of depression, from 1 to 10? 8

What is your current level of anxiety, from 1 to 10? 8

What is your current stress level, from 1 to 10? 10!!!!!!!!!!!!!!!!!!!!!!!!!!!

What are your strengths? I am excellent at computer programming, website/mobile application design/development, nonfiction writing, constructive literary analysis, advanced mathematics, academic research, and business management. I can write and speak conversational Spanish and have elementary proficiency in French and Italian. I recently became a regional finalist for the Future Leaders Essay Contest, and found out yesterday that I won Pennsylvania, ensuring that I will travel to Washington, D.C. this summer for a summit to meet with the forty-nine other winners.

There. That laundry list of talents would impress anybody. It'll show Therapist #8 that I'm more than my diagnosis of *major depressive disorder, reoccurrant, severe, without psychotic features.* I'm ambitious, talented, and tired of people who underestimate me because of a few glitches in my brain chemistry.

"Carter and Ashley Harper? I'm Dr. Maryn Locke."

Mom and I turn our heads toward Locke. Her appearance bursts with color, from her honey blonde afro to her deep green eyes to her bright yellow skirt to her blue heels. Somehow, the cacophony of colors works with her dark brown skin and inviting demeanor.

I'm underdressed in my boots, skinny jeans, and checkered black and white hoodie. Mom, as always, is pressed and professional in a skirt suit, her hair slicked back into a ponytail.

I flip my intake forms upside down on my lap. Mom stands and shakes Locke's hand. "Hello Dr. Locke, I'm Ashley Harper, Carter's mother. Thank you for finding the time to fit us into your schedule."

"Oh, of course!" Locke winks at my mom. "Happy to help out a fellow Quaker."

"Right, I saw you went to UPenn!" Mom conducted a full background check on Locke, from how long she's practiced to her college major to her Yelp rating. The two jabber on about the culture of their alma mater as Locke brings us into her office. The room is overflowing with plants, tiny electronic candles, and framed photos of island destinations abroad.

While Mom's in the room, Locke runs over the standard stuff about confidentiality *unless there is an imme-*

diate *psychiatric emergency.* And we can't forget about how Locke will do her best, but *therapy will not cure my mental illness.* We sign a bunch of *confidentiality and select information release* waivers before Mom goes back out to the waiting room, kissing my forehead before her departure.

I want her to come back. Mom's departure means it's time to dig into the hellscape that is my brain.

Locke smiles that smile therapists to invoke trust in patients. It sets me on edge. The only reason she'd need to gain my trust is to ask me invasive questions.

"Hello, Carter. I noticed you didn't participate much when your mother was in the room, so I'll go over a few key points again. Everything you say in this room is confidential. The exception is if I believe you are an immediate danger to yourself or others, which is why I had you and your mother sign the emergency release forms for Harrisburg Hospital and Community Osteo-pathic, depending on your locale at the time."

"I know," I say. "I've seen seven other therapists." I slump back in the sofa.

Locke nods and flips through my intake forms. I feel naked all of a sudden, like she's seeing my black lace bra and plain cotton undies, rather than the outfit I chose semi-carefully this morning. Or worse—like she's seeing into my soul. "Yes, which is why I strive to emphasize that this is a safe place for you to speak," she says. "I understand from your mother that you haven't always been the most cooperative patient?"

I shrug.

"Well, I'd like to hear your voice. If you continue to hold all that pain inside, you'll cave in on yourself and cause so, so much damage. I don't want that for you, or for any of my patients."

I perk up oh-so-slightly. Is Locke truly interested in learning about my problems? Therapists #1-7 either didn't care in the first place or didn't care once they realized I wasn't interested in treating myself. Maybe Locke is trustworthy, but it's more likely that she isn't. I'm not holding my breath, unless I decide my next suicide attempt will be by asphyxiation.

"Now, let's go over your intake information, shall we? I want to make sure I have a clear picture of your mental, emotional, and physical health."

We review the basic information about family history, medical conditions, and medications. We hit the first snag when Locke asks, "You say that you still have suicidal thoughts sometimes?"

The direct question catches me off guard. "S-sometimes."

"Sometimes is better than frequently," Locke says. "Before your suicide attempt, how frequent were your suicidal ideations?"

"My what?"

"Suicidal ideations are thoughts of suicide with a lack of direct intent. For example, if you had thought of overdosing on your antidepressants and fantasized about what it would like if you were gone, that would have been a suicidal ideation. You taking the pills and writing the note showed direct intent to commit suicide. I'm required to report suicidal intent, not suicidal ideations."

I frown. I don't like not knowing psychological terminology. I'm supposed to be the expert on suicide, after all. And I never knew the difference between which suicidal thoughts a therapist had to report and which ones they didn't. It's nice to know that if I felt like saying I want to blow my brains out *but won't actually blow them out,* that statement wouldn't warrant an immediate phone call home. I never told my other therapists about the suicidal thoughts, because I couldn't risk Mom finding out that I want to die.

Too late for that. Too late to avoid hurting her, so at least I can be honest about my thoughts of death and what they do to me.

"What was the question again?" I got sidetracked, which isn't normal for me.

"Sure." Locke repeats her inquiry about my suicidal ideations.

"Oh. Yeah. Uh, pretty often."

Locke won't let it go. "Approximately how often? Daily? Weekly? Monthly?"

I cup my throat. "Daily. More than daily. A lot."

Locke scribbles in her notebook. I'm a lab rat, trapped and viewed for other people's satisfaction. "And now?"

With a shock, I realize that my ideations have lessened. "A few times a week, but they're...less intense than normal."

I...haven't been thinking of killing myself all that much. What's going on there? What happened to suicide-happy Carter? I would assume this change was due to my silent pact to my mom, the pact to not attempt again. But that's the thing about silent pacts: you only have to show external changes, not internal. I didn't have to stop the majority of my suicidal thoughts, not really.

No. Something with my brain chemistry has changed.

I don't know how to feel about this. On one hand, having fewer thoughts about death is nice. On the other hand, who am I without the dark cloud hanging over my head? I don't know who I would be without major depressive disorder. Could I survive college and live long enough to receive a PhD? Could I find real friends, not the pseudo-friendships I've made with the POPS? Could Hudson and I get back together, get married—okay, *no*, that's not happening. He's made it clear that I'm not his endgame, even if he did email me again to ramble about some science program he started. Slater told me he's interested in me, but I really doubt it.

Who am I? Who could I be?

"You look like your whole world changed. What happened?" Locke crosses her legs, causing her knee-length skirt to shift up a bit. Without missing a beat, she pulls it down with one hand. I wish I could be that in tune with my body, rather than flipping between indifference and simmering hatred of my larger frame.

Reluctantly, I explain my pattern of thinking, the spring of hope that's welled up.

"Don't you think that's a good thing? To recover from your mental illness?" Locke asks.

I shake my head. "Depression is half of my personality."

"And what's the other half?"

I nod toward the intake forms. "I listed my strengths in there."

"Okay, let me read." Locke scans over my list. I straighten my spine, ready to be showered with compliments about my academic prowess.

"You've listed your academic, creative, and technical skills. Which are fantastic, but this wasn't meant to be a job application."

I slump in my chair.

"What about your personality traits? What non-intellectual capabilities and strengths do you have?"

"Uh."

Locke smiles at me, despite ripping me to shreds two seconds ago. "It's okay, Carter. This happens quite often. Especially with secondary school students. Achievement is what your generation has been taught to value, mostly because of my generation's pushing that onto y'all and the advent of social media. Those platforms are excellent tools and constant comparison traps all in one."

"But I like academics," I say. "And I'm not on social media. I actually wrote an essay about—"

Locke ignores what I'm about to say about the Future Leaders Essay Contest. "Yes, but do you enjoy the praise you gain from your scholarship? Or the pursuit of knowledge itself?"

She's got me there. "A little of both," I admit.

"Exactly. And that's part of the cycle I hope to break my clients from. Liking hobbies and activities for their own sake, rather than because they've been force-fed to you. If you enjoy academics, fine. But if you don't, if you're only doing this for approval…it's worthless, in the end. Your pursuits only hurt you if they don't explicitly make you happy."

Interesting.

"I apologize, I veered off-track a bit. What personality traits and non-intellectual strengths do you have?"

Still drawing blanks. "I don't know." My intelligence is my dominating feature, though I'm not exactly showing my capacity for critical thinking at the moment.

"That's okay, Carter. We can figure that out in upcoming sessions." Locke checks her watch. "Which reminds me, we have five minutes left. I know this session was more intake, less actual therapy, and I apologize for that. It's the nature of our practice to know as much about the client's past before we can plan a course for their future."

I nod.

"If you would like upcoming sessions, that is."

"Me? I'm deciding?" Previous therapists assumed that I would come back next week, despite my clear reluctance.

"Yes. If you don't want to work with me, I won't force you onto my client list. However, I feel like we could work well together."

Surprisingly? Same. "I'll come back next week."

"Excellent. And I'm going to give you some homework. On your way out, I'll ask the secretary to print out a self-values inventory for you to fill out. I want you to bring that to your next session. There's more to you than you believe, Carter. Academics are fine, and wonderful, even. But every well-rounded person has more than their talents to rely on. They have core beliefs, personality traits, and values. I'll see you next week."

As I leave Locke's office, a snaggle of something

creeps into my stomach. It's small, but it was a feeling buried so deep inside me that I'd believed it to be gone forever.

Hope. And for real, this time. Actual living, breathing hope.

Well. What am I supposed to do about that?

CHAPTER 24
ABBY

I'D BEGUN to think Daddy was so absorbed in his case that he wouldn't call to check in.

Silly me.

The call comes in the morning, when Mother is still asleep and I've just finished my run. Daddy knows enough about our idiosyncrasies for this timing not to be a coincidence. Though it's still really late or very early over in California, depending on your perspective.

"How's it going?" Daddy asks with a yawn.

"Did you go to sleep?" I ask, trying to distract him.

I can almost hear him rubbing his eyelids. "No. This case is taking the life out of me. Turns out that...."

I prepare my breakfast as Daddy gives me the salacious details of the case, which ended up being more complex than he thought. Turns out, the guy really might be a victim of malpractice. Daddy's still not buying it and is waiting on crucial records from the defense to argue his theory. The case has grown boring to me, and I suddenly can't wait until it ends.

The tedium of the case isn't the only reason I want it to be over, though. Mother and I are getting along as well as can be expected, but that doesn't mean we're getting along. Fights over the television, arguments over what we eat for dinner (my healthy meals aren't healthy enough for her), and fracases over my friends coming over erupt nearly daily. That's progress, actually—when Mother first started living here, we fought at least once a day, usually more. We're falling into a rhythm, trying to find our way into a mother-daughter relationship.

Daddy finally stops talking about his case, as he's mistaken my silence for interest. "How's it going with, er, your mother?"

"Fine."

"Fine?" He knows both of us well enough to know that "fine" isn't a word I'd use to describe our relationship.

I laugh in spite of my bleak mood. He's so *hesitant* to bring up the elephant in the room. "Okay, awful. But you stuck me with her."

"Yeah, uh, I'm sorry about that."

"I'll live." I hate that I said that. I hate that phrase now. *I'll live.* I've seen what happens when people don't want to live.

Which brings us to the other elephant in the room. Mother says she didn't tell him about Carter. "I will if you want me to," she claimed, "but that decision is up to you."

I've got to say, it's a large improvement from the way she acted the last time an awful thing happened to me.

Daddy and I chat a bit more about school before hanging up. Right when he does, Mother comes to the kitchen. No coincidence there.

"I didn't tell him," I say to myself as I serve our agreed-upon breakfast of egg whites for her, real eggs and cheese for me, grapefruit juice for her, orange juice for me, and yogurt for me, nothing else for her. I personally believe that a great day begins with a great breakfast, but if Mother wants to keel over in the middle of her morning meetings, that's her decision.

"Didn't tell him what?" Mother asks. She bites an egg. "Too cold."

Yeah, because you're used to being in Hell. "About...you know. Carter."

Mother shrugs. "It's best that way. In fact, it's best that I was here, instead of your lily-livered father."

"He's not weak!" I argue.

"He's strong in his own ways," she semi-agrees, "but not like this. He doesn't understand darkness, especially of the female persuasion. He would never understand what led you to hurt that girl. I do."

I only half-understand what she's saying, but I totally see this as an opening. I sit down at the kitchen table. "Why did you...do what you did? In ninth grade?"

190

The spray paint—
The neighborhood—
The women who formed a circle
 'round me, a fortress—

Mother's quiet for so long that I'm afraid she won't answer the question. Finally, she says, "When I love someone, I love and protect them to the point of self-destruction. To the point of *their* destruction. But I don't expect you to understand that."

I do, I want to tell her. *I do understand that.*

But we still are not close enough for her to see the piece of herself that I inherited.

CHAPTER 25
CARTER

ACCORDING to my period tracking application, my period shouldn't arrive until next week. And yet.

I check the clock on my phone. Lunch ends in ten minutes. I could wait to head to the bathroom until then, but I have t-minus five minutes until we're facing a *Carrie* situation. I place a bookmark between the pages of my AP Gov textbook. I pack my backpack, taking special care to place my Emergency Period Kit on top of my notebooks, textbooks, pencil case, and copy of some book about the neuroscience of trauma that mom shoved in my hands yesterday.

I pass Abby as I leave. She's alone, absorbed in annotating *The Bell Jar* by Sylvia Plath. I know she isn't doing well because no one who reads *The Bell Jar* for fun is happy.

I hope the lunch supervisors won't give me a hard time about leaving early. I was raised to follow rules and listen to (if not necessarily respect) authority figures. The lunch supervisor closest to the door allows me to slip out without incident.

I'm an estimated twenty paces away from the bathroom when I realize somebody is following me.

Goosebumps break out on my flesh. I should have known it wouldn't be so simple to escape the POPS and their cruelty. What other reason would someone have for following me to the bathroom? I doubt they have to pee in the exact same bathroom at the exact same time as me. If the past month has taught me anything, it's that coincidences don't often exist. Events that may seem like fate are likely the result of somebody's screw-up.

I hate that I'm too scared to turn around. If I turn around, I'll know who's there. I shut off the soothing parts of my brain and allow my anxiety to bubble over. Anxiety isn't a good feeling, but it's more familiar than this strange swirl of emotions called "recovery."

I calculate potential escape routes. Back to the cafeteria? That's my best chance at safety, though me and my stalker are too far away for the glut of witnesses there to be much good if they decide to strike. Make a run for it? If my annual Presidential Fitness Tests have taught me anything, it's that I fail them for good reason.

I'm debating leaving school altogether when a familiar, high-pitched voice beckons me. "Carter! Wait up! Got a sec?"

Kelsey. The POPSiest POPS to ever disgrace my presence.

She knows I heard her, so there's no point in running away. I steel myself, taking meditative yoga breaths. *You can do this,* I hype myself up.

I turn around to face a diminutive blonde as charming as an angel before she turns on you like the predatory devil she is. "....Ay," I say. I'm too stunned to gurgle out the "ohk" in "okay."

Kelsey grins. Despite my loathing her, I can't help but be dazzled. Only a tiny bit. Charisma, rich and locally famous parents, and physical attractiveness aren't like to draw me in when I've seen the monster beneath the pretty-girl mask.

"I wanted to talk to you for a bit," says Kelsey. "We haven't gotten the chance to catch up lately!"

"I, uh, have to pee," I say. I begin walking backward. It's semi-true. I'd rather not explain my menstrual problems to Kelsey.

She matches my steps. She's an apex predator, hunting me. "I'll wait."

"Um, alright," I say before darting into the bathroom.

Unfortunately, no matter how much I want Kelsey gone, I can't speed up replacing my bloodied boy shorts, which I save with strategic toilet paper use and a plastic bag from my lunch sandwich. I have to jump a little to shove my ass back into my jeans once I'm done.

Dammit, where are the clothes for girls with fat asses and thick thighs? Where are they?

Sometime during this process, someone enters the bathroom. I pray it's not Kelsey, though I know good and damn well it is. She's impatient enough to barge in on my tiny moment of privacy.

I emerge from the stall. Kelsey's fiddling on her phone.

"That took a while," she says.

I say nothing as I wash my hands. Two spots of blood cling to my left, which I meticulously scrub off with a double dollop of soap. Other than that, no noticeable evidence of my period. Kelsey would have made fun of me by now if there was any other telltale mark of menstruation.

"How are you, Carter? Since you returned to school." Kelsey places her phone upside-down on the bathroom sink. It isn't like her to make idle conversation.

"Okay?"

"You were gone an awfully long time."

Being alone with Kelsey is a bad idea. She can shove my head in a toilet, crack my skull against a mirror, call me a fat friendless nothing as she has so many times. Fear roots my feet to the floor. If terror could plant seeds, a garden would grow from this dingy tile.

The bell rings. I point my thumb toward the door. "I'm gonna be late." *Stop talking stop talking stop talking.*

Kelsey shrugs. "Who cares? Class will always be there."

"True." Is it a good idea to agree with her? Maybe I should fight, claim she's wrong. I need a social guide-book because I've never been aware of the rules of the game.

"I know we've had a rough past, but I'd like to start over. You helped me out the other day, after all. Maybe you're not as bad as I thought you were." Kelsey beams, like I'm supposed to accept her bad apology.

A rough past is the understatement of the century. Abby may be the person who primarily bullied me, but Kelsey's doled out more than her fair share of cruelty. Almost worse, she sits on the sidelines and laughs, drawing more attention to Abby.

My lack of an answer points to "no."

"Why not?" Kelsey asks, painting on a look of concern as she leans against the bathroom tiles. Kelsey pretends to have raw emotion. Too bad robots like her don't have feelings. "I really am sorry, you know. I mean, I felt terrible when—" she (fake) sniffles— "I found out from Mei you tried to kill yourself because of me. Like, just...do you know how that feels?"

My blood runs cold. Time stops, and I am lost in my panic.

Do I lie?

Deny?

Run?

Hide?

Abby should be the only person who knows I tried to kill myself. And she kept that secret from everyone but Slater because she needed a ride from the hospital. Why would she tell Kelsey? It must've been Slater who told.

"I was in Florida," I lie again. "For my grandfather's funeral. Making arrangements with my mom." *Stop shaking stop shaking stop—*

Kelsey shakes her head slowly. "Carter, come on. Funerals don't take that long to plan. It's okay. Nobody else knows but Mei, Slater, and Abby."

The worst four girls to know I tried to die by suicide.

"H-how...wh-who...?" I don't realize I'm stumbling out the question, I'm so shook.

Kelsey checks her already perfect fingernails. "Mei came to me, crying, after Slater told her. I told her your near-death wasn't our fault, so she needed to get it together. That traitor Abby's the reason you did it, right?"

"Uh..." It was Mei's fault, though. She co-created the rumor. Even if she's sorry now, *she and Abby still nearly killed me.*

Kelsey's intense chartreuse eyes pierce into me, like she's willing me to say yes.

"I guess she was?" I'm surprised by my own answer, that I'm so afraid of this pint-size blonde that I'm making things up.

Kelsey beams. She places her hand on my shoulder. I will myself to stop trembling. As per usual, my stress response system refuses to listen to my frontal lobe.

"I'm so glad you were able to admit that. That's an important step," Kelsey says. "And I'm sorry about that silly little rumor Mei and Abby started about you. It all got out of hand. You know how it goes." Kelsey waves a hand dismissively.

No. I don't know how it goes, what it's like to destroy lives for fun.

"I-it's f-f-f-f—" I'm so terrified my stammer is out in full force. "Fine." There. A word. Good girl. I take deep breaths again to center myself.

Time to grovel.

"Please don't tell anybody," I say. I clasp my hands in prayer position despite not giving a crap about God. "I'm sorry for blaming you. You're right, everything that happened is Abby's fault."

"Don't apologize." Kelsey seems genuinely upset. She twirls her pressed-to-death hair. "You must've gone through hell."

I nod.

"So, were you in a psychiatric hospital? That must have sucked." Kelsey practically coos with sympathy. This time, I can't tell what's fake or real.

I nod again. My stay at Winterwood did, indeed, suck.

Kelsey's expression drips with sympathy. Like she

gets it. Like she's experienced depression, bleakness, never wanting to wake up again. Why would she? She has looks, money, status, athletics. Brains, if she chose to exercise the intelligence I know she has.

"But, anyway," Kelsey says. She's chipper, bright, back to her normal self. "I'm glad we got the chance to talk. And don't worry, I'll keep your secret."

Yeah, right. From now on, that's the only thing I'm going to worry about. "T-thank y-you. Thanks."

"In fact, I want to offer you something." Kelsey reaches into her Kate Spade purse. I wince, both from the brand name and from her grabbing something. Is it a gun? Is it a knife? Or perhaps a dead rat? A vial of poison?

My brain works on overload until she pulls out a thick piece of paper from an envelope.

"I want to invite you to my party," Kelsey announces. "It's the biggest party of the year, and a loser like you should be grateful for the invitation. No offense. But you know I'm right."

Yeah, this is worse than a dead rat. At least I could throw a dead rat away. This teal invitation, topped with a ribbon, is too pretty to discard.

"Here ya go," Kelsey says. She sticks out the invitation. Hesitantly, I accept it and read.

THE ANNUAL SPRING SHITFACED
EXTRAVAGANZA

THIS SATURDAY · 8 PM to 1 AM

819 Saddlebrook Drive, Harrisburg, PA

COME CELEBRATE SPRING BREAK AT KELSEY MAXWELL'S EVENT OF THE YEAR! DON'T TELL YOUR FRIENDS! THIS PARTY IS INVITATION-ONLY.

AMENITIES

FULL BAR (FREE FROM 8 TO 10 PM, $10/DRINK AFTER) · FREE SWAG BAG FOR FIRST 50 PEOPLE, $10 SWAG BAG FOR NEXT 50 · PHOTO BOOTH

ENTERTAINMENT & SPECIAL GUESTS

<u>EMILY RHODES</u> (TAYLOR SWIFT'S SECOND COUSIN) · <u>LOCAL DJ $ SQUARE</u> · <u>SOPHIE MILLER-COX</u> (WAS IN A DELETED SCENE OF *THE KARDASHIANS*)

<u>RSVP ON MY INSTAGRAM, WHICH YOU SHOULD ALREADY BE FOLLOWING.</u>

No one under the age of 14 or over the age of 18 will be allowed entry aside from the entertainment!!!

What in the fresh hell is this? Who has the time,

money, and energy to host a five-hour party-slash-Ponzi scheme ($10 for a swag bag...bruh)? And to design custom invitations for this nonsense? Who throws a rager in the middle of April? Whose parents let them get away with this—okay, I know the answer to that question. After meeting her mother at the parent meeting, I wouldn't be surprised if I saw her at the party.

"It's super exclusive," Kelsey says as I continue to decipher what I just read. "Only a hundred people are invited each year. That's invitation number 98." Sure enough, there's a silver 98 in the corner.

"One hundred?" I marvel. I'm also wondering who number 99 and 100 are. Who at this school is more of a loser than me?

"I always invite a few losers and poor people for my charity work. I count it under National Honor Society hours," Kelsey says. "You're lucky to have made the cut this year."

A chortle bubbles up. I squash it when I realize she's dead serious. "That's me, Little Miss Luck," I murmur.

"Absolutely!" Kelsey says. She checks her phone, which has been lying on the sink during our entire conversation. "Ugh, I really do have to get to class. Miss Parker will chew me out if I'm late again. She's a pain in the ass."

Kelsey gives me that expectant look again, but I can't agree with her on this. I won't indulge in talking about someone who cares about me.

"Anyway," Kelsey says, sounding annoyed. "You can RSVP on my Insta."

"Why are you doing this?" I blurt. "Why me?"

Kelsey looks at me like I'm a complete dolt. "I'm giving you popularity. You tried to kill yourself because you're a loser, so I'm helping you get some social status. You're welcome." Kelsey shrugs. "Besides, you did us a solid by keeping us out of trouble." She measures her next words. "I always remember the people who don't betray me."

Kelsey finally leaves the bathroom. My breathing returns to normal now that I'm no longer under her steely gaze. I'm alone again, blissfully alone. There's a difference between being alone and my normal lonely, and man, I need to be alone right now.

The next bell rings, but I can't bring myself to dash to gym class. My interaction with Kelsey was surreal.

I'm tempted to crumple the invitation and throw it away. If Kelsey believes the potential of popularity will override her triggering my suicide attempt, she has another thing coming.

Yet I'm still afraid of her. So the invitation remains with me.

I follow the typical sequence of pre-running stretches in silence, concentrating on the movements of my body and not the ceaseless chatter around me. My body twists and bends as I command it, a welcome change from my normal flopping and flailing and huffing and puffing. I've kept up with my yoga sessions, and it shows. Though as I glance at the toned calves and defined biceps of the girls surrounding me, I'm reminded that I'm nowhere near fit.

"Harper. Ready to put in an effort today? Especially because you were FIVE MINUTES LATE?!" Mrs. Clarke barks. Unfortunately, even with my new class time, I'm still stuck with her.

"I guess?"

"Don't get smart with me." More yelling followed by the *purp* of her whistle. "Now, GO!"

"I'm not—okay," I say before breaking off into a jog. Sometimes, it's best to let adults say what they want to you, no matter how abrasive. Some people need to be right 24/7.

"She can be a hardass," Mei says from next to me. I do a double take. Why is she speaking to me? To ferret out more secrets?

"Yeah," I agree.

Mei continues to jog at my side for the next two laps. I don't slow down, lest I give her a reason to make fun of my slow pace.

You're already slow compared to her normal speed, I remind myself. I've seen her in gym class before. Mei and the other POPS are unusually athletic. It's yet another trait they have in common, along with beauty, what we traditionally consider intelligence, long hair, thinness, creative talent, and money.

Bitches of a feather fuck lives up together.

"Keep it up, Harper," Clarke yells. "You didn't stop yet!"

I'm mid-eye roll when I realize she's right. Interesting. Maybe all that yoga has increased my lung capacity.

Mei cocks her head to the side. "Water break?"

I shake my head no. "We can—" Ow. "Talk—" Ow. "Here." This is so the wrong time to get a stitch in my side. "I need to sit down." I grip the right side of my waist.

"Transient abdominal pain?" Mei asks.

Is that what it's called? "Yeah."

Mei follows me to the bleachers. Before Clarke can scream at me again, Mei says, "She's got a side stitch." Well, why couldn't she have said that in the first place? Sometimes being around overachievers is a real pain in my ass.

"Five minutes," Clarke says.

"That'll be enough time," Mei says.

"For—" Ugh. "What?" UGH! My side hurts.

"Push your fingers against where you're feeling the most pain," Mei says. She demonstrates, pushing the side of her four-pack. "It should help relieve some of it and speed up recovery. I do it all the time in track and field."

Though I'm reluctant to do so, I follow her instructions. Huh. That works. "Thanks."

Mei shrugs. "I owe you one. Kelsey told me she told you about what I knew about *your grandfather's funeral,* and that she invited you to the party."

Right. "She did. Both." The invitation still burns a hole in my backpack.

"You should—"

The teacher blows her whistle. "Harper! Xiang! Back on the track!"

Mei scowls. "I need to go practice. We can talk later," she says. She takes off before I can tell her we have nothing to talk about.

I walk slow for the rest of gym class. The stitch in my side disappears halfway through, but I don't want to risk it coming back. Meanwhile, Mei laps me several times. Showoff.

Mei allows me to change out of my gym clothes after class before bothering me again. "You should go to the party," she says. "It'll be fun."

"Fun," I say. If your idea of fun is fidgeting nervously at an unsupervised party with people who nearly killed you, then yes, the party will be the highlight of my year.

Mei reapplies her burgundy lipstick without bothering to look in a mirror. She knows she's perfect. For the first time in years, she offers me a smile. "We want you there. Despite what Kelsey's selling you, we know it's a useless apology. But it's something, which I can tell you firsthand is better than what she typically offers."

Mei leaves me to speak to her actual friends, leaving me confused about what just happened. Like. What does Mei have to gain by trying to coerce me into going? Aside from pulling some stunt to humiliate me at the party, which could happen.

Except....

Mei seems sincere enough, and Kelsey, in her own odd way, did too. They want to give me access to the most exclusive event of the year to improve my social status and make up for the bullying that nearly killed me.

The situation is almost laughable.

Still, it's an intriguing concept. Kelsey's popular, and she doesn't have problems. Same with Slater and Mei. Abby's issues didn't begin until she was ousted from her clique. Kelsey and the POPS hold so much power, and nobody messes with them. I have zero power, and everybody messes with me.

Is being popular a shield? Is that what I've been missing? Is that the key to my salvation?

Popularity. Huh. Why not try it out?

I search for Kelsey's Instagram. Cursing myself out all the way, I fill out the Spring Slobbering Whatever RSVP form in her bio.

Let's do this.

CHAPTER 26
ABBY

MY ANXIETY IS OFTEN SOOTHED by baking.

I'm spending the afternoon refining my specialty recipe, vanilla layered cake with lemon and blueberries. It's sweet, with a bit of a bite, and perfect for mending broken relationships. I'm still trying to decide if I want to give it to Carter, Kelsey, or Mei. I'm not on the best terms with any of them, and I don't even *like* Kelsey and Carter, but I need more than one friend (Slater). I don't know why Slater's still tolerating me, but I won't complain about that. I enjoy her company.

My mother is lounging in the living room and hasn't cooked a day in her life, so I figured this would be a good way to stay away from her ~~because I think I'm growing to love her again~~ because she's annoying and Machiavellian. As I frost the cake, my mind runs around to the same topic I've pondered all week: tonight's party.

In my previous life, I would be with Kelsey at this moment. We'd be blasting Top 40 hits while decorating her house. Laughing while greeting whatever D-list guests she scrounged up this year. Retreating to her bedroom to have sex in the middle of the party, washing my mouth out with Listerine right after so nobody could claim it smelled like vagina.

Some of my best memories were created at that party. It's always a good time, aside from my massive hangovers the next day. Last year, Slater, Mei, and I all claimed we were having a sleepover at Kelsey's to avoid questions from our parents. It's not like Kelsey's parents are around enough to care. In the middle of the afternoon, when my hunger overtook my headache, I made us all pancakes. Kelsey swore they were the fluffiest she'd ever tasted.

My heart pounds as I walk across the street. Nope. Nope. Nope. Not thinking about this. I'm here to deliver this cake to Carter. Out of the three people I have issues with, she might be the most forgiving. Besides, I was really mean to her and should properly apologize for it.

And, alright, maybe I want to check in on her. She seems to have bounced back fine, which is likely fake. People don't recover from trauma that fast.

when they destroy you from the
inside out

you can smile and fake happy all
     you want
those of us who have stood on
     that path
know you're a liar.

Carter doesn't look out the peephole before answering. When she sees me, she squeezes her eyes shut. "Whatdoyouwant," she says in a rush.

"Why do you look nice?" I blurt out.

Carter's wearing a navy baby doll top that highlights the blue undertones of her deep brown skin. She tugs at the mid-thigh length hem, which, if she does enough times, will cause the rayon-spandex blend to tear. She's paired the top with slate leggings that shimmer and two-inch black suede ankle boots. Carter's geekdom is reflected by a tiny necklace that's purple and silver and does not match the rest of her outfit. Come to think of it, she wore it all the time before junior year started.

Overall, making an effort for once makes her look kind of hot, if dorky girls with half-finished makeup jobs were my type. (They're not.)

Carter's cheeks grow ruddy. Another tug at the hem. "Uh, is there something you wanted?"

"Carter, who is it?" her mother yells. I glimpse into their house, though I don't see Ashley anywhere. The last time I was here, admiring the décor wasn't my priority. The small foyer is the only visible area, and its walls are lined with two bookshelves. They're half filled with books, the other half being decorative items that add balance to the room. I recognize a few poetry and fiction titles. There's also abstract art on the canary yellow walls. That color seldom works, but they managed to pull it off.

"It's Abby!" I yell.

"Leave before I beat—"

Carter steps outside and closes the door.

"I baked you a cake." I thrust the cake in front of her.

She skitters back like a terrified cat. "Why?" Carter lifts an eyebrow. She points at the cake that I'm still freaking holding, by the way. For a mix of common household ingredients, this thing is heavy. The glass pan isn't helping.

"I made it because you like to eat." I snap before remembering I'm trying to be nicer, at least for now. I may have sworn off teasing her, but I won't be a Goody Two-Shoes.

Carter's face falls. Argh, I've accidentally called her fat.

"That's not what I meant. For once," I say before she can pull receipts that oh, yes, I've meant that in the past. "Look, I wanted to say I'm sorry. I shouldn't have been an asshole to you the...well, you know when. All the other times. I'm...dealing with things."

"So am I," Carter points out. She grips her throat.

It's a strange gesture, almost like a silent plea for help. I've seen her do it a few times since she came back from the hospital.

I shrug. "Well, duh. So, let me in?" I flash the grin that awarded me "Best Smile" in last year's yearbook.

Carter stares at the cake and becomes lost in her own world. If I had anything to do today, I'd be irritated with how long it's taking her to make a simple decision. Or maybe it isn't so simple. She's considering letting somebody who terrorized her into her house.

I take the lead, since this modest mouse isn't going to. "I messed up. And I know we haven't had a good relationship in the past—" Carter snorts "—but I don't know. You aren't the worst. I guess." I huff, annoyed at my own vagueness. "I wanted to see if you wanted to, like, do something? Hang out?" Even the thought of hanging out with her

Carter still looks confused. "I have plans tonight. For the rest of the night."

"What do you have to—no." The anger that I'm trying to stamp out is back in full force. The one day Carter decides to look nice is this Saturday? There's no way, and yet.... "You are not. Going. To the Spring Shit-faced Extravaganza."

Carter's face lights up and the ghost of a grin is on her face, like she's won some prize over me (again). "I am. I take it you're not?"

"Does it *look* like I am?" I stomp my foot, knowing

I'm close to throwing a tantrum. How dare Kelsey invite Carter to the party I practically owned? I was the princess, while Kelsey was the queen. That's how it worked. And she replaced my invitation with Carter Harper's, a designated 95 to 100? Last time I checked, Carter's still a loser who can't dress!

The door opens. "Carter, come on, I have to finish your eyeshadow—Abby?"

This situation could not get any worse. Slater's holding an angled brush, drenched in one of my favorite eyeshadow shades.

"Why the fuck are you here?" I ask. And why is she using so much shadow with a brand known for its high color payoff—*not the point, Abby.*

"I was doing Carter's makeup," Slater says.

"Is that why her eyeliner is so smudged?" I point toward the offending eye.

Slater inspects her work. "It doesn't have setting spray yet!"

"SETTING SPRAY IS USED TO PROTECT LOOKS THAT ARE GOOD."

Slater rolls her eyes. "Is that cake for anyone? Cause I'll eat it."

"We know you would eat me if you could," I snap. "It's mine."

"What happened to being nicer?" Slater leans against the doorframe.

"What happened to not going to the Shitfaced party in solidarity with me?" I say.

Slater blushes. "I had to help Carter."

"Uh-huh," Carter confirms.

I point at her and then Slater. "Fuck the both of you." I spin around on my sneakers and march back across the street.

"I take it that didn't go well, considering you brought your cake back," Mother says as I enter the house. I hadn't realized she noticed me leave. As evidenced during my Year of Hell, she tends to only see what's wrong with me if I point it out to her.

"Do you want some?" I ask. I don't want to look at my failed peace gesture anymore. If Mother wasn't here, I'd just bring it over to one of the neighbors who stood up for me when I couldn't stand up for myself.

Mother frowns. "I don't eat carbs."

"You could make an exception."

Her rock-hard face softens a smidge. "Fine. It does smell good."

I smirk. "Come on, let's go to the kitchen."

Mother watches me as I set out the plates and utensils. Hell yeah, I'm eating some of my own cake. Marie Antoinette didn't die for me not to.

"How are you, Abby?" Mother asks. "I never see you."

"Fine," I say.

213

Mother doesn't know enough about me to be able to figure out that I'm lying.

"Truly?" Mother asks. "Your father would not have dragged me back to Harrisburg if he believed you were well."

I practically toss her slice of cake to her. "Since when do you care?" I ask. "It's not like you ever visit."

Mother barks out a laugh. "Well, isn't that convenient! I put my life on hold again and you still can't summon a scrap of gratitude."

"Nobody asked you to almost go to jail for me," I say. I snatch my pan of cake for the second time of the day. "And nobody asked you to tell the entire neighborhood." Finally, we're getting it all out into the open.

I came home early from school that day, thanks to yet another vicious bout of nausea. Climbing out of the car, we saw a small crowd of neighbors causing a commotion near our home.

"I thought Tom was painting," Mrs. Yang muttered to Mrs. Chelsen. Her dyed blond hair whipped around her in the wind. In this neighborhood, a little bad weather doesn't get in the way of gossip. "Who would've thought somebody was vandalizing the house?"

"You got that nonsense mixed up with a paint job?" Mrs. Chelsen snorted as she blew out a puff of smoke. She saw me next to her and jerked her head toward the defaced garage. "You see this shit? Unbelievable."

I didn't know it was my life that they were dissecting. I

didn't know yet that I was the subject of gossip, in the worst possible way.

"The spray paint was anonymous," Mother says in the present. But she can't pull me back, because I'm two years away from this place, the day I realized how monstrous mothers could be.

Yes, the spray paint. Bright red screaming "PEDOPHILE." Daddy went into the house to scream at Mother while I, well....

"My reaction wasn't anonymous. You should've known I'd freak out," I say to Mom. "I begged you to not call the police. I didn't want it reported because I knew nothing good would come out of it, but you took my power out of my hands. You had to have realized I would react the way I did."

I walked closer and closer to the garage door, unsure if this was a bad dream or a real-life nightmare. I blew chunks before fainting in my own vomit. I woke up in spurts on the way to the hospital. Mrs. Chelsen and Mrs. Yang drove me there. It should have been my parents, but they were too busy screaming at one another to be concerned about me.

And the two women knew. There's no way they didn't know.

Mother is still calm. I want to slap her, curse her out, make this robot react like a normal human being. "I did what had to be done."

Seriously? "You didn't need to tell the entire neighborhood that *he* raped me!" I scream as I run upstairs.

This is why I don't want my mother around. We're too similar. Too blamey, too ambitious, too stubborn. Too much for everybody else, and a terrifying force of nature when we are combined. We were doing so well, and then I had to go digging up how I felt rather than remembering that *she loves me, she loves me, she does.*

I sit on my floor, inhaling the cake. I seldom binge eat, but today was stressful and this cake is delicious. The subsequent sharp pain in my stomach tells me that was a mistake. After I'm done, I slip off my sneakers, socks, and bra. My hair goes into a thick ponytail holder.

Carter rejected me. The loser, the punchline, the dork.

Slater chose to help Carter. That means they're friends. Carter has forgiven Slater and Kelsey, not me.

I crawl into bed and groan. If Carter can't deal with me, why would Kelsey want to? Why would Mother? Maybe I am as awful as recent events say I am.

I sit up straight in bed.

No.

If Kelsey can earn back Carter's forgiveness, so can I. I want Kelsey to speak to me again. I need my best friend back. I've lost everything since I lost her: some "friends," my actual best friends, my social status, a thousand social media followers.

I know how to start: by crashing Kelsey's party. Despite the security at the door, it shouldn't be too hard. Then we'll make up, kiss it out, and I'll become popular again. Then Kelsey will make Carter back into a loser, and order will be restored in our kingdom.

I drag myself out of this queen-size bed and start again.

CHAPTER 27
CARTER

I HAVE to be careful as I take my place as a sellout.

I examine the exterior like Mom taught me. Kelsey's house is ostentatious yet boring, tucked within a housing development where all the homes around it look nearly the same. Just like the POPS—all a different variety of the same stuck-up, mean girl.

"Remember the steps?" Slater asks as she veers into a parking spot marked *RESERVED*. While doing my makeup, she provided a crash course in how to behave around Kelsey—checking my body language, hiding my depression—and how to interact with people. In our last session, Therapist #8/Locke gave me some solid advice for social anxiety as well.

"The steps are...." I take a moment to remember. "Use hand gestures to show expression when my words are lacking. Try to center conversations around easy topics like pop culture and groaning about class. Don't gaze into space. People don't take it well."

"I'm shocked you remembered all that." Who does Slater think I am? Some lazy punk who doesn't pay attention in class? I have a 3.97 GPA for a reason. Or *had.* My grades have slipped since February, and I now have a 3.6. Embarrassing.

"Yeah, well." I shrug without giving any real explanation. Thanks to my lack of social graces and hatred of the people in this house, I'm already over this party. Though I am curious to see how the POPS have fun. I've been on the outside for so long that I can't help but wonder what it's like to be *in.*

I tug on the tunic Slater discovered in the depths of my closet. She let me borrow her heeled boots and a belt. One of the three items in my jewelry box, the test tube pendant Hudson gave me for our one and only anniversary, was deemed "perfect" for my outfit. I didn't protest as Slater latched it.

I smiled as I looked in the mirror, for once. I know I'm not a belle of the ball beauty like Kelsey. Nor do I possess the haunting ice queen characteristics of Abby. I don't have Mei's toned figure. I can't fathom having shiny, waist-length hair like Slater. But there's something interesting about me. Something worth looking at. Something worth loving. It's easy to forget that, when my apparent ugliness is often thrown in my face.

Abby, Kelsey, Slater, and Mei's antics could break anyone's piddling confidence.

Though maybe they've stopped. You did score an invite to "the party of the season," Rational Carter muses.

My new semi-positivity streak is getting on my nerves.

"Let's do this thing!" Slater sings. My heart gallops as she locks our arms together.

Slater rings the doorbell. Kelsey answers, a paper crown atop her head and a shot glass in hand. She screams and raises the glass in the air. A bit of her drink splashes onto me, warm and irritating.

"My bitchessssssss! You made it!" Kelsey drags out the 's' like the snake she is. She steps back and examines my outfit. "You look good. How?"

I don't trust myself to speak, knowing I'll stammer and stutter and Kelsey will roast me for it. Luckily, Slater speaks on my behalf. Normally I'd be pissed about her doing so, but there's nothing normal about my life right now.

"Me," Slater says.

Kelsey raises her overplucked eyebrows. "Since when do you color-coordinate?"

Slater taps Kelsey on the nose. "I learned from the best."

"Hmm. Fine," Kelsey says. Though I'm not the one who was interrogated, I'm relieved for the inquiries to be over.

Kelsey steps aside so we can enter her "home," if this McMansion stuffed to the brim with teenagers can be considered a home.

The party of the season is an understatement. Bass from the makeshift DJ booth in the backyard reverberates through Kelsey's palatial home. The French doors are open, and I spy a pool. I almost wish I'd brought a bathing suit before I remember that the POPS love to make fun of my weight. Plus, Kelsey would make an ignorant comment about Black people not being able to swim. Ah, well. Maybe another time. If there is another time. As it is, though Slater did her best to help me blend in with the POPS, I stick out like a sore thumb in this strange, parent-free playland. As we navigate the party, when people look at Slater, they admire her. They look at me with pity.

Though I was admitted to this party as a charity case, I don't have to be one for the whole thing. I can be fun. I can be cool. Give me a chance, and I'll prove it.

Kelsey sweeps her arms out, once again forgetting the drink in her hand. "Well? Is it everything you imagined?"

I didn't imagine ninety-nine other people grinding on each other on the glitzy dancefloor, and/or cannonballing in the pool. "Of course!" I say brightly. "Thank you for inviting me."

Kelsey smiles. "No prob. Like I said, I owe ya one." She owes me way more than that, but okay.

"Is the pool heated?" I whisper to Slater as we meander to the kitchen.

Slater looks at me strangely. "Uh, yeah. Have you been outside? This might as well be called the Winter Shitfaced Extravaganza."

I chuckle. "You're right." The weather is too cold considering it's spring. Thank you, politicians and billionaires who don't care about climate change.

We pass the packed living room. The guests are in various stages of drunkenness, from stone-cold sober to, uh, Kelsey. Mei waves from her seat next to a Black boy on the floor, who I recognize as Troy. We worked on a group project once, and he was nice. I wave back. So, this is what it's like to have friends. Though Mei's more of a grudging acquaintance than a friend.

"Help yourself." Kelsey points to the two rows of liquor bottles tucked within the wet bar. Seriously, where the hell are this girl's parents? I know one is a CEO and the other is a socialite, but the lack of adult supervision has me shook. "What do you want?"

I have an idea. I've had alcohol before, when Hudson and I snuck bottles from his mother's cabinet and got tipsy. I felt a fuzz and a sparkle in my chest that day, and I remember having fun. Alcohol could help me get that feeling back. And if I get that feeling back, I could be accepted, if only for a night.

"Vodka?" I suggest.

"Uh, are you sure that's a good idea?" Slater asks. She scrunches her face in concern.

"Yes." *No.*

"Fine with me. Vanilla or cherry?" Kelsey asks.

"Cherry." I spot the bottle, grab it, and swig straight from it. The vodka burns, but not as much as the prospect of being here without it.

"Carter—" Slater's voice is drowned out as I focus on the vodka. "Yeah, okay, you're cut off." She takes the bottle from me.

"You're no fun," I mumble.

"Neither is you passing out on the lawn later," Slater snaps at me.

Kelsey lets out a baying laugh and shoves me. "Good girl. Now go out there and talk to people. You've been a re-rel—" Kelsey frowns, trying to find the right word. Drunk girls are so senseless, I swear.

"Recluse?" Slater asks dryly.

"Yeah! Thanks! Anyway, you've been a recluse for way too long. Mingle, bitch. I need to talk to Slater."

"I guess," I say, though I want to stay with Slater. She's my safety blanket.

"You'll be fine." Slater's brows furrow, like she's not sure of that at all.

It's fine. I got this. No need to worry.

Time to get social.

I walk to the dining room. Nobody's there, despite the ten-person table and dimmed lighting to nurse premature hangovers. I don't get why the crowd in the living room don't come in here so they can breathe. Dining rooms must be uncool according to the unofficial popularity code of Harlow High.

I know I should go to the living room. Isn't that the point of all this? To ingratiate myself with the rest of the POPS? To "mingle, bitch"?!

I sit down at the dining room table instead. What was I thinking, trying to be popular? That's for girls in low-budget teen movies, not me. I've never been someone who can be social just by trying. It takes so much work for me to even try to hold a conversation: I can't be the life of the party.

I rest my face on my fist. My elbow presses uncomfortably against the table. I'm there for a solid ten, fifteen, twenty, thirty minutes thinking about how bad my life is and waiting for the alcohol to hit me before people trickle in. Mei, her boyfriend Troy, Amy Ryan, and some other girl whose name I can't place come in giggling about some girl's outfit.

Their conversation stops when they see me. I shift uncomfortably.

"Hey," Mei says. She sits at the table and pulls out her phone. Troy, Amy, and Girl #3 share a loaded look before following suit.

What do I say? Social interaction is my weakness. At best, I am awkward. At worst, I am offensive and branded as psychotic.

"Uh, how are you guys?" I ask. *Smooth, Carter.* I add finger guns for punctuation.

Amy snorts. "Fine." She glances at Mei, who refuses to look her in the eye. Rather, Mei continues to play with her phone. Troy looks uncomfortable and smiles at me.

"What—you—what—typing?" Why can't I talk right? I might be bisexual, but I can at least talk straight.

Mei doesn't bother looking up. "I'm checking my stocks."

"At a party?" Troy says. He slings his arm around her shoulder. "Babe, come on."

Mei smiles at his touch. "Apple's headed for a crash and I need to call my broker to sell my shares when it hits." Mei finally puts her phone away. "Luckily, that crash isn't happening tonight. Who wants Jell-O shots?"

"Me!" I raise my hand, happy to have found an opportunity to bond with the cool crowd.

"No," the table says in unison. I break into a cold sweat.

"...Right," I say. I get up and leave. It's fine. She doesn't have to say the real reason, that I'm too much of a loser to do Jell-O shots with them.

Whatever. I can make my own Jell-O shots, thank you very much.

"What's with her?" Girl #3 says when she thinks I'm gone.

"My guess? Kelsey got her drunk," Mei says. "Five bucks says she falls into the pool."

The living room is less people-heavy than when I arrived. The French double doors leading out to the pool, meanwhile, are wide open and offer a view of Kelsey's huge pool. Hmm. Pool. Sounds like a fun idea.

Before I head out to the water, I notice a girl with long, black hair texting in the corner. She looks like she belongs here, despite being uninvited.

Abby.

My vision clouds and I grip my arm to chase out the memories of *her writing the note her picking up my Prozac herherherherher I don't want to react I can't react how drunk* am I?

I thought she was kicked out of the popular clique. Why is here? Who let her in? Should I get away? Do I stay? Goddammit, I can't think when I'm drunk. Am I drunk? Yeah. I'm drunk.

Abby glances up and sees me staring.

Too late to run. Her gunmetal blue eyes are a shot to my system. "Oh. It's you."

"Why are you here?" I ask. More like whine. Argh, wine sounds cool.

Abby puts her phone in her back pocket. She looks wild, uninhibited, out of place. "I belong here. Unlike you."

"Fuck off." Whoa. Where did that come from?

Abby laughs. "Holy shit. Are you drunk?"

"Mehbe." My legs wobble. I lean against the wall. I hope I look sexy, in case any cuties walk past. Though with my luck, I likely look like a shaking dolphin.

"There's no way. Carter Harper, brown-noser extraordinaire, is wasted." Amusement dances across her face, replaced by horror. "Wait, aren't you on antidepressants?"

"Yeah?"

"Carter, you're not supposed to drink with those."

"Wait, what?" I vaguely recall a warning from Psychiatrist #3 about alcohol and my medications. At the time, I was fresh out of the hospital, and didn't want to listen to anyone but my mother.

"How did you not kn—whatever. You need water. ASAP." Abby yanks on my arm. "Kitchen."

"Ow!" Still, I follow her.

"I almost killed you once, I'm not letting you die again," Abby mutters. She's still yanking my arm.

Kelsey, Mei, and Slater are talking and laughing in the closed-off kitchen. Though people wander in and out to grab drinks and food, they're the anchors. They're the stars of this party, perfectly placed in the center. It makes you fall a little bit in love with them. Or that's the beer goggles talking. Vodka goggles. Antidepressants goggles?

Abby opens one of the cabinets and retrieves a mug. "Hey, gals. Nice to see you again."

Kelsey's pissed. "How the hell did you get in?"

Abby fills the mug with water. "You used the same rent-a-cop from last year, you incompetent wench. He knew who I was and let me in without an invitation." Abby places her finger on her chin. "Hmm, did you give away the #1 invitation this year? I guess you wished you had only ninety-nine problems, but now this bitch is one."

My instant reaction is to sing the rest of the song since my mother named me after Jay-Z. (Look, she was in high school when I was born.) But this environment is too white for that outburst.

"I would kick you out, but you don't have a life. Consider yourself a charity case." Poison and malice are written on Kelsey's lips.

"Good thing I was here to take care of your wasted 'friend' who, FYI, is the real charity case here." Abby hands me the water, which I guzzle. Water. Yum. Love the stuff.

"We're not fr—can you get out of here!" Kelsey screeches.

Abby rolls her eyes as she leaves the kitchen. "Gladly."

"Fuck up. Wait, off. Fuck off!" Kelsey says. She points at Slater. "Did you know she was coming?"

"Do I look like I did?"

"Mei?"

"She's not even talking to me!"

"Carter?"

I hesitate. "No, but I think it's my fault she's here."

Kelsey gestures for me to sit at the kitchen island. "Explain." The music is so amplified at this point that she has to yell. Kelsey snaps her fingers at Slater and Mei. "You two. Sit."

Some drunk member of the Actively Disinterested who wandered in sits at our makeshift command center. "Not you. OUT."

"Bitch," he says.

Kelsey throws an empty plastic cup at his retreating head. "THIS IS A FEMINIST HOUSEHOLD," she yells. "Now explain, Carter. I gotta pee."

In a rush, I explain what happened this afternoon. Abby bringing me a cake and getting angry when she realized I was coming here. Slater and Mei interject when necessary, though Mei wasn't there when all this happened.

While recounting the story, I'm torn. Is this my information to share? Should Slater dissect Abby's facial expression? Should Mei analyze Abby's words? Should Kelsey look like a girl with a plan? If we put our powers of deduction together for good, we'd be unstoppable.

My head hurts.

"Why is she here?" Kelsey whispers when we're all done. "Why couldn't she have stayed home?"

"Why? Now that she's here, can't she—" What's the

right word? "Stay?" Yeah. That one. Good job, National Merit Semifinalist.

Kelsey's eyes grow dark. "No. I have to destroy her."

"Huh?" I ask. They've lost me.

Slater rubs her temples. "Y'all, there is zero point in hurting Abby at this point. She hurt herself by crashing the party. Just kick her out."

Kelsey shakes her head. "It's not that simple."

"Except it is! Your life doesn't need to revolve around schemes," Slater says.

Kelsey snorts. "Are you in love with her, Slate? Or are you showing off for your new buddy, Carter?"

Slater glares at Kelsey. "Have you considered that I'm trying to do the right thing here?"

"Why do you want to be mean to Abby? You two were best friends." I sniffle, trying to suck the snot back in from Drunk Carter's ugly crying jags. Gross.

Kelsey rolls her eyes. "Yes, Carter. We were best friends." She studies me and smiles again. "Be grateful, okay? We're hurting the girl who caused you to stab yourself. Or whatever."

"Don't bring up her sui—You know what? Forget this, I'm out," Slater says. She gets up from the table. "I'm going to find Abby."

"If you do, we aren't friends anymore," Kelsey threatens.

"I don't care!" Slater roars. She leaves, and Kelsey

follows her. After a moment's hesitation, Mei does as well.

"Shit," I mumble. I sit at the counter for a second, trying to figure out the best way to game this. Where's Abby? How do I tell her? Can I warn her?

Only... I don't know anything. I'd still need to weave through the crowd. Kelsey will be *pissed* if I bail on her. She surely expects me to witness Abby's humiliation.

How can I sit there and watch somebody else get dragged the way I've been?

I can't.

I have to.

No. I don't.

I wade through the crowd to the living room, where loud voices make their way toward me. The booming music is pulsing and mingles with the voices and my head hurts and I want to go home.

I can't go home. While I contemplated what to do, this party has gone to hell.

CHAPTER 28
ABBY

THIS HALF-BAKED PLAN of mine went wrong from the start.

At least slipping into Kelsey's house was easy. The hard part was dealing with mocking stares when I entered the living room. Even Kelsey's charity cases knew I wasn't invited. Nobody spoke to me, and for once, I was too intimidated to speak to or make fun of other people. I was relegated to sitting in the corner, playing a game on the BRAIN/ZAPP app. Lights danced all around me, the effect of Kelsey's unfortunate love of disco balls, reflecting on my body-shimmer-dusted skin.

Forget that. These assholes don't get to treat me like dirt. Slater doesn't get to help someone else succeed socially. Mei doesn't get to pretend we're no longer friends, despite us not having an official falling out. Kelsey doesn't get to ignore me, then invite my former worst enemy to her party.

I know everything about Kelsey. The beautiful, the ugly, and the downright awful. With a few clicks, I can revert her life back to the hellish past she thought people could forget. And s, I do. Within one minute, I'm surrounded by gasps and laughs. They're not in my direction anymore. I solved that problem with one well-timed social media post.

Before I can leave to deal with the damage I've wrought from the safety of my own home, Kelsey drapes herself all over me. "Are you sure we're over?" she whispers in my ear. I almost drop the shot glass I'm holding. Her hot breath smells like rubbing alcohol. She's worse than Carter when inebriated. Drunk Kelsey is prone to mood swings and frequent changes of opinion.

"Back off," I say. Kelsey staggers away from me. She opens her mouth to say something else.

A random screech sounds in the distance. "Ab—!" Carter's voice cuts off when she trips on the kitchen entrance and falls onto the carpet. "Never mind," she mumbles into the floor.

"Come on." Slater appears out of nowhere and pulls Carter back up.

"But I need to tell—"

"Girl, you're not sober enough to have that conversation."

"So-dah? Where?"

"For God's sake—" Slater drags Carter back into the kitchen.

I blink. Why did Carter scream my name? Does she know something? I need to talk to her, but she's too far gone and Kelsey's too close.

"How many times do I have to tell you I don't want you, Kelsey?" I project my voice so other people can hear our torrid drama.

"You used to." Kelsey starts to pull down the strap of her slinky dress. I grab her hand and yank it back up. I ignore the tingle in my palms as I protect her from exposing herself.

"Past tense." I'm about to call her out further, maybe boast about what I just did, when Mei storms up to me. Her bangs fall in her eyes, an unusually messy look. Through the fringe, sandy eyes flash and eyebrows scrunch to mirror their anger.

"You are the most vile, petty, daughter of a *bitch!*" She punctuates each word by jabbing her shiny, polished nails in my face.

Mei's not wrong about any of it. What I did was awful, but I'm desperate. Desperate to fully divorce myself from Kelsey, who enjoys toying with me the way we used to toy with other people *together*. Desperate to get my place back in Harlow's social hierarchy, if for no other reason than to topple Kelsey off the pyramid.

And look, as far as secrets go? I didn't reveal the worst of what I know about Kelsey. I could've told the world that she's a pillow princess, or that her mother said she regretted giving birth to Kelsey when Kelsey was in elementary school, or that she sucked my ex-boyfriend's dick before we dated. (Which, ew?)

In reality, I'm doing her a kindness. I could out her as bisexual, remind everyone that she's a slut, and taunt her about being an unwanted daughter. Instead, I'm reducing her to being nothing.

Again.

"Relax, Mei. We all know Kelsey used to be a loser." I smirk at Kelsey and open the pictures I swore on my grave would never get out.

Too bad. Kelsey dug my grave. It's about time I fight back by digging hers.

Kelsey leans over to look at my phone. "What are you—?" Her face drains of color as she looks at herself in fifth grade, bloated, unfashionable, and sad. The Kelsey people pretend to have forgotten, that Kelsey herself has attempted to leave behind. The daughter her mother couldn't connect to, leaving permanent scars.

Kelsey, drama queen that she is, reflects on her loserdom as the worst days of her life. She has vowed never to go back to the insecure girl she once was. Her current head-bitch-in-charge status can't last, though. Every peak must have its valley. Tonight, I'm starting Kelsey's push down to the Marianas Trench of high school girl politics.

Kelsey screams like a banshee. A loud, wailing yell that stops the DJ from playing a Lizzo remix.

"I HATE YOU!" Kelsey tries to shove me, but Mei holds her back.

"She isn't worth it," Mei whispers. "You're drunk. Let me handle this one." Aww, look at Mei, cleaning Kelsey's mess once again. Mei's the fixer in the group, the one who ensures we look perfect while doing dirty deeds.

Slater and Carter rush into the room. "What the hell?!" Slater asked.

"While you two were dicking around, she ruined me!" Kelsey wails.

"I can't believe you'd betray your best—ex-best friend like this," Mei says. "I don't care if you two are fighting. This is cruel."

"Hey, remember when we almost killed your new 'friend'?" I whisper. Though I doubt my cryptic language points to Carter's suicide, I keep my voice low because people's phones are out and if anybody knows the importance of controlling a fight, it's me.

"They aren't friends!" Kelsey exclaims. "The little bitch tried to defend you!"

At least someone did. "I'm the only one who gets to call her a bitch!" I lunge at her. Once again, Mei stops me. "Stop it, Mei! Don't you see what she's doing?"

Mei's face crumbles in pain. The rest of the party fades to white, and it's only us, locked in this battle of wills and friendship. "I'm sorry," Mei says. "But Kelsey saved me."

"What are you talking abou—are you serious? You really mean middle school? When you two got makeovers? Kelsey may have saved you, but she ruins everything else!" I scream. Now I know what to do, ripped straight from the Kelsey Maxwell Playbook: cover a bubbling scandal with a bigger one. "So you've traded being my subordinate to being Kelsey's? You'll never one-up her, no matter how much you want to. And considering how many times you've complained about her 'narcissistic, needy, greedy, self-serving ass,' you're the last one entitled to judge me." I navigate to my screenshots folder. "In fact, I think I have some screenshots here, hold on—" If she thinks I won't go there, she knows nothing about me.

"At least my parents love each other," Mei says, glossing over my accusations. Yikes. She needs to deflect, deny, leave, anything but concede. "How many times did yours get the cops called on them because of their loud-ass arguments before they divorced? Seven? Sounds like a record—"

Oh, fuck this. I interrupt her mid-sentence by throwing my Sprite (disguised as vodka) in her face before leaving the house. The jeers of my classmates follow me out the door.

"You coming?" I shout at Carter, Slater, Mei,

anybody who wants to follow me. I can't be alone, not right now.

Not the way I was when *he*—

Footsteps fall behind me. I don't turn around to see who decided to hitch a ride home with me. All I know is that Kelsey isn't behind me, because she got her revenge at last. She told Mei about my parents' verbal abuse toward each other. The abuse that created a toxic environment that made me pray they'd divorce. Thank God I never told her about *him*.

I protected Kelsey's secrets, the things she decided to hide from the world to preserve her social standing. She couldn't even offer me the same courtesy.

Tonight was a failure by all means. I didn't get Kelsey back. I drove her as far away as possible, and she did the same. There's nothing left for us. We've finally, irrevocably hurt each other beyond repair.

CHAPTER 29
CARTER

I STUMBLE up the walkway as Slater and Abby hold onto me. As the night grows older, it becomes clearer and clearer that guzzling eighty-proof vodka was... doing too much.

"Where are your keys?" Slater asks.

"Purse zipper side thingie," I say. "Why isn't there a name for that?"

"It's a pocket, you prick," Abby says.

Slater fumbles with my keys before she can find the right one to unlock my front door. We move past the foyer into the living room, where Mom's watching a rerun, bucket of popcorn in hand. She squints her eyes. "Abby? Why the hell are you in my house?"

Abby and Slater try to hurry me upstairs. "Uh, it's all good, Ms. Ashley! Carter and I made up! Right, Slater?"

"Yeah, they're fine," Slater says.

"Well, alright," Mom says with a healthy dose of skepticism. She knows, likes, and trusts Slater, so she returns to watching her show.

And Carter screws things up in three...two...one! "Mei told people that Abby—"

"Oh my G—*shut up!*" Abby whispers.

Mom crosses her arms and stalks over to us. "Are you drunk?" she asks me.

"Yeah," I admit. "But I'm more fun that way!" I pop my arms into the air and kind of just dangle them there.

"No, you're not." Mom points at me. "You. Upstairs. We'll discuss this in the morning." She turns to Abby and Slater. "You two seem sober enough. We'll discuss your part in this now."

"Thanks, Carter," Abby says. I pat her on the head before running upstairs. Once in the bathroom, I retch until I can't feel my throat anymore.

I am *never* drinking again.

Too exhausted to worry about my unsalvageable outfit, I take it all off and crawl into bed. As I pull my hot pink and black comforter over me, Mom yells at Abby and Slater downstairs.

Twelve hours later, I awaken with a headache, but nothing too awful. I think I got most of the toxins out last night. I put on a pair of pajamas, since I'm not planning on leaving the house today anyway, and walk downstairs.

The smell of breakfast food seduces me to the kitchen. Breakfast. Yeah. Good idea.

"How's your hangover?" Mom asks as she flips the sizzling turkey bacon.

I shrug and sit at our kitchen island. "Tolerable." Mom pushes a heaping plate of scrambled eggs at me. "Thanks." I scarf them down, barely registering the hot eggs, cheese, and mushrooms scalding my throat.

"Now, there are a few things we need to talk about."

"Hmmkay," I say. The food's still in my mouth.

"One: you're grounded. For the rest of the school year. You're only going home, to therapy, and to school."

"Wait, what about GSA?" I started attending meetings, sitting in the back and not participating. It's okay, I suppose. It gets my name on the roll call, which is all Principal Adams really wanted. Also, it's an activity for my college applications, so National Honor Society isn't my only school-sanctioned extracurricular.

"Oh. That too."

"And to the grocery store?"

"I gue—now you're messing around with me!" Mom laughs, then grows serious again. "I just don't want you to go to any more parties. I don't care about a little drinking, but I sure as hell don't want a repeat of last night."

"No problem," I say. "Alcohol and parties suck major dick."

"Which leads me into my second question." Mom

sits. "Do we need to take you to Planned Parenthood? I hope you don't, but we can go today if you need Plan B or to get tested."

I spit out my orange juice. "What? No!"

"Slater and Abby said the party is known for—"

"All I did was drink!"

"Carter!" Mom says. "This is serious. You shouldn't have been drinking with your antidepressants. Do you want to die? Is that what you want?"

I pause. "No," I say. "Not anymore."

I don't know who's more surprised by me saying that: me or Mom.

KELSEY

omg i'm so hungover

are you??

KELSEY

hello????

KELSEY

ugh i guess your phone is off

or slater gave me the wrong number

—NEW GROUP CHAT STARTED, 11:15 A.M.—

SLATER

uh, we all need to talk
about wtf happened last night

> **CARTER**
>
> why am i in this

SLATER

first of all, you were the drunkest
one at the party. also, like it or not,
you were involved in the drama last night.
barely. but still involved.

> **CARTER**
>
> .

SLATER

can everyone meet at my house today?

MEI

WTF, I'm not friends with Carter.

SLATER

ye but I am!!!!!!

> **CARTER**
>
> I'm grounded anyways

ABBY

Alksjdfhkasjdhlfjsadf who the
FUCK gets grounded anymore?????

SLATER

people who aren't white
and fine, we'll just meet
at your house

CARTER

wait i didn't say I wanted
y'all to come to my house

SLATER

see you soon!! xoxo

Mom is a terrible disciplinarian, considering she lets
Abby, Slater, and Mei come in without much fuss. Abby
and Mei are as far away from each other as possible—I
wonder how Slater wrangled them into being in the
same room, considering what went down last night.

"Can we get this going? I have a date with Troy in an
hour," Mei says. She's curled up on the barrel-backed
club chair I tend to frequent. She's the only one of the
POPS not to show any signs of wear and tear after her
night of partying. Hair: flat. Bootcut jeans: crisp. White

heels: too high to imagine stepping into. Slater and Abby, meanwhile, rolled in with unwashed hair, t-shirts, and leggings.

I cross my legs at the ankles. I learned long ago that my thighs are too thick to cross at the knee.

"Yeah. We all have some things to discuss about what happened last night," Slater says.

From my perch on the chair opposite Mei, my eyes dart around the room, searching for each girl's reaction.

Slater stares sternly at each of us in turn like a deeply disappointed parent.

Mei chews her shellacked lip.

Abby's face grows taut, like she's constipated.

The girls become statues, bitter due to remembering all the reasons we're sitting in this room. The magic has faded, and they are once again fractured.

"Okay, let's start with Abby," Slater says. She turns to Abby, who's sitting rather close to her on the couch. "Why did you release Kelsey's ugly elementary school photos?"

Abby snorts. "I was upset at Kelsey for inviting Carter to the party and not me. I'm upset at Kelsey for a lot of other things, too, which don't need to be rehashed here. The end."

Slater rolls her head back. "Sure, that makes sense."

"Slate, honey? I'm a teenage girl. I won't always behave rationally," Abby drawls.

"Y'don't have to be a dickhead all the time, though," Slater counters.

Mei jumps in. "Honestly, you throwing vodka in my face was so uncalled for. I'm putting that in the Rumors Notebook." The what?

Slater directs her attention to Mei. "I didn't even get started with you. At least we already knew about Kelsey's hot mess of a past life. Thanks to you, the whole school will know about Abby's parents nearly killing each other by Monday. If they don't already."

"Whoa, how did this become about me? She threw vodka in my face!"

"Yeah, and then you threw her family issues in everyone else's! How'd you find out about that, anyways?" Slater turns to Abby. "You only told me, right? I think she only told me."

Abby looks annoyed as hell. "Why would I bother telling anyone else? You and Kelsey only know because she you saw them cursing each other out. And you only know about To—" Abby freezes and her eyes glaze over. I've never seen her like that before. Like she's...afraid of something.

Or someone.

"To—what? To Mars?" Mei says.

"Shut up," Slater snaps. She rubs Abby's back. Abby's ice now, ready to crack at any moment. "Abby, honey?" Slater. "He's not here, Abs. Not anymore."

My brain works overtime trying to figure out what Abby means. To where? And who's *he?*

Wait. He. To—

Tom. Tom?

No. It can't be Tom. Abby couldn't have been the one he hurt.

Except maybe he was.

Everyone in the neighborhood remembers when Tom's house nearly burned down, when someone tagged his garage with a nine-letter word that destroyed his reputation.

Mom heard about a girl fainting when she saw the tagged garage, but the other moms in the neighborhood refused to say who it was. She wasn't upset about that; she'd been impressed with their commitment to protecting her.

Abby got worse around that time. She got worse and worse until she threw a dead frog at me. I didn't know why she lashed out; she always had, so I didn't delve into why she was targeting me yet again. Now I wonder if she's the girl Tom raped. If she is...maybe she stayed strong and cold and hard because she *had* to. I'm not excusing her for what she did. I will never do that, no matter how quasi-friendly we've gotten recently.

Abby seems to snap out of her spell. "Where were we?"

"You *throwing vodka in my face!*" Mei says.

"It wasn't even vodka," Abby interjects. "I threw

Sprite in your face. The vodka would have burned your eyes out, right, Carter?"

I refuse to respond.

"Oh, yeah. Carter." Slater glares at me. "Vodka. Never again, you hear me? I don't know how much you had when I wasn't lookin', but you shouldn't have been that drunk."

"She's on antidepressants, Slater," Abby mutters.

"Fine. I just...what's going on with you?" Slater asks me, like she knows me well enough to see changes in my behavior. "I'm surprised you even wanted to go to the party. Why did you go?"

"You *helped* me," I whine. I wanted to fit in for once in my life, ha ha, very funny.

"For no reason," Mei interjects. "Why is Carter the key, anyway? Why are you, Abby, and Kelsey obsessed with her? I don't *get* it!" Mei turns to me. "No offense. You're fairly pretty and would look better if you used a good face serum that fixed your slight hyperpigmentation. Your wardrobe sucks, but you have an hourglass shape. Like Meg Thee Stallion, but plus size." Uh, thanks? I have zero clue if she's complimenting me or not. Though Meg is hot. I would let her if she asked.

We consider Mei's question, me most of all. Yes, Kelsey wanted to "make it up to me" since she nearly caused my death. She doesn't need to invite me to parties and send me texts I ignore.

I shift in my seat, trying to center myself the way Dr.

Locke's taught me. *Imagine you're somewhere else. Tune it out. Tune out their words—or, er, stares. Do not give your oppressor the power to hurt you.*

"The key isn't Carter," Abby says slowly. "The key is me."

Mei rolls her eyes. "Don't flatter yourself."

"Think about it. Kelsey practically admitted that she's in love with me. And Kelsey's love isn't...the best. You all see how possessive she is. How many friends do each of you have outside of the group? Close friends, real friends?"

"Well, that's not because of Kelsey. It's because we're better than everyone else." Mei flips her pitch-perfect hair, as if to punctuate her point.

"And who told you that?"

Mei's silent.

"Kelsey. Right. She hates three people: girls poised to take her place on the popularity ladder, our other friends, and girls with a better shade of blond than her. Remember when she eviscerated Jennifer Baker?"

"Who's that?" I ask. The name sounds familiar.

Abby shakes her head. "You don't want to know."

I drop the issue.

"Carter was the key because Kelsey saw Carter and me growing closer because of the...you know," Abby says. "She wanted to take away somebody who was—er, is—starting to mean something to me." Abby settles into the couch. "She figured I'd snap after finding out you were going to the party. And voila!—that's exactly what happened."

I look down. I hadn't realized that I was just a pawn. It makes sense, though. What else am I good for, to these girls? Despite Abby's claims of us growing closer (before she blew it), I know I'm nothing more than a charity case to the POPS.

Guilt has a funny way of skewing people's perspectives.

Slater looks worried. "Kelsey is using Carter...to get to you?"

"Duh, that's what I just spent ten minutes explaining."

"Kelsey wouldn't do something so douchey," Mei says.

"God, Mei, you're stupefied with loyalty to her!" Abby yells. "Don't you get it? Kelsey doesn't give a shit about anybody but herself. She never has, and she never will. When she loves somebody, that love is conditional. She dumped me because I didn't tell her about Carter's suicide attempt or that my nightmare of a mother was coming in town."

Mei's silent again. She stands, grabbing her purse from the floor in one swift motion. "I'm not dealing with this. Abby, I forgive you, and I hope you forgive me because I didn't mean to screw you over. But I'm not listening to you talk shit about my best friend. Do it on your own time."

I follow Mei to the front door. "You seem okay," she says to me as she leaves. "Not as much of a blockheaded loser as I'd thought."

That's the best compliment a POPS has ever given me.

Slater gets up to leave as well. "We worked out about half our issues, which is what I was hoping for." She points to Abby and me. "Are you two cool?"

"Uh...." Abby still hasn't apologized.

Abby sighs dramatically. "I'm sorry I was such a bitch to you at lunch. And at your house. And I'm sorry I took your cake and accidentally called you fat. I've been dealing with a lot of stress, which led to me taking it out on you, I guess."

"Uh...okay," I respond. Granted, it's not the most graceful apology, but it is an acknowledgement of her wrongdoings.

"But—" Abby starts.

Nevermind.

"Are you done now, Carter? Are you done trying to be popular, to be something you're not? You don't fit in, and you know it."

"Abby—"

"No, Slater, she needs to hear this." Abby stares me down, but her glare doesn't seem heated with anger for once. In fact, she seems almost...caring? "You're not one of us. And that's fine. Do your science crap, get a ton of scholarship offers, we all know you're headed down that path. But don't play games you don't know how to play. I know how to do this and I still got burned. You pretended to be totally innocent, but admit it: you wanted to be us, even for just a minute. You wanted that power, to be someone you're not." Abby looks me up and down. "And if you take that power, it'll consume you. And we all know what happens when you get hurt."

Yeah, no need to rehash *that* scenario.

"I'll ask you one more time. *Are. You. Done.* Because I can't lose—" Abby swallows her words.

I realize that she's trying to say she cares.

"Yeah," I whisper. "I'm done with this."

Turns out, maybe I can't lose me, either.

CHAPTER 30
CARTER

AFTER SCHOOL TUESDAY, I sketch ideas for a proposed BRAIN/ZAPP user interface design tweak. It'll be a small adjustment, moving some icons here and there and switching out Arial for a less ubiquitous font, but the changes will have a measurable impact on user satisfaction. We've had a huge uptick in subscribers since the article, so I need to step my game up. I can't do this all alone anymore, and I'm considering hiring more help than my part-timer in Singapore. I'm also working on a ZAPP/PACK for sexual assault survivors. I can't believe I haven't created one before, but after seeing Abby's reaction the other day, I realized that people need this.

Rape. Domestic violence. Divorce. It turns out Abby and I are both traumatized, and the girls who should have supported each other tore each other apart. (Well,

I didn't do much tearing. Perhaps a rip.) I thought Abby was perfect, yet here she is, as vulnerable as me.

Which, in a way, is a revelation I needed since my foray into popularity was the disaster of the season. I semi-appreciate what Kelsey tried to do for me (even if it was a weird ploy to get back at Abby), but it's clear now that popularity doesn't solve anything. No, I'll stick to being a loser. Or whatever I am nowadays, since I'm no longer the POPS's chew toy.

Overall, as I reflect on recent events and work on my craft, I'm content in this moment. I find myself able to think past my depression.

Wait a sec.

I haven't had suicidal ideations for a while. I waited for them to come back, but they've been tempered. I peruse my memories, trying to consider the last time I wanted to kill myself. I know that in the days following my suicide attempt, all I could think of was death, but since then, I haven't given death more than a few passing thoughts. And since the POPS became my sort-of friends, I got new meds, I've gotten some new hobbies, and people stopped bullying me, well....

Am I...recovering?

Do I...want to recover?

I throw down my pencil in frustration. What am I supposed to do with this feeling? My purpose for so long has been to die as quickly as possible while mini-mizing the damage done to those I care about. But this?

Seeing that there's a path through this darkness? How can I deal?

I grow increasingly anxious. *Breathe in, breathe out.* I pace around my room. Cue a Spotify playlist full of soothing thunderstorm sounds. I complete a quick session of vinyasa flow yoga. I sit on the floor and meditate while inhaling my "Stress Relief" aromatherapy oils. I pull out the "personal massager" I smuggled in from CVS and, well, do my thing. I even try positive journaling.

Positive. Motherfucking. Journaling.

There. Basically all the coping mechanisms I've learned, exhausted. None of it calms me down because this situation is too weird for me to handle.

I reach for my phone and scroll through my limited contacts list. I could call Mom, but I'm tired of being the cause of her worries. She deserves some uninterrupted time to work, and I deserve some uninterrupted time to freak the hell out. I could call Slater, but—crap, I missed last week's GSA meeting, so I can't ask her for help. She'll ask why I wasn't there, and I don't want to admit I went home after school to nap (I can only handle so much socialization). I could call Mr. Atkinson or Miss Parker—they both gave me their phone numbers as a lifeline after I tried to die. I could text Mei, but she has cooler things to do than listen to my problems. Or I could visit Abby—okay, I'm scraping the bottom of the barrel.

I know who I should contact, though I'm still scared.

If you don't want to turn to the ones you care about, at least turn to her.

Maybe Rational Carter is right sometimes. *Sometimes.*

KELSEY
Why didn't you say hi at lunch today? :(

KELSEY
Carter?

KELSEY
CARTER.

"You consider not being depressed anymore an emergency?"

Okay, I hadn't realized how ridiculous that sounds until Locke laid it out like that. Now I want to go home and crawl into bed. Or, like, not crawl into bed. Read a book or something. Spring has arrived after a series of global-warming-related false alarms, meaning I can read on the patio without cold biting my skin.

"Uh, I'm sorry. I know this is a waste of your time."

I'm balled up on her Therapy Couch, as if constricting my body will hide my newfound shame.

"I apologize if that came out wrong. I didn't mean that you are ever a waste of my time. I admit, though, this is the first time I've had a client schedule an emergency appointment with me because they're recovering from their mental health issues."

I bite my lip, savoring the tiny bit of pain because this is the first time I've deliberately hurt myself in what feels like forever and *wait a minute, that means*—

"I'm not self-harming, either," I blurt. "This is weird, right? This is weird!"

"Carter, how long do you believe you've had major depressive disorder? Or any other manifestation of depression?"

Locke's voice brings calm to my chaos, and I'm able to think more clearly. "I was diagnosed in—"

"Not your formal diagnosis. When *you* first realized something was wrong."

This is always a fun story to tell. "There was a PowerPoint on mental illnesses and their symptoms in sixth grade health class and bam! Depression fit. Way too much. I fell into a research hole, cried, had to tell my mom when she found me crying. She took me to Therapist #1, and my life has sucked since." I consider this. "Actually, life sucked before that. But like. We reached extra levels of suck."

"Of course it was a PowerPoint," Dr. Locke mumbles.

"I like spreadsheets, too."

"No matter what, it makes sense that you believe your personality is tied into your mental illness. You've had depression for at least six years."

I frown. "Actually, since fourth grade. At least, that's what I think."

"Eight years."

Oh. That *is* a long time for a seventeen-year-old. Nearly half my life has been spent under unceasing dark clouds.

"Let's try an exercise. I like to get interactive in my sessions, and I don't believe we've had a chance to try this yet."

"Okay...."

"Close your eyes."

I comply, fighting against my natural urge to open my eyes to shelter myself from the moves of my enemies. But this isn't an enemy. It's Dr. Locke, the first therapist I've trusted. One of the women working to save me from myself, a member of the community of allies I am slowly building for myself.

"Breathe in, with seven breaths. Breathe out for another seven. Good. Be present in this moment. Grow still physically, mentally, and emotionally. Don't allow your brain to wander; allow it, for once, to rest." I'm about to doze off when Locke continues. "Let us drink in the possibilities of the future. Let us discover the strength in ourselves, in our values, in our communities. Let us unleash the visions of what we wish to enter our lives. Let us create a future of spiritual and financial prosperity. Of education, of learning, of love in all its mysterious shapes. A future of hope. A future at all."

I allow her words to draw me into a trance as I clear my mind. This exercise has me constructing a new reality rather than considering my current one, so I can see why it's helping more than all the yoga and meditation and masturbation I did earlier.

And construct, I do. I imagine surviving the year. Leaving Harlow High School for good, transferring to cyberschool or private school to exit the environment I'm finally ready to admit is toxic. Spending my summer at a college summer program, making an effort to speak to students as odd as me. Celebrating Christmas with my mother and having our annual tradition of visiting my grandmother's grave.

I imagine graduating from MIT, my dream school for as long as I can remember. Or Howard or Princeton or Drexel, other schools I've aspired to go to, but didn't think I'd live long enough to attend.

I imagine continuing to develop BRAIN/ZAPP, expanding it from an iOS/Android app to an actual company.

I imagine, I imagine, and in these moments, I believe. These are dreams I never dared to consider too closely, for fear of living long enough to see them through.

I think harder and harder until Dr. Locke's soothing Southern lilt brings me back into the present. "Carter? Are you still with me?"

I open my eyes, still slightly hypnotized from the soothing of her voice. This is why I don't meditate—I'm naturally sleepy, and this makes it worse.

"Huh? Uh, yeah." I shake off my remaining sleepiness. "That was...something."

"Care to elaborate?"

I tell my therapist all about my innermost dreams and desires. As I delve deeper, Locke's smile grows wider and wider until she's grinning like a whole fool.

"Don't you see, Carter? You do have hope. Your life has aligned to show you what you needed to learn: the power of positive, nurturing relationships, quality mental health care, antidepressants, and a somewhat clear purpose for life can work wonders." Locke places a palm on her chest. "Though your suicide attempt obviously was not a good thing, you can still see that positive events have happened after you took charge of your post-attempt life. You created the life that you loved, and you're doing damn good things with it."

I bask in her words. You know, she's right. My life has changed in the past two months. Not being bullied anymore. A failed experiment in popularity. My blossoming friendships with Abby and Slater. Bonding over trauma with Abby. Finding a therapist who seeks to understand my pain. Taking antidepressants that work rather than lying useless in my liver. Oh, yeah, and trying to die by suicide after so many tiny deaths by society over the years. They're all adding up to a changing Carter.

And to her, I say: bring it, bitch.

I've never backed down from a challenge, whether it's trying to be popular for a night, calculating an (almost) lethal dosage of Prozac, or striving for a 1550 on my SATs last year.

I sure as hell won't give up on myself without a fight, now that I'm worth fighting for.

CHAPTER 31
ABBY

SINCE SLATER WAS SO CONVINCING when she begged me to join the GSA, here I am, seated next to Carter. The rest of the GSA alternates between giving me dirty looks and looking scared. Last year, they *all* would have been scared.

I have lost my power. It sucks to be on the other side of things, to know that people hate me because of my past popularity. Kelsey continues to rule the school with an iron fist, despite the slow loss of her friend group. Even Slater's stopped talking to her after the party.

"I cannot believe you told Kelsey to fuck off," I say to Carter. Carter showed me Kelsey's increasingly desperate texts, which were alarming yet amusing.

Carter shakes her head. "I didn't *say* that. I just ignored her. God, she's going to come after me again."

"I don't know," I admit. "This could swing either way."

"Like me," Carter mumbles.

"What?" I ask. Did Carter admit that she's bisexual? I mean, that would explain why she's here. I don't think she's out of the closet, despite me revealing everything else I know about her.

I think I'll stop doing that. No: I *have* stopped. I don't want to hurt people anymore if they don't deserve it.

Carter doesn't deserve it.

Slater comes in the room. She looks polished today, for Slater. Her hair is straightened, and she's ditched her signature knit beanie. "Oh, look who decided to show up," she says. Slater plucks me on the head, and I swat her arm. Carter looks horrified. I don't bother explaining to her that this is how my friends and I show affection: by hurting each other in small ways.

"I didn't have any homework today," I lie. "Also, you made me do it."

"Sure you didn't." Slater squeezes onto my lap, which is no small feat in these tiny seats.

"Okay, maybe not."

She plucks me on the nose, something she usually only does with girls she *likes* likes. We're best friends, though. She doesn't feel that way about me, the way I've started to feel over the past few months—a slow, aching burn for her that I refuse to acknowledge. My life is complicated enough without falling for another best friend. I won't hurt myself like that again. "Told ya," she says. "Glad you're here, though. We're launching a cool project today that you might be interested in."

"I can't wait to see it." I mean that. Whenever Slater does something, she does it big.

Carter lets out a snort, and we turn our heads toward her. Before I can ask what's so funny, some girl in my poetry class whose name I never bothered to learn interrupts. "Slater, are you ready?"

I almost come for her awful outfit (purple and green? Together?) and audacity to interrupt us before remembering I'm trying to stop being mean to people. I can still do it inside my head, though, and I almost get the same rush of endorphins I do when talking about people face-to-face.

"Ready." Slater slides off my lap and bounces to the front of the room. She cups her hands like a megaphone. "TIME TO GET QUEER!" The room hushes, captivated by her. I don't blame them. "Alright, y'all, I know we planned to discuss recent public policy developments for LGBTQIAP+ students, but we're going to push that back. This March, the school board approved a special fund for initiatives supporting mental health and diversity. The funds can be used for any after-school or weekend activity."

March. Does this have something to do with Carter's suicide attempt? I sneak a peek. She seems as confused as I am.

"Our lovely treasurer and I applied for one," Slater says, presenting Jessica Ames, who I may or may not have made out with at last year's Spring Shitfaced Extravaganza. Jess gives a mock bow. "And we got the grant to sponsor a community wellness fair to promote mental and physical health."

The room's silent. What's a community wellness fair?

Slater sighs. "There'll be free food, okay?"

The room breaks into cheers and applause. If there's one thing high school students love, it's free...anything.

Slater turns around and starts writing basic details on the whiteboard. Thanks to the school's lack of funding, it takes her four tries to find a marker that works.

COMMUNITY WELLNESS FAIR

- The Saturday after next, 9 AM to 4 PM (IT WAS THE ONLY TIME AVAILABLE BECAUSE THE SCHOOL YEAR IS ALMOST OVER DON'T @ ME)
- Free food and music (vendors to be determined, tho we want the new grilled cheese place)
- Booths from school clubs, with most of them being from our club. PLEASE MAKE

TOPICS SCHOOL APPROPRIATE (this one is for Abby)
- You can use this for Key Club and National Honor Society hours because it's the end of the year and half the members don't have enough hours yet

I smirk at Slater's callout. I would be the one to create a booth about how to get a girlfriend, or something. Not that I'm doing so well in that department.

Slater starts passing a clipboard around. "There are three sign-up sheets here: for the publicity and planning committees, general volunteering like setting up, and the opportunity to create your own booth or join one."

The list makes its way to me as Slater continues discussing minute details. I sign up for the publicity committee, determined to put my aggregate 8,249 social media followers to good use. I also volunteer to help set up, buy refreshments, and break down at the end of the day.

I pause when it comes to creating my own booth. The tables so far center on books about health, feminism and intersectionality, queer-friendly local organizations, and HIV/AIDS prevention. Even Carter's in on it: she's planning a booth based on self-care techniques for mental health.

I want to create a booth to make sure enough people

sign up. I'm one of the last people to wield the clipboard.

Damn it. I know the booth I want to work on. I'm still more afraid than I care to admit. I'm still navigating my identity as a semi-known survivor.

This is a way to care for others. Make amends in a way.

Care for yourself, make sure you feel safe.

My hand trembles as I try to decide. Neither option is good or bad, which is part of why I'm having a hard time.

Another hand quiets the vibration. I turn my head to see Carter staring. "If I can do it, you can. We can work on our booths together."

I offer her a small smile. You know what? Screw it. Carter's right. As long as I don't focus on my experiences and give general resources instead, I should be fine. And if not, I can always leave in the middle of the fair, though Slater would kill me.

I write:

ABBY WALLACE
SEXUAL ASSAULT AWARENESS AND RESOURCES

Slater scans the lists, nodding. She wrenches her eyes away from the clipboard and stares at me. My cheeks grow red. I cover my face with my hair. Then she smiles, and the world is aligned again. "Proud of you," she mouths.

The rest of the meeting blows by as Slater asks each person about our booths and starts to plan the fair. Before my eyes, the event takes shape.

It's beautiful. It's magnificent.

And maybe I should say something about it.

CHAPTER 32
CARTER

KELSEY

I heard that Abby was at your
house the other day.
JSYK, she has herpes. It's sick.

—*NEW MESSAGE TO ABBY WALLACE, 8:30 A.M.*—

CARTER

hey I know we're not really
friends so I apologize for asking
this in advance, but
do you have herpes?

ABBY

A) No.
B) If I DID it wouldn't MATTER because
it's TREATABLE and only jerks

judge women by their STI status!

C) What????

> **CARTER**
>
> I'm not the one who said it!!!!
>
> I figured kelsey was lying but idk

ABBY

I mean if I had herpes

That means she does too :)

also lmfaooooooo. why is she texting

you. she doesn't even LIKE you.

(no offense)

> **CARTER**
>
> Ok first of all did not need that info
>
> not offended bc the feeling is mutual
>
> how do i get rid of her

ABBY

You could always put a hex on her O:)

I DON'T GET why Mom's pulling me out of school for the day to take a field trip to Princeton, New Jersey. It's not like we can't visit colleges during the summer.

Whatever. I could use a day away from Kelsey's increasing neediness. I didn't realize accepting her party invitation would also mean she'd try to be my friend, which, yikes. I asked Slater about how Kelsey even got my number, and Slater said Kelsey likely swiped it from her phone.

Why are she and the POPS obsessed with me? Abby (who I suppose is an ex-POPS) sat with me at lunch twice this week. Sure, we don't talk, and I eye her throughout lunch to make sure she doesn't have a sudden change of heart about treating me like a human being, but she's there. Surprisingly, her presence isn't as disquieting as I'd anticipated it being. Slater alternates between sitting with Abby and sitting with Kelsey, Kelsey's new boyfriend (Abby's ex, Caleb, she told me while laughing at Kelsey's desperation), and Mei. Mei's nice enough, but we aren't friends. More like acquaintances who happen to share mutual friends.

I can't run from Kelsey forever, despite my best efforts. I just don't know what'll happen when running doesn't work anymore.

Mom says, "Carter, take out your earth pods."

"AirPods," I say as I pluck them out. "You're thirty-four, not ancient."

"Three years ago, they were earbuds," Mom says. "I can't keep up with y'all. But we're here."

We pass unremarkable trees on a residential street until the campus of Princeton University approaches. I've loved this place since I was a kid. We visited when I was ten and I was struck by the historical buildings, the friendly tour guides, the environment of learning. I always wanted to go back. I have the grades to get in, don't get me wrong. My lack of extracurricular activities is what would give me zero chance at acceptance. I could write a triumphant essay about my return from near-death to impress admissions. Which might do the trick. College admissions officers love tragedy porn written by women of color.

Mom lets out a sigh of contentment. "I love it here. Their buildings are my favorite."

I can see why. They're composed of layers of brown bricks, jutting skyward in tandem with their ornate carvings. This creates a haunting, lingering effect. No wonder droves of students apply to enroll, even though most know they can't stack up to the Ivy League's constricted ideas of who deserves to attend elite institutions.

"The architecture is Gothic style, right?" I ask as Mom slides into a parking space. Mom teaches me about architecture and interior design every chance she gets. I enjoy the mathematical aspects of architecture, which is something she struggled to overcome. It's hard to imagine that my mom wasn't always the math wizard she is today. Chemistry, physics, and software engineering, my love languages, are beyond her sphere of understanding despite my best efforts.

"Yeah, you would know," Mom says, eyeing my

black skinny jeans, plaid Docs, and off-the-shoulder sweater (also black). Wow. Callout.

"Rude."

"I said what I said." Mom pulls her tablet out of her leather tote and reviews her calendar. "Alright, we're headed to the engineering quad. I know that's not what you want to major in, but still it involves computers." Mom vaguely points in the direction of where we're going.

We walk through the campus. Clusters of students lounge around, either chatting or silently studying, occasionally lobbing questions or theory at one another. Many are taking advantage of the warmth and have lugged their books outside. Despite my usual apathy, I'm admittedly excited to see so many people who care about learning. I only somewhat get that in my AP classes; it's clear who's in AP for the love of it rather than for the prestige.

"I arranged for a classroom visit before our campus tour," Mom says.

I break out into a huge smile. "Which class?"

"I have never seen a child so excited to skip school for more school," Mom says, shaking her head. "Something about engineering stats? There weren't a lot of options." Sweet.

Some of the students look at us funny as we head to the back of the lecture hall, wondering why some girl with deep purple hair (I got a new weave in last week-end) is joining the class mid-semester.

I've endured worse. The college students aren't looking with jest or malice, just confusion. Which is okay. Almost.

For the next fifty minutes, I'm swept away, learning new concepts of probability and statistics expanding on the AP Stats course I took last year. I use my phone to record the lecture, determined to transcribe it later, and scribble the practice problems. I need a bit more practice to unravel their complexities but can probably puzzle out the math on the car ride home. Meanwhile, Mom resumes work on the proposed downtown apart-ment complex she's been working on forever. At this point, my mom's role is to select sustainable, fiscally responsible construction materials.

My phone buzzes thrice, but it's easy to ignore. I doubt it's anything more than a random email from school or about BRAIN/ZAPP.

After class, the actual students leave as soon as possible, save a few who speak to the professor. The actual students are as confuddled as me about the last problem, which makes me feel better.

I figure I should seize the opportunity. "Can I talk to the professor?" I ask as Mom and I pack our things. "I wanted to ask about a problem."

Mom looks horrified. "You understood all that?"

I shrug. "A bit."

"Well, go ahead. We still have some time before the tour."

I take nervous steps to the front of the lecture hall. The same old pattern of thoughts reappears in my head. *They'll laugh at you you're a weirdo who the hell shows up at PRINCETON with PURPLE HAIR you're nothing—*

I shut them down with an affirmation Dr. Locke gave me in our last session. *People will laugh at you no matter what you do. At least do something worth laughing at.*

While in line to talk to the professor, I check my phone.

Oh, come *on*.

KELSEY
Ugh, Mei is so annoying.

KELSEY
She got this ugly haircut this weekend
(chin length, with bangs) and I told her
how ridiculous she looks
and now she's not speaking to me

KELSEY
Like hello????????
I care about how my friends look!

Who cares? Gossip and backstabbing are far from fascinating. I hate the minute ways people destroy each other and I want no part in the drama.

I text Abby to see if she knows why Kelsey keeps talking to me. If anybody knows what goes on in Kelsey's brain, it'd be her ex-best friend. I'm hesitant to text Abby twice in one day, but I like to think she dislikes Kelsey more than me at this point.

CARTER

help

why is kelsey still texting me

ABBY

How often is she texting???

CARTER

[Screenshots sent.]

ABBY

WTF LMFAO

I think it's bc her friends are leaving her

She ROASTED Mei for her haircut

(she's right BTW but I

know better than to say it)

CARTER

i see.

does she have…better options?

ABBY

Obvs but she probably thinks you're such a
loser that you won't reject her.

"Hello! Are you Carter?" The professor's voice
yanks me out of my reverie. I'm still getting used to
Abby's caustic style. It's reassuring to know that she
really is like this with everyone, though I clearly got
the worst of her personality before the suicide
attempt.

I slide my phone into my back pocket, embarrassed
to have been caught red-handed. "Yes, I am. Harper." I
smile at him. "Thanks for letting me observe your
class." My stammer, which shows up when I'm unfa-
miliar or uncomfortable with somebody isn't on display.
Come to think about it, it hasn't shown up as much
lately. "I did have a question about problem five, if that's
okay?"

"Please, be my guest."

I show him my paper. According to the professor, I
screwed up because of a mathematical concept I
wouldn't have learned until I took the prerequisite for
this class. Not knowing what I'm doing is a new,
thrilling feeling, one I'd like to capture more. Is this
what college could be like?

After thanking the professor, I chatter to Mom

about the class as we head out. "What he said about joint probability distributions made sense, since—"

"Before you tell me about what you learned, let me state the obvious and tell you I have no clue what you're talking about, but will listen to and support you, even though I can't comment on any of it because you're far more brilliant than me."

"I know," I say before recapping the class. "Thanks again for bringing me. But could you tell me why we came here? We could've toured Harrisburg University or Millersville."

Mom smiled. "Because there's so much more out in the world, beyond Kelsey, high school, and Central PA."

Ugh. Kelsey. I remember to put my phone on silent, only to see another text pop up from her as I do. Why am I her latest fascination?

"College does seem nice," I say softly.

Mom notices me spacing out, as moms always do. "You good? You went into another world there."

"Yeah," I say. I'm not convincing her, because she gives me The Black Mom Look that makes me cave. "I was thinking about next year."

Mom nods. "You know, you could take college courses if you left Harlow. You could go to HACC or Harrisburg University." Mom mentioning Harrisburg University strikes the same nerve she'd hit earlier. I'd researched their early college program for my senior year.

I admit this to Mom, but hasten to say, "I'm not considering the program anymore."

"Carter, why didn't you tell me you wanted this?" Mom asks. "We could've been gotten you in there."

I look at the grass. "It was too expensive." The main reason I shuttered that dream was the tuition. We're pretty well-off, but Mom was expecting another year to save for my education. The science and technology-oriented program doesn't accept federal financial aid.

Mom's face falls. Determination quickly takes the place of sadness. "I've never let that stop us from doing anything, and you know it. I can make that work. You donate half your app earnings to charity, anyway; you could help pay for this, too."

Oh! I hadn't considered BRAIN/ZAPP. Mom has insisted on paying as much of my college tuition as she can when the time comes, so I'd never thought about it. I'm annoyed at my own privilege: she's paid her way since she was in high school. It's only fair that I contribute to my own education if I have the means. Thanks to the unprecedented success of BRAIN/ZAPP and the 37.132% surge in subscriptions this year, I do.

Mom barrels on, trying to convince me. "If college doesn't work out, we tried. You can stay here, do freelance, get a job, or whatever you want to do. But you'll succeed. The one thing you've always cared about, no matter how depressed you get, is your schoolwork. I doubt college will change that."

Mom's right. Even on days where dragging myself out of bed was a struggle, I still managed to do my homework before returning to sleep.

"I think this could work," I say. Then my face falls. "Applications are probably closed, though."

We've finally reached the tour group, a cluster of overly eager teenagers. "We can check with your guidance counselor," Mom promises. "As soon as we get back."

Butterflies flutter in my stomach. I could still fail, even now.

But what if you succeed and live up to your full potential?

"Ready to get started?" Our tour facilitator is the same breed of overly preppy student ambassador I've seen on every other college tour I've attended. Why do colleges send the most annoying students they can find to sell us on their programs?

I stare at my phone, needing a distraction from Little Miss Preppy, my self-deprecating thoughts, and the thought of potentially attending college next year. As we tour, Kelsey keeps texting me. Her texts grow more and more annoyed. I'm ready to snap at any moment, a rare feeling for me. Unlike Abby (sorry, girl, it's true!), I'm not super disposed to anger. I want people to leave me alone, and I'll give them the same respect.

But Kelsey. She continues to talk about her friends, ex-friends, and everyone in between, and I've had enough. I need to do something, anything, to get this asshole out of my messages.

I do something really, really inane. I stand up to Kelsey Maxwell. (Over text. Can you imagine doing so in person?)

KELSEY

abby looks like hell today
that's so sad

KELSEY

WHY ARE YOU IGNORING ME.

CARTER

kelsey it's not that I don't
like you but please leave
me and my friends alone

"You good?" Mom asks. We've fallen behind on the tour.

I put on a fake smile. "We're good." Unless I've released the kraken. Then no, I'm not good at all, and I've fucked myself over once again.

To be sure, I block Kelsey Maxwell from my phone and from my life. I don't know how to truly escape the girl who causes destruction in her wake without remorse, but this is a solid start.

CHAPTER 33
CARTER

I SCAN the lawn as Mom and I finish setting up my booth. The first band, a local indie outfit called Valid Scientific Theories, are tuning their instruments and completing a sound check. I'm half-tempted to ask if any of them care about the scientific method or if they merely wanted a cool indie/rock band name. Kelsey, our emcee, flirts with one of the bandmates. I look away, lest she catch me staring.

I'm still waiting for Kelsey's revenge for me leaving her. She hasn't even looked at me for the past week. Maybe she was just playing tricks on me again when she barraged me with text messages, trying to see if a loser could fall for it. If so, I'm in the clear.

Abby's worried Kelsey isn't done with me yet, though. That makes me anxious, since they devised the playbook on How to Break a Girl together.

The sweet smell of bubbling crepe batter wafts over

from the designated refreshments area, which includes paid food trucks and several tables of free food and drink. Next to the refreshments area are several inflatables for the kids whose parents dragged them to the fair. Though let's be honest: the high schoolers are going to be in the bouncy house by the end of the first hour. There are also a few lawn games scattered around, and an open relaxation space for mingling and sitting on the grass.

Booths are arranged in a U shape just beyond the few chairs near the stage. Each booth is draped in a different shade of the Pride flag. My booth's tablecloth is purple. As for my own booth, I downloaded and ordered resources from the Crisis Text Line, The Trevor Project, and To Write Love on Her Arms so people will have takeaways. I prepared two posters. One described the most common types of mental illnesses, including LGBTQIAP+-specific statistics, and the other is about self-care and self-love. Mom and Dr. Locke helped with the last one. I still rely on other people to build myself back together after falling apart. I have a support system, so I ought to use it.

I step back and admire my work. Yes, I went a little deeper than I expected to. That's what happens when you find reasons to live. You want to do your best with everything because, as it turns out, your next moments aren't your last. Who knew!

Abby's booth is similarly extra. We asked to be

placed next to each other; Slater was happy to acquiesce.

"I'm so proud of you." Mom envelopes me in a hug.

"Thanks, Mom. And thanks for helping out. This means a lot. Especially since you woke up early," I tease. Listen, she'll wake up for work, but if she's not getting paid for something, she's like "nah."

"Girl, you know I'm going to bed right after work." Mom pulls out her phone. Oh, no. Here we go. "Let me take a picture for the 'Gram!"

Yes, she calls the app the 'Gram. My mom is more into social media than I am. And I'm supposed to be the Generation Z, cell-phone-obsessed teenager.

I give in and smile for her one hundred followers. I can imagine the caption: "My baby Carter killing it at the #HarlowCommunityWellnessFair! Come out and support the cause, y'all!!! #Blessed #MyOnlyBaby #TheOnlyGoodThingDarrylEverCreated."

"Abby! Get out the picture! This is for my social!" I turn around and see Abby giving me bunny ears.

"Sorry, Ms. Ashley," Abby says. She hugs Mom, who's become something of a distant aunt to her. "Someone needs to set her wild ass straight," Mom explained to me last week, when I asked why she let Abby hang around more and more. One time I walked in from therapy to see Abby giving my mom *cooking lessons*.

I hate it here.

"It's all good. In fact, lemme get a shot of you two together." Abby throws her arm around me, juts her denim-shorts-clad hip out, and beams. She's nothing if not dramatic. I resume my normal, kinda awkward position of a stiff smile and spine.

"Perfect." Mom kisses me on the cheek. "I'm gonna go to work. Love you. See you, Abby."

"Love you," I say as she walks away.

"Your mom's awesome," Abby says as she straightens out brochures.

"Yeah." I leave it at that, because I can't return the compliment. Abby's mother scares both of us. Luckily, she couldn't be here today because her weekends are reserved for house showings. "You ready for today?"

Abby shrugs on her too-big motorcycle jacket over her cranberry cami. Wait—that's Slater's jacket. They could not be gayer if they tried, and I don't even think they're together. (Yet.) "Nope. You?"

"Nope."

"Awesome. Let's be nervous wrecks together."

"Sounds like a plan." I turn to the stage, where Slater is about to speak.

After Slater talks a bit about the origins and creation of the fair, she hands the microphone to Kelsey (Abby and I look away). Then, a flood of community members comes in and the show begins. I talk to parents, teenagers, and even the mayor about mental health issues, often resorting to the short speech I prepared. I don't stutter or stumble over my words more than thrice per person. My training with the POPS helped.

At least I got something out of that disastrous relationship aside from a stomach ulcer.

Spinning my negative experiences into positives is a huge step, albeit a mentally draining one. Abby and I switch off and cover each other's booths for ten minutes whenever one of us needs a break.

In the middle of the fair, Abby and I beg some floater volunteers to cover our booths for half an hour so we can eat lunch. Abby heads to the crepes stand while I'm tempted by the pizza in a cone. We grab soda and water, then settle into the grass near the stage. The latest local band assaults my eardrums. I liked the others, but I don't know what Slater was thinking with the Gray Mosquitoes.

"How does it feel to use your childhood trauma for good?" Abby asks. She bites into her crepe and groans. "Yes. Food. I love you."

"Don't tell Slater. And I kind of like using the evil of depression for good."

Abby snorts. "Well put. And for the last time, Slater and I are *not dating*."

"Uh-huh."

Abby laughs at my sarcasm.

This is so weird. We shouldn't be getting along. We

shouldn't be growing together, her becoming softer as I grow stronger.

We've got to be trauma bonding, as Locke said. That's the only explanation that makes sense.

We don't talk for a bit, too focused on our food. I'm so into inhaling the remnants of the second cone that I don't notice Kelsey creep up to us until Abby asks, "Don't you have somewhere to be? Like hell, along with Ronald Reagan?"

"I'm not even *homophobic*," Kelsey says, ignoring the fact that she's everything-else-phobic. "Just...ugh! Never mind." She swings around, her low ponytail cutting through the air. She struts away from us. See, if she was nice, I'd point out that pizza sauce got on her hair.

"I'm so tired of her," Abby mutters. "Can't she go away?"

I don't respond, suddenly terror-stricken by Kelsey's appearance. I saw how she eviscerated Abby at the party. Does she care enough to do the same to me? Aren't we "even" now? When will this anxiety over her antics end?

I spy Kelsey approaching Mei, who's testing her kickboxing skills at an experiential booth for a local fitness center. Kelsey grabs Mei's slender wrist and yanks her away. They proceed to argue, Kelsey waving her arms wildly. Mei backs away from her. Kelsey is persistent. Finally, Mei turns and walks away from Kelsey. She heads toward us.

"Carter, why did you have to go rogue?" Mei plops next to Abby, but not before setting her leather purse on the ground to sit on and protect her black jeans from the grass. "Now Kelsey's a paranoid mess."

"Did you seriously lay your Michael Kors in the grass?" Abby asks.

"Sorry?" I say.

Mei rubs her temples. "I get it. She can be a handful. But ugh. Now that I'm her only close friend, she's *blech*. I need a break. And she doesn't confide in me."

"Too bad," Abby says.

"Anyway, I'm going to grab a snow cone. Be right back." Mei leaves as fast as she arrived, abandoning her Michael Core or whatever.

"Harlow Hawks! Thanks for coming out today!" Kelsey's voice surprises me. "Shout-out to the Gray Mosquitoes, whose name may be obvious, but their music is psychedelic and original." The Gray Mosquitoes' lead singer hangs her head in shame as Kelsey's callout. Honestly? Her band's music is so bad that she should.

Kelsey charges on. "Slater García-Svensson, the wonderful organizer of this event and the President of the Harlow High Gender and Sexuality Alliance, asked me to give a shoutout to today's participants."

"No I didn't," Slater says, joining our little group. She plops next to Abby, because *of course she does*.

"Thank you to Principal Adams, who approved the

grant funds for the GSA to do this," says Kelsey. Principal Adams, standing to the side of the stage, stops mid-gourmet-grilled-cheese-bite and gives her a thumbs-up. "To Pizza Cone Zone, The Harrisburg Crepe Place, and Mmm...Cheese!, for bringing their food trucks here. And, of course, to the people who've created our booths about so many important topics."

"Does she even care?" Mei returns and sits on her purse again. Abby glares at Mei's bony butt, which makes me snort.

"No," Abby, Slater, and I say simultaneously.

"There are booths about sexual assault awareness, for arts and crafts, from our local Planned Parenthood and other organizations," Kelsey continues. "But I want to talk about one close to my heart. The mental health booth."

That delicious pizza in a cone feels like it'll come right back up.

Slater whips her head toward me. "Why is she calling your booth out?"

I'm as lost as she is.

"You see, my friend, a while back she tried...I'm sorry, it's just so hard." Kelsey dabs fake tears from her smoky eyes. "She tried to kill herself because people at our school were bullying her so bad. So she created this booth to help other people."

This can't be happening.

"Oh, hell no." Slater tears toward Kelsey and shouts, "Don't you DARE!"

But she's already too late. Nobody is ever fast enough to stop the indomitable Kelsey Maxwell.

Kelsey points to me. "Shout out to *you*, Carter Harper!"

CHAPTER 34
ABBY

I THOUGHT I couldn't hate Kelsey any more than I already did, yet here we are. I turn to Carter, but she's gone. Panic creeps into my chest, and I struggle to breathe. *No. I will* not *lose her again!*

"WHERE DID SHE GO?!" I scream. I don't mean to yell in Mei's face, but I can't apologize to her because *I lost Carter again and she could hurt herself.* I stand and scan the confused, whispering crowd. No sign of Carter. She must have bolted the second Kelsey said her name. Mei and I stood in shock for a minute, unsure of what was happening.

One minute was enough to *lose her again.*

Ms. Ashley is going to kill me.

Mei's eyes grow wide. "I don't know!" She gets up from the ground and follows my lead.

"You don't have to pretend to care," I snap as I powerwalk around the fair, frantic and aching to find my...person, or something. "I'm sure you planned this with Kelsey. Congrats. It worked." I no longer know who to believe or who to trust. Our alliances have constantly shifted this year, leading me to think that Slater, my parents, and maybe (*maybe*) Carter are the only ones on my side.

Mei shakes her head violently. She's growing hysterical, which scares me because she's always the one with the cool head. "Do you seriously think I'd bother staying around if I knew?" she protests. "I don't want her to die. I don't care if we aren't friends, she can't just *die* and it can't be our fault if she does."

Fair point. "Just help me find her before she leaves." I practically trip over people in my haste.

"You've seen her in gym class! She couldn't have run far!" Mei yells.

Slater joins us. "Principal Adams says I have to stay and repair the damage Kelsey caused. AKA, stop the inevitable PR crisis." Slater's furious and ready to fight someone.

"It's okay. Mei's helping me find Carter."

Slater blinks. "...Huh?"

"Can't I do *one* good thing without people questioning it?" Mei asks.

Slater and I shrug at each other, and Mei and I run off. "My money's on the parking lot," I say, huffing. This high-speed chase is already too much for my lungs, untrained from months of apathy.

The sobs reach our ears soon enough. As awful as it sounds, her cries are a relief: at least she's alive. Carter is behind the wheel of her car, heaving and wheezing. Her hands grip the steering wheel.

I yank Carter's car door open. "Carter. Backseat." Carter obeys, in too much of a daze to do anything else. "Mei. Passenger side." Mei does so, scrolling through Instagram. She gasps.

"Kelsey," Mei whispers. "She...." She shoves her phone in my face in lieu of an explanation.

I see Kelsey's username and the caption:

Want proof? Here it is. And I bet you thought I lied.

The camera is aimed to the bathroom ceiling. The audio, though, is clear. Carter and Kelsey are talking. Kelsey accuses Carter of attempting suicide, and Carter admits it.

No.

No.

No.

There was proof all along. I almost laugh at my naïveté. Kelsey does nothing without making sure she's covered.

"W-we w-were in the bathroom," Carter says in between cries. "D-did she p-post it?"

"Yeah," I whisper. I hand back Mei's phone. I can't

bear to watch anymore or look at the comments. "Carter, we're taking you home, okay?"

"Mom," she cries. "I n-n-need to see my mom. She's at w-work. She's doing o-overtime. For me, crap, for my medical bills, it's for me...."

"Give me the address." I veer onto the main road.

Carter does. "I was thinking about driving the car into the trees. You know, the ones near the s-school? I can't face this again. I can't do this again."

"You are not driving into a forest. That's a shit way to die, okay?" Carter's not dying on my watch. Not again. "You can still get better. You *are* getting better."

"I was so close. I thought I could be happy."

We illegally park on the streets downtown. I'm not in the mood to find or pay for proper parking. Mei and I hold Carter as we walk. Carter sways to the side, too sad to move, and we give up and half lift her up. Mei grumbles the whole way, despite her being the physically strongest of all three of us.

We make it to the fancy office where Carter's mom works. Mei and I drop Carter into a chair. Carter closes her eyes and mumbles under her breath.

"We're here to see Ashley Harper," I say. "It's about her daughter. Carter."

The receptionist looks at Carter sprawled on the chair. "Er, yes. What are your names?"

"Abby Wallace and Mei Xiang."

He dials an extension and talks to Ms. Ashley for a bit. Soon enough, we're cleared to head upstairs. Mei and I drag Carter around like a rag doll all over again. Miraculously, we make it to the twenty-second floor. Carter's mom is waiting outside the elevator. She ushers us to her office. We dump Carter on the comfy-looking leather sofa and sit in front of Ms. Ashley's long, teak desk.

I'm impressed by Carter's mom's office. It's the second home of someone who's in charge and knows it. Photos of her completed blueprints decorate the walls. The L-shaped desk features two huge iMac monitors and gold accessories. Behind the desk are pictures of Carter, her and Carter, and people who look like relatives.

Ms. Ashley stares at Carter, tenderness and fury in her gaze. "Explain."

I give her a rundown of what Kelsey did. The stage, the video, the blackmail, everything. Mei fills in missed details. Then I show Ms. Ashley the video.

"I will...." Ms. Ashley shuts her eyes and inhales. "I can't say it in a professional setting." Her phone rings. "Give me a second." She puts on a fake smile. "Good afternoon, this is Ashley Harper at Zinn and Mueller. How may I help you?" She glowers. "Yeah, Dr. Asshole, she's in my office because your school couldn't keep track of her. It's about time that twat got suspended. She better be expelled."

Mei and I exchange a glance. Is she talking about Kelsey? Is the witch burned at last?

Ms. Ashley slams her phone down. "A suspension and revocation of after-school activities for the rest of the year? That heifer gets suspended and can't *do the school announcements* while my daughter is messed up for the rest of her life?"

I slump back in my seat. "Not surprised. Our school lets people get away with anything."

"Clearly." Ms. Ashley rubs her temples. "I don't know what to do anymore. It's too late in the year for Carter to transfer schools, and we don't know if she's been accepted to her new school yet."

I have a brief flash of confusion. Carter didn't tell me she's planning to transfer. It does make sense, though. I'm surprised she didn't leave school in the thick of the bullying.

"She's got to do something. She won't go back to Winterwood. She hated it there," Ms. Ashley continues.

Before I can point out that "she" is right here, Carter does so herself.

"I can go." Carter's voice is groggy and thick with tears.

Mei and I turn our heads toward her. Carter's folded into herself on the couch, a faux fur blanket wrapped around her. I'm impressed by her mother's taste and wonder why Carter ended up being so...Carter.

Not the point at all. (But I'm right.)

Ms. Ashley rushes toward Carter. She swipes Carter's purple-ish hair away from her face. "Carter, baby, you don't have to go to Winterwood again. We can find another option. You can stay at home through this."

Carter gives the tiniest of nods. "No, Mom. I've got to...try. I mean, like, did you see me when I tried? I've been trying. So hard." Her voice grows stronger as she speaks. "I won't let her take my recovery away from me. I'm doing better. I want to keep doing better." Carter pauses. "Even if, fine, that means leaving school. If I have to see Kelsey again, I might stab her in the throat."

I smile. That's my girl. As I've grown softer due to her influence, she's grown stronger due to mine.

"I'll do that myself," Ms. Ashley promises. "Are you sure about Winterwood?"

"Yeah, Mom. We can...I've got to go there now, or to the ER. I don't want to go back to where I was. Please. I can't go back."

Carter's mom rests her forehead on Carter's. "We're going to get you through this, baby. We all love you too much to let you go."

Without her saying the words, I know that list now includes Slater. And me (sort of). And Mei (sort of).

Mei and I shut the door and leave mother and daughter to plan Carter's new life.

CHAPTER 35
CARTER

IT IS day three of my second stay at Winterwood Psychiatric Hospital. Mom and I agree that it wasn't Winterwood that was ineffective; it was my approach toward treatment.

Plus, they had a bed open.

There is no more waking up with screams; my sleep grows more restful, especially because of the newly prescribed Trazodone that knocks me out the second I take it. Elizabeth, my new and nosy roommate, and I are awakened by a nurse at six for weights and vitals.

Breakfast is eggs. Protein is nice and healthy and could help balance some neurotransmitters. The eggs taste like glue, but so does half the other food here. I douse them with salt and pepper (the only seasonings available, so you know this place is majority white) and focus on conversations with Elizabeth rather than this lumpy mess they call food.

Before school comes process group. I'm actively listening. When I open my mouth, though, the thought of ten other teenagers knowing what I'm thinking is too much, and I clam up. The facilitator says he understands.

Yet again, school is the highlight of the day. My teachers sent Mom my assignments for this week, and Mom, in turn, sends them to Winterwood's secondary school teacher, who prints them out and gives them to me, along with whatever textbooks I need. She's supposed to guide me, but it's not like I need guidance in any area of my life but my shoddy mental health.

Lunch comes after. I spend my time sometimes answering Elizabeth's probing questions. I pick at my food. I'm starving, but this food isn't drumming up a desire to eat. Elizabeth says I'm being bratty, and I should eat what I'm given. She's been here so long she's used to it. This is my second round of inpatient. I'm not used to it yet, and don't want to be.

Now, a slew of therapy.

I have a new-new psychologist, though I'm going back to Locke after I'm out of here. This dude wants me to try something called dialectical behavior therapy, which is a switch from negative to positive or mixed thinking patterns. Locke, who's updated on my care and checks in with me during daily ten-minute phone calls, agrees with him.

Then a snack, usually fruit.

After, a walk around the grounds for people up for it. I am because being in my room gets boring, even with all the sleep I'm getting. The other patients chatter and bond during these walks, while I stay to myself and observe nature.

We do talk sometimes. I notice myself being more social this time around, but not social enough to be one of the girls surrounded by friends. That's okay. I have my own circle of semi-friends now, even if they're the reason I'm here in the first place.

No matter that Abby and Mei ultimately saved me: I can't get over the ways they destroyed me. I try to keep my distance, despite being irrevocably drawn to them.

Next is the other highlight of my day, which came as a surprise: art therapy. Despite sucking at it, getting out of my head and focusing on creating is fun. As a bonus, I'm not expected to talk to people. Today, I create a painting of a brown girl screaming, desperate words floating from her mouth.

I'm free to do what I want after dinner. I rotate between reading and watching old Disney movies and talking to Mom, Abby, or Slater. Mei hops on the phone with Abby or Slater sometimes.

Overall, I'm giving inpatient a real shot this time.

I heal for the long battles ahead of me.

CHAPTER 36
CARTER

KELSEY and I return to school on the same day, at the same time.

The silence is startling as we both reach for the door at once. We lock eyes. I'm not as intimidated by her today, partially because Abby insisted on styling me "so you don't look like you just spent a week in a psych ward, *God*, Carter. If we're going to be seen together, you have to care about your appearance at least a little."

As brash as her delivery was, I realized she was right. Besides, I needed a shield on my first day back so people wouldn't find more reasons to make fun of me. The entire school knowing you tried to kill yourself makes you develop protective measures like that. Abby, Slater, and Mei swear that people don't think I'm a freak, and that Kelsey's cruelty at the fair overshadowed my suicide attempt. I don't believe them, but I also don't have reason not to believe them. Sigh.

"Hello," I say to Kelsey. *I will not give her the power to hurt me. I will not. I refuse.*

She huffs. She yanks open the door, hitting me in the shoulder. Um, ow. I didn't give her the power to, but she hurt me anyway. Rubbing my shoulder, I enter the school, expecting laughter to hit me. I put in my earbuds, crank a rock album, and head to my locker.

A tap on my shoulder interrupts the singer's quasi-screaming. I pluck out an earbud, wondering who dares to interrupt.

I don't know who this white girl is. She's kinda cute, though, with soft features and kind, soft eyes. I stand up a little taller.

"You're Carter, right? Harper?" the random blond girl asks in a melodic voice.

I nod. I'm entranced by her, as I tend to be when I see pretty people.

Blondie passes me a note. "Just...read it, okay?" She leaves before I can respond. Curious, I open the note.

Hi Carter! <3

We don't know each other, but I saw the video
Kelsey posted before it was removed for not
meeting Instagram's community guidelines. I'm
sorry all of this happened to you. Kelsey's actions
were cruel and unwarranted.

I saw that you ran the mental health booth at the school wellness fair, which is really cool! That's a great way to be involved in activism. I started volunteering at my dad's hospital after my sister died by suicide a few years ago.

If you ever need somebody to talk to, I'm here. I don't know what you've experienced, but I know what it's like to have suicide impact your life because of my sister, Rose. I think you would have liked her.

If no, please know that there are so many of us who love and support you!

Sending love,
Lilly F. (phone # on the back!)

I'm a speed-reader, so Lilly's still in the hallway when I'm done scanning the note. "Lilly!" I yell, walking toward her.

Lilly turns around, her face open and inviting. "Yes?"

"Thank you," I blubber. I hold up the note, like she doesn't know what I'm talking about. "Thank—thank you."

Lilly smiles. "Anytime." She walks away again. This time, I let her. It means a lot to me that a stranger cares whether I live or die.

"Yo, Harper!" Troy (who is now the latest boy to claim the title of Mei's ex) passes me and offers me a fist bump. Awkwardly, I give one back. Odd. Cool, but odd. And while wading my way to class, I see smiles, not frowns or indifference. Perhaps I don't need to be afraid of school, after all.

Maybe I'm no longer the weirdo.

Perhaps I'm the hero.

"You're still a nobody," Abby informs me at lunch. She, Mei, and Slater are seated with me today, since Kelsey's back and they don't want me to face her wrath alone. Surprisingly, we've been able to keep up a conversation. "But you're the nobody who got Kelsey Maxwell suspended. Though they fear her, people still hate her, and that counts for a lot of your semi-permanent clout."

"It's still good that people aren't being dickheads." I tear open my package of grapes. My health seems to dip when I eat crappier foods, so I'm trying to nourish my body with more fruits, vegetables, and meat. I may have more energy, but I high-key miss having fruit snacks at lunch.

"Obviously. Just wanted to make sure you don't think you're popular."

Four months ago I would've teared up at her

words. Now that I'm in her circle, I know that this statement is affectionately abrasive rather than intentionally cruel.

"She's kind of popular," Mei says. "Amy called Carter a bad bitch in homeroom." She's copyediting the latest issue of the school paper, mostly checked out of our conversation unless she mutters about how incompetent her writers are. She's only sitting with us because Kelsey didn't bother showing up for lunch today, and Troy's table smells like "boy sweat and late-night masturbation." Abby said something about a blush brush after that, which I don't think I want to know about.

"A bad bitch. Wow. The ultimate compliment," Slater says. She and Abby are seated super close, meaning I may be onto something with my hypothesis of them being into one another. I wonder how Kelsey feels about that, now that we all know she was in love with Abby.

I've summoned the devil herself.

"Ew. Since when are you all friends?" Kelsey screeches. She folds her arms over her t-shirt, which bears the words OVER IT. Subtle.

"We're not," Mei says, despite being friends with Slater and having made up with Abby.

Out of fear, Mei hauls ass back to the POPS table in the center of the room. I can't blame her for that; still, the rejection stings a tad. Mei looks back at our table, surely expecting Kelsey to join her. Kelsey doesn't, choosing to berate us instead.

"It's not your concern anymore, Kelsey." Abby looks at Kelsey like she's an irritating speck of dust she'd rather not have to deal with. I remember being the recipient of that look. Not a fun experience.

"Nice try, babe," Kelsey says. "Or, aww, I guess you're not mine anymore. You're with Slater. How adorable!" Kelsey turns to Slater. "Do you know how many times I fucked your girlfriend?"

Slater drapes her hand over Abby's shoulder, accidentally (or...maybe not accidentally) grazing her boob. "She's not my girlfriend yet, but I still plan to beat your record."

Abby blushes so hard it looks like a tomato's burst on her face. I manage to suppress my snort. One thing you can say about Slater is that she really doesn't care anymore.

Abby starts in on Kelsey again. "You realize I'll win Prom Queen, right? You...."

Blah, blah, blah. Same old mean girl crap. I'm over it. I tune out of the conversation and become hyper-aware of the tables around us staring. Yes, this is a show, and we are the performers. I hate this. I was hoping to be done with this. I breathe deeply to quell my anxiety, then switch to drumming my fingers on my thigh as a distraction of sorts. It works until Kelsey decides to direct her malice toward me.

"I suppose you've forgiven Abby, Carter?" Kelsey asks in the syrupy voice that signifies she's about to do something douchey.

I don't respond. I don't want to, after how cruel she's been. Abby is (or was?) trash, and she's done more to me than Kelsey ever did. But she showed exactly who she was when she tried her best to help me post-attempt, when she saved my *life*. Meanwhile, Kelsey spilled the tea about my attempt when she *knew* how vulnerable I was, how I tried to kill myself because of her and her friends.

Kelsey still sought to destroy me. And for what? Because I refused to play nice with a girl who never apologized? Because I decided to be friends with the girl she loved, thanks to Abby's and my shared, weird connection?

No. I'm over those games. My friends are popular; I don't have to be.

"Carter?"

More silence.

"CARTER!"

Since Kelsey screams like a banshee, the cafeteria grows silent. Yet nobody stops this confrontation from happening. Great. Have we learned nothing from my suicide attempt?

"Oh my God, just leave the girl alone," Abby says.

"Why?"

"Because she's never done anything to you, for starters," Slater says.

"Also, for the last time. NOBODY WANTS YOU HERE," Abby says. "Aren't you supposed to have a life? Why are you still talking to people who want nothing to do with you?"

"Oh, shit!" someone interjects.

"I'm NOT!" Kelsey says. She flips around and tries to leave the cafeteria.

Tries, because somebody (Abby, Slater, an unknown entity?) trips Kelsey. She lands flat on her (also flat) ass.

The cafeteria erupts in an uproar. They're...laughing. At...Kelsey. The former queen of Harlow High.

But it's as painful as if they were laughing at me. While I wanted the POPS to stop bullying me, I didn't want their malice to be imparted onto other people.

Even my sworn enemies.

That's why, though the voices in my head scream *DON'T DO IT YOU POTATO HEAD,* I approach Kelsey and reach out my hand to her. No one deserves to be laughed at like this, not even Kelsey.

She glares at my hand for what feels like forever. "Go to hell," she growls before picking herself off the floor.

Welp, I tried.

"Why did you try to help her? No one would blame you for letting her stay there." Abby stares as Kelsey stomps out of the cafeteria. Jeers follow her as she exits, the very picture of a defeated girl who refuses to be kept down. You can almost admire her tenacity, if that tenacity weren't rooted in a desire to wreck the world around her.

"I would blame myself," I say softly.

Slater reaches over and squeezes my shoulder. "I know what you mean."

Abby rolls her eyes. "You guys are pussies." She turns to Slater. "Speaking of, what did you mean by—"

"Going to my locker, I forgot something," I announce. I do *not* want to be part of this conversation, so I leave the conversation and go to the library. After my attempt, when I first saw the librarian (who was used to me browsing the aisles for new science books), she said I could eat lunch in here if I needed to and wrote me a permanent pass. Surprisingly, I've never had to use it until now.

I settle myself at a table. I work on catching up with the assignments from my extended absence. I'm getting tired of this mountain of homework, since it feels like I'm being punished for trying to get help.

I'm also contemplating teenage girls and the power we create. How we manipulate that power and can use it to destroy others and ourselves. Kelsey's the prime example of someone who does that, with (the new and improved!) Abby coming in a close second.

I'm over all of this. And, though they may be power-hungry themselves, as long as my new friends let me be, I'll be fine. Let Kelsey find a new clique. Let her reconstruct the balance of power she's had all these years. If what happened at lunch today is any indication of things to come, people are done with her dictator-lite, social-climbing, harm-causing methods of gaining popularity. Now that Abby's the accepted queen bee/alpha/whatever, I think there will be more peace at Harlow High School.

Anyway, if the college application Mom and I submitted works out, Kelsey will no longer have the power to hurt me. Nobody will. At college, there's no time for the games of schoolgirls. My visit to Princeton University proved that college students are too focused on the long game (or, uh, partying and avoiding responsibilities) to pay too much attention to misfits.

At least, I hope so. I've been proven wrong so many times, with so many things. But there are still embers of hope within me, and those embers will light the way when my self-doubt doesn't.

CHAPTER 37
ABBY

MOTHER and I turn the corner of Broadway and Prince Street to visit our now-favorite café. I'm visiting her the weekend before prom to catch up, see the sights, and get acquainted with the city where I'm considering staying this summer.

This semester's taught me that anything is possible. Enemies can become friends, lovers can become adversaries, and parents can be supportive.

We grab our normal orders: a caramel latte for me, an espresso for Mother. After walking the city all day, we need the pick-me-up before I cook dinner. Our arms are laden with designer shopping bags (Kate Spade and Saks Fifth Avenue and Lululemon, oh my!), including one containing a prom dress that'll make Slater's heart stop when she sees it. Mother agrees with me, though she didn't say that in quite so many words.

On the Uber ride home, we pass yet another tiny

indie bookstore. This one advertises an open poetry night at seven. It's five now. I could drop my things off at Mother's place and make it if I take the subway.

I have enough poetry to do it. Thanks to the unbelievable number of irritations in my life, dozens of poems have piled up in my Moleskine notebook this semester. I have so many feelings bubbling in my heart, ready to burst. I need to express them before I explode.

I did open poetry nights before *him*. Daddy took me, and we'd get coffee either before or after. After, so many of my poems were centered around *him* that I didn't want to let strangers into what happened. Then, when I felt ready to go for it again, I had so much schoolwork that I didn't bother going back to the community poetry night that was a haven in eighth and ninth grade. I took over the vice presidency of my school's dying, weirdo-filled Creative Writing Club last year to try to engage again. After churning out so many meaningless poems that avoided what I truly wanted to discuss, I quit.

I won't let *him* take another thing away from me. I'm ready to reclaim what's mine.

Once we're inside the loft, I rush to my laptop. Hesitantly, I leave my door open in case Mother wants to talk to me. This is a relationship-repair trip, after all.

"I thought you wanted to cook dinner," Mother says. She hesitates outside the bedroom designated as mine. I'm sort of shocked that Mother gave me my own space rather than relegating me to the sofa. She must be serious about turning over a new leaf.

"I do, and I will," I promise her. I'm still engrossed in my text document, perfecting the cadence of my chosen piece. I keep testing out new turns of the phrase, desperate to find the best one before it's time for me to slip out of the house. You can't rush poetry unless you want it to flop.

"Are you doing homework?"

We sound like a parody of a mother and daughter. More like two strangers trying to understand each other's interests before deciding if they are worth one another's time.

I pause. I could tell her about my poetry. Will she laugh? Demand to see my poetry, to see if my words make her look bad? The anxious thoughts run through my brain faster than the speed of light. Or something.

Because Mother has never shown interest in my hobbies before, I say, "I write poetry."

"What types of poetry?" Mother invites herself to sit on my bed. Like the rest of her apartment, it's stark white. There are occasional flashes of red in her decor, like the abstract painting hanging in the foyer. I try not to think of the dripping paint as blood.

"Mostly free verse." I minimize my work-in progress. I spin around in my IKEA desk chair to face Mother. "Sometimes it rhymes. It's based on whatever I'm feeling at the moment." I hesitate before pushing my luck to its limits. "I'm going to an open mic tonight. If that's cool." Asking my mother for permission to leave the house is strange. It's not like she or Daddy care where I go.

Mother smiles. She doesn't have much practice with happiness, so it looks more like a grimace. "Could I accompany you? I would like to hear your poetry."

Oh. That backfired.

So here we are, riding the R local uptown. The stark black and white poem contrasts with my champagne-colored tunic that flows into black leggings as I attempt to memorize it on the train.

We're late due to my nitpicking. (At her house, Mother told me to "finish the poem so we can eat." Thanks for the love, Mother.) I pay close attention to the craft and language of poems about grief, a birthday party gone wrong, and watching a movie with an ex. Some are told slam style, some are timid recitals, but all come from a place of vulnerability.

Too soon or not soon enough, my turn comes.

I step onto the stage and try to ignore the thin layer of dust collecting on it. Bookshop griminess is a boon to some of these artist types, but it only makes me sneeze.

As my ex would say, "This one is for *you*, Kelsey Maxwell!"

true love bites after it ends, leaving a seemingly permanent mark deep, dark, mottled with bruises representing something that could have existed

but was taken too soon by a jealous girl, so unsure of her own position in an arena of treachery

my stomach clenches with the memory of your convoluted adoration, our twisted conversations

I was merely a trophy to you. you did not love who I am, choosing to crush my spirit like a flower ripped from its stem

—I will never again allow somebody to shift my entire being the way you did

The truth rings through with every word as I bare my secrets to these strangers and my mother. I don't know which one is worse. The clapping after my performance quells my worry. As good as it feels, though, the applause doesn't tell me the most important opinion of all.

As we wait for our (late) train, I finally ask, "So what did you think?"

Tears glisten in Mother's eyes. Okay, this is unsettling. "It was beautiful. I hadn't realized you were talented. Your rawness and vulnerability...you have a gift, Abby. I hope you share it."

"Maybe I'll become a poet for a living." I say it to

scare my business-minded mother. She grows pale. I resist my urge to snicker.

"Abby. You're good at poetry, but please don't make it a career. Poetry doesn't make any money. Stick to business or finance. Perhaps accounting."

I laugh at her practicality. That's the mother I know and (am starting to) love.

CHAPTER 38
CARTER

PRINCIPAL ADAMS ACCEPTS my request for
a meeting with Abby and me after school. I'm surprised
Abby agreed to do this, because it's admitting she's done
wrong. Publicly, no less.

"Yes, Miss Harper?"

"I wanted to talk about the bullying assembly," I say.
My hands are clasped around the five-page proposal I
furiously typed and printed this week. Abby said it
looked good, and she meant it, because I've dragged her
into this, too. Two is better than one, considering my
garbage public speaking skills.

"The one we already gave? The one you had no
interest in?" Adams asks.

I grit my teeth. *Please don't make this discussion any
harder than it already is.*

I snap the rubber band on my wrist. I haven't self-
harmed for over a week, but my wrist still begs me to

cut into it every day. It tingles at the worst moments, like a phantom limb that doesn't know when to quit. The buzzes on my skin are a siren's song, eager to cause me harm for no good reason. My skin should want to protect itself, but it's gotten so used to pain that it doesn't know how to cope without it. I know I'll relapse one of these days. Snapping a rubber band against my skin when the urges are coming on helps, but I'm just biding my time until they overwhelm me. And when that happens, I'll restart the cycle.

"No," I reply to Adams. "If you can get me a meeting with the Harlow Middle School principal, I'd like that school to consider letting me speak to those kids. Or pre-teens? Tweens?"

Abby sighs. "What Carter is trying to say is that we'd love the opportunity to try to mitigate bullying among middle school students. We think that two people, the bully and the bullied, standing up to say how it's affected our lives would drive the point home."

See, *this* is why I needed her to be here. I'm typically good at speaking to adults, except for when it comes to the things I really, really need to stand up for myself about.

Adams's eyebrows shoot up. "Huh. Can't say I'm not surprised." You and me both, my guy. "What brought this on?"

I shift into reading from my proposal. "The bullying that turned from childhood taunts to malicious attacks on me began in middle school. Early intervention could be key to stopping some bullying there, because I know it happens. And humans learn best through story-telling. Seeing somebody who legitimately almost died from bullying could help the next person who comes across the POPS."

"The *what*?" Abby and Principal Adams ask simultaneously.

I slink in my seat. "Never mind. Just...read the proposal."

Kelsey may be too far gone to save, but what about the next generation? What about the next Carter Harper? The thought of going into a middle school and preaching about tolerance shakes me, I won't lie. But not as much as the thought that there could be another eighth-grade girl sitting alone at lunch as her class-mates either pretend not to notice or outright mock her. Another girl crying every day after school because people won't accept her for who she is. Another girl trying to asphyxiate herself after school, wondering why she can't complete the attempt, why nobody seems to care.

Who knew I had maternal instincts?

"I already see an issue with your proposal," Adams says. "I doubt middle school students would want to hear about your...attempt. Or have the emotional matu-rity to understand."

"Don't underestimate them. I started trying to kill

myself in eighth grade." Adams begins a strange coughing fit. "Middle schoolers need to know what suicide is and how to prevent it as much as high school students do. Maybe even more. I'd really recommend you look over what I'm trying to say to you, and to them." I take another deep breath. "So if you want your poster girl for bullying, you've got her."

CHAPTER 39
CARTER

"THE AWARD WINNER IS...." Mr. Atkinson opens the envelope. He chuckles. "I'm sure this will come as a surprise to nobody. Carter Harper!"

A polite smattering of applause emanates from the room. I focus on not tripping on my wedge heels on the way to accept the Prize for Excellence in Language Arts. Once again, Abby and my mother insisted on dressing me, which explains these ridiculous heels and my periwinkle, knee-length layered dress. Mr. Atkinson smiles as he hands me the certificate and twenty-dollar gift card to Barnes and Noble.

I smile back before hurrying off the stage as fast as these wedges will allow me to.

"She's not even a senior," someone at a neighboring table mumbles as I walk back to my seat. I try to let it slide off my back. People will talk shit about you, no matter how much you beg them not to. I'm doing my best to learn to deal with it.

"Jesus, that's the fourth one," Mom says as I slide back in next to her.

"It could've been the fifth," I mumble.

I'm annoyed at myself rather than the awards committee for that one. My fifth award would have been for being third in the class, an honor that went to Mei. Abby and I compared notes last week, and it turns out I'm now seventh in the class and she's eleventh. "Sorry," we sheepishly said to each other—this has been a rough year. At least I'm not dead.

"You know I'm proud," Mom says. She kisses me on the forehead. I smile.

Mom and I are seated at a round table with Abby and her mother, and Mei and her parents. Slater was supposed to be here to accept an award for photography but had unbearable period cramps.

"Your daughter is quite accomplished," Abby's terrifying mother states. The parents devolve into a compliment-fest about each other's children as the next round of awards are handed out. Abby, Mei, and I exchange looks of annoyance. No matter our differences, we can always agree on how extra our parents are.

Mei swings her head around the room, like she's been doing for the past hour.

Abby lays her hand on Mei's. "Mei. She's not coming."

Mei slumps in her seat. "I figured. I just...."

"I know."

I shift in my chair. The "she" in question is Kelsey, who was rendered ineligible to be recognized at the annual school awards ceremony due to her recent suspension. It's not like someone who basically attempts to murder someone at a school event can be considered a credit to the institution.

Mei still hoped Kelsey would come to the ceremony to support her, now that Mei's taken Abby's place in Kelsey's life and they're true best friends. But why would Kelsey come here when she knows the girls she feels have betrayed her are here?

At least Kelsey's let us be at school after that weird incident in the cafeteria. Abby thinks that's because the social tides have turned against Kelsey, and people don't respect her like they used to after she outed my suicide attempt. Since there are two more weeks of school left before I leave Harlow, I don't expect this temporary truce to change.

Then again, it's not like Kelsey herself has changed or is willing to. I still need to watch my back for these next two weeks. I'm a bundle of stress thinking about it.

Abby turns her attention back to me. "Carter, did you reconsider coming to prom with us? We'd need to tell the limo driver so we can have enough soda in the back and add you to the route. Though you could always crash with me and Slater at the hotel."

"Nobody wants to do that," Mei mutters. Her parents look appropriately scandalized at the prospect of two teenagers spending the night together unsupervised, even though they're *still friends* and *working things out*. Meanwhile, Veronica remains unbothered, since it's not like Abby's lax parents care about her spending the night with her likely girlfriend.

Speaking of parents, under other circumstances I'd be touched at Abby and Mei including me in their prom plans. Not so much when my mother, who loves dresses and formal events even more than my new friends, can overhear this conversation.

"Carter, I thought you were ineligible for prom because you're still a junior," Mom says.

"What? No, Ms. Ashley, anybody can go! I've attended prom since I was a freshman," Abby replies.

Abby is not comprehending the death glare I'm shooting her. Prom just isn't my thing, okay? It's another asinine social event that will end in drama. Worse, there's dancing. It's bad enough that we're forced to square dance with ugly boys in gym class, a Pennsylvania tradition that will not die. Who wants to dance with people for recreation? Who's sick enough to want that?

"Ohhhhhh, wait a sec. Sorry," Abby mouths. I don't think she's sorry at all, considering that she's been asking me all along to go to prom. She leaves the table to accept her award for Excellence in Creative Arts

(Poetry). One student from each grade submits their work for the award each year.

"Do you want to go to prom?" Mom asks.

"No!" Though there is this tiny part of me that dreams of being beautiful, just for one night. Wrapping up my high school experience in spectacular fashion. Maybe I should go....

Before my mother can interrogate me further, Mr. Atkinson announces that he will now hand out the final award of the night. It's the big one I've dreamt of earning since my freshman year of high school. I'm tempted to tune out, only some feeling inside of me tells me to sit up and pay attention.

"The Kateryn Wynn Ritter Excellence Award is given to a junior or senior student who fits the following criteria: has maintained an 'A' average throughout their time at Harlow High School, has a demonstrated record of academic and extracurricular achievement, and has contributed to the school in an immeasurable way.

"There are several students who fit these criteria," Mr. Atkinson continues. Including me, aside from the last bit. "The awards committee unanimously agreed to grant the honor to one student. This student, if you know her, is unconventional in many ways." I doubt it, at this cookie-cutter, popularity-obsessed school.

Abby jabs me in the thigh. "Ow," I mumble. She needs to cut her nails, for Slater's sake and mine.

"I can say from personal experience that being her English teacher for the past three years has been a delight. She always brings fresh insight to her academic arguments and won the honor of representing our school in Washington D.C. through the Future Leaders Essay Contest."

Wait.

"She has completed her community service requirements for the National Honor Society with the utmost dedication and grace. She contributed to the First Annual Harlow High School Community Wellness Fair, with a well-crafted booth offering resources for mental health help."

Mom squeezes my hand.

"Without further ado, it is my honor and privilege to award Carter Harper the Kateryn Wynn Ritter Senior Excellence Award."

I'm near tears as I approach the stage for the final time. I almost can't believe I'm being recognized for the blood, sweat, and tears I've put into my academic work over the past three years. Yet the trophy—yes, a trophy, not a paper certificate—bearing my name says otherwise.

"I knew you'd get it," Mr. Atkinson whispers as he hands me the trophy and *holy shit this is an envelope which means a check not just a Barnes and Noble gift card— I'm about to go bananas at Target.*

"Thank you," I whisper.

Mr. Atkinson grins before turning back to the audience. "Traditionally, the winner of this award says a little something. However, Carter here is shy, so I won't force her into that. Off you go!"

The audience offers a polite chuckle. I stand in place for what feels like forever, weighing the pros and cons of making a tiny speech.

"Actually, I would like to say something. If that's cool," I tack on.

I do have some public speaking experience now, thanks to the bullying assembly Abby and I gave at the middle schooler last week. It was basically a live episode of *Beyond Scared Straight*. Some of those kids looked like they were about to piss their pants. I don't know if what I said struck a chord with them, or if it'll make a difference. But if I helped one person, it was worth it. I even got a couple of thank-you notes after the assembly, which was nice. They seemed sincere, though Abby swore that two were total bullshit.

"The floor is yours." Mr. Atkinson steps away from the podium so I can take his place. A roller-coaster-like swoop of nervousness takes root in my stomach. *What do I have to say? Who cares about my words?* The weight of my trophy reminds me that, hey, some people do care.

And that's when it hits me like a spark of light. I know what I need to say.

P"I didn't expect to survive the year," I begin. "As

many of you know, I at—" I stumble over the words. "I attempted s-s-suicide in February. This led to the worst semester I've had...pretty much ever. But I learned a lot, and made some friends along the way, and, well, I'm still here. I learn every day that that's likely a good thing." I pause before wondering what conclusion to give. "If you need help, contact the Crisis Text Line at 741-741." I've had the number memorized for years, never allowing myself to dial the sequence for fear of people thinking that I can't do it alone.

Now I know better. Seeking treatment isn't weak. It may be the strongest act a person can commit.

In a haze, I make my way back to my seat. The flood of congratulations at my table doesn't touch me due to my lingering terror. If that bumbling speech were an academic paper, I'd deserve a failing grade. But for my first real go at public speaking, I give myself an A+.

CHAPTER 40
ABBY

A FEW MONTHS AGO, if you'd told me Carter Harper would inspire me to do anything but not wear cashmere with flannel, I would've thrown my Starbucks in your face.

I'm proud of her. She deserves to be in the spotlight for something other than being the poster child for the National Suicide Prevention Lifeline, a comment I probably should not be making but is real as hell.

Carter was the star of the awards ceremony, angering seniors who felt they earned more than her. But really, who's *literally* survived more than Carter this year? She fought her way out of a coma, narrowly avoided another suicide attempt, and kept her grades up through it all. Yeah, they slipped, but not enough to derail her chances at Yale, MIT, Johns Hopkins, Howard, and all the other non-name brand schools she wants to go to. Now that she, you know, is interested in living.

Yesterday, she admitted she's not coming back to high school next year. She got into Harrisburg University's STEM-focused dual enrollment program. While I'll miss her (yeah, yeah, get your jokes in now), she's still right across the street.

Everyone in our friend group will be busier than ever next year. I retook my SAT and scored in the top fifth percentile, meaning college is once again a real possibility. The vice president of the GSA is also switching schools, so Slater asked me to step in next year. I declined, instead asking Wes, the current president of the Creative Writing Club, if I could take over again. He accepted gratefully, because he just wanted to write, not lead.

I know how he feels. Before this year, I didn't want to lead in any meaningful way. Rule the school, of course, but that wasn't leadership. That was pure evil disguised as a bid for power. Now I know how to use my natural skills—and, okay, what Kelsey taught me—to make changes that are meaningful.

I'm not naive. I know I'm going to have to fight Kelsey more since we both want to be the alpha female at school. I know I'll still be a mean girl until Slater and Carter (and maybe Mei...but maybe not) can beat it out of me.

I'll be damned if I don't try, though. I'm a better

person than I've ever been. Even Carter has noticed, and she's the person who almost died because of me.

I shudder.

That's when I make the decision, one I should have made a long time ago. Only how was I supposed to know how bad things could get?

I lie awake and replay her speech. Then I slip out of bed, grab a blanket and my laptop, and walk downstairs. I sit on the angular sofa, which hurts a bit. Thank you, Mother, for having me inherit your practically nonexistent butt.

A twinge strums in my belly. I miss my mother. After our storied history, it's nice (and weird!) that there's anything left for me to miss.

I put my headphones on and crank up my *ABBY WALLACE CAN DO ANYTHING* playlist, which is a curated mix of pop, indie pop, and electronica. There's also some alternative rock (Carter and Mei), post-grunge (Carter and Slater), house music (Slater), and folk pop (Mei) populating the playlist.

I furiously type and click and huff in annoyance until I'm ready to pass out.

On one hand, I want to gather my friends in the morning and feel their strength around me as I complete this monumental task. On the other hand, I need to know if I can seek help on my own, rather than being influenced by other people. Maybe that's my problem: I care too much about what people think. It's why Kelsey was able to lead me for so long with me being happy just to nip at her heels.

It's funny how Carter has the opposite problem. She has to figure out how to be helped by other people, since she's closed herself off for so much of her short life. That's why we're so stubbornly, inconceivably drawn to one another. We can teach each other how to be independent, or how not to be alone. I can help Carter use her creativity, while she helps me see logically. Both together and apart, we can fix ourselves from the damage we wrought on one another through the bullying and suicide attempt (though, really, that wasn't Carter's fault I'm so destroyed from that). If I've learned anything this semester, it's that just about anything can be healed.

That's why I forward Daddy and Mother the names and addresses of some potential therapists, both in Harrisburg and New York City. I add no context. Though they're impossible when it comes to mental health, they will surely understand that all the problems in my life have led to this moment.

Something is off in my brain, and I need more than the help of my friends to solve it.

CHAPTER 41
CARTER

THANKS TO ABBY and Mei's inability to shut up, I'm stuck planning for prom all week. It took a lot of coaxing and the promise that I wouldn't have to wear a new dress for my friends and mother to drag me to the annual Harlow High School junior prom. Abby even offered to find me a cute girl to date. Not gonna lie, I briefly considered her offer—but in the end I decided to go to prom dateless. If I'm going to do this thing, it'll be with my friends and not a fake date.

I'm standing in Slater's fairytale-esque backyard, grinning like a fool as my way-too-hype mom, Slater's too-beautiful-for-the-world mother, and Abby's tearful father take photos of me and Mei and Abby and Slater.

I'm going to kill Slater, Mei, and Abby for putting me through this. (Though all the glam *is* a bit fun.)

Abby's number one on my shit list. Her pre-prom photoshoot took place near the river. She said, and I quote, "If you take the pic from far enough away, the water looks blue, which matches my dress." She looked like a model, her aquamarine floor-length gown clinging to the few curves she has. She posed near the water for nearly an hour; meanwhile, group shots took fifteen minutes because the rest of us were hungry and wanted to hit up Sheetz before the dance.

Really, I can't complain too much. I'm just thrilled that I have friends, even if they still feel like enemies sometimes. Still, I can't shake the feeling something bad will come of me being friends with popular girls, though I myself have slipped back into relative obscurity now that Kelsey's gone and Abby's declared me absolved of the social crimes she previously persecuted me for. I'm not a target and not viewed as a victim, just the way I like it.

Forgiveness feels strange, though anger feels stranger. I can't continue to hold a grudge against Abby and the POPS for leading me to my near-death. A grudge feels like poison seeping through my heart, seeking revenge on the bastard who created the pain. But I can pretend to forget about their harm and be normal during moments like this

Moments like tonight, when I'm dressed to kill.

I chose one of my only nice dresses, a black number that shows off my boobs a little too much and falls to my knees. Abby, when I consulted her yesterday, thought the "drab funeral dress" wasn't worthy of "the biggest social event of your life, at least act like you love yourself for one night, my God, Carter." She forced me to wear a black petticoat to fluff it up and ombré black-and-grey tights underneath. Then, she ordered me to pin my oceanic hair into a high bun complete with one of her silver headbands.

Surprisingly? I love it. It's like I'm darkness manifested, sweeping into this POPS parade.

"What do we do?" I whisper to Slater, Mei, and Abby. We've arrived at prom, and the lights and decorations and dancing are already overwhelming me.

"Talk? Dance?" Slater says. "I know you're a hermit, but it's okay to have fun."

"I'm not a—" No use arguing, she's right.

I survey the room and realize I don't know most of the people here. And I don't know the names of most people I do recognize, aside from my friends. Until recently, I was so wrapped up in thoughts of death that I barely acknowledged anybody else's existence. This wasn't how I wanted my high school experience to go. I wanted my time here to be decent, not a series of events that led me to constant suicidal ideations. Instead, I hid myself away, succumbing to my major depressive disorder and social anxiety. I wanted nothing to do with anybody.

It's okay. College is my second chance. Even if I remain the same girl, there will be no POPS to drag me down. I won't be the same girl, though. I've changed so much since February that I almost don't recognize who I've become. But lack of recognition is not always a bad thing. It can be a sign of change, a sign of greatness.

Kelsey appears in my line of vision. She's looking at us, pissed off and beautiful in a ruby red dress with a poufy skirt.

"Look, it's your boo." Slater gently nudges Abby in the ribs.

Abby scrunches her face. "More like the Wicked Witch of the East Harrisburg School District."

Kelsey spots us and walks our way. Why, why, why? Leave us alone.

"You look like a puff of toxic smog," Kelsey says. "An improvement."

"Don't talk to me like th—"

My attempt to stand up for myself is drowned out by Abby doing it for me. "Aww, Kels, you look like a period," she says with a smirk. Thanks, I suppose.

Kelsey scoffs. "That's not a good comeback."

"And you thought the toxic smog thing was?"

"Yep." Kelsey scans our faces. "Can I talk to all of you? My *ex*-best friends?"

Abby, Slater, and I exchange glances.

I can't believe I'm on the other side of what could morph into a showdown. There are four of us and only one of Kelsey. No matter how much I hate her, I don't want to start public drama that leads to someone ganged up on. Humiliated. Degraded. Perhaps that's why I say, "Okay."

"Wait! I'm coming," Mei says. "If you kill each other, there should be a witness."

"Clowns," Abby mutters as we leave the hotel ballroom.

"Let her say her piece so we can move on," I reply.

Mei checks out her floor-length shimmering purple dress in a mirror we pass. "Carter's right. For once."

"Thanks?" I say to Mei's backhanded compliment.

"Alright, what the fuck do you want?" Abby asks once we're in the deserted hallway.

"I know why you decided to go against me," Kelsey says. "But I never got an explanation from Skittles Explosion and My Chemical Hoe-mance." She jabs two fingers toward Slater and me.

Slater surveys her colorful dress. "Maybe that's why your ex likes to taste my rainbow," she says. Abby and I try, and fail, to hold back our snorts. "You're too control-ling, needy, naggy, and did I mention controlling? I did, right?"

"You did. Twice," Abby says.

"I hate you people," Kelsey mutters.

"Why? Because we're not your puppets anymore?" Abby asks. She imitates a ventriloquist with her arms.

"Puppets? You're, whoa, you're serious." Kelsey tilts her head back and laughs. "I was helping all of you! What you call control, I call assistance. Why do you think I got on you so hard about your weight and wardrobe, Carter? And Abby about being out of control with her panic attacks and messy-ass family life? Mei and her grades slipping? I helped you! All of you!"

"It's true," Mei says. "Kelsey has an odd way of showing it, but she does care about us."

"Whose side are you *on?*" Abby asks, echoing exactly what I'm thinking.

"The side of being tired of being caught between my friends. Ugh, forget it." Mei stomps back into the ball-room. Fair point. I don't even like Kelsey, and I'm strained, standing between these warring girls.

"Kelsey. That's not help," I say. "That's not love. Tearing people down has nothing to do with us, and everything to do with what you think of yourself. A pathetic—" YIKES, that last part shouldn't have slipped out of my mouth

Kelsey bares her teeth. "Don't you ever call me pathetic. I'm not the one who keeps going in and out of psych war—"

Somebody's hand strikes Kelsey's face, but it's not mine. I turn to Slater, steam practically coming out of her ears.

Abby snorts. "Nice one."

The rest of Kelsey's face floods red to match the handprint. "I'm not going to bother acknowledging that, because it was clearly a mistake."

"Nah," Slater says. "I'd do it again." Slater shakes her hand out and mumbles, "Ow."

"Back to the point. Every bad leader in history has fallen," Abby says. "Only, you're still young. You still have a shot at redemption before you go to hell."

"Redemption, my ass," Kelsey says. "I'm still the best. This intervention, or whatever this sad after-school special is, won't change that."

"*You* dragged us out here! It's not an intervention!" Abby half-screams.

"Then what will make you change?" I ask, desperate. Because something's got to. Not even for me, since I don't even go here anymore.

"Nothing," Kelsey says. "Special announcement, Carter. People like me never lose. Even when we've lost."

"Sure about that?" Abby says. "Last time I checked, loser-ass Carter"—thank you, Abby—"is better off than you."

"Alright, I've had enough of your fantasies," Kelsey says. She starts walking off. She half turns her head so we see her profile, eyes on the ground and blond hair covering most of her face. "You know, Abby isn't any better than me. So enjoy this while it lasts, Slater and Carter. Because it won't."

"You're wrong!" Abby says as her ex-best friend walks away from us. "But thanks for the propaganda ideas! I'll be sure to use them when I run for student council president next year."

Kelsey doesn't reply. She's gone.

Hopefully forever, but probably not. I have a sick feeling that Kelsey isn't done with wreaking havoc on Harlow High School.

I suppose that isn't my problem anymore, as long as I can convince Abby, Slater, and Mei not to tell me about whatever devious antics they pull. I'm done with the girl politics and well-crafted wars of adolescence.

I couldn't be more relieved if I tried. Pettiness isn't in my nature. I'd rather create, learn, and grow.

CHAPTER 42
ABBY

"DON'T WORRY ABOUT KELSEY," Slater murmurs to me as we slow dance. "She can't touch us anymore."

I nestle my head into her shoulder. "Yeah, she can." I'd been naive enough to think the games were over after we pulled a *Mean Girls* at lunch.

After Kelsey tried to gaslight us again, I marched to the bathroom. I sat on a bench and shed silent tears of contempt. Kelsey can never let me be happy. She always has to have the upper hand.

Then I stood up.

I smoothed out my dress.

I checked my hair and makeup.

Then I went back into the ballroom because that's what prom queens do.

"Would you believe me if I said I feel bad for her?" Slater says.

I wrench my head to meet Slater's concerned eyes. "No, because she's a demon."

Slater scoffs. "Wow, I can't wait to see how you talk about me if we break up." She spins me around.

"Have you blackmailed my friends?" I ask as I dip her.

Slater considers it. "True. But think about it. She's used to getting everything she wants. Look at her parents, her money, her popularity. When she lost the most important thing, she lost herself." Despite the seriousness of our conversation, I smile as I look back into her green-ish, brown-ish eyes. I can't believe I can stare at them without abandon whenever I want. I can't believe this magnificent activist, artist, and leader is my girlfriend.

Well, we aren't putting labels on it yet. I need some time to figure things out without the pressure of a relationship, thanks to the damage I took from Kelsey.

(Slater's my girlfriend, though.)

"Getting what you want is no excuse for taking things from other people," I say. Slater gives me such intense side-eye that I'm forced to recognize the irony of my own words.

Before we can argue further, Principal Adams interrupts. "We've tallied the votes and are ready to announce your new prom king and queen!" He tries to sound enthusiastic but falls flat. Doesn't matter—the student body has enough excitement to make up for his lack of pep.

"Can the nominees please come to the stage," Dr. Adams demands. Slater squeezes my hand before I float away. I line up with the rest of the prom court. Kelsey's not here, of course. Her eligibility was snatched away with Carter's pride at the fair.

I scan the crowd and beam at my fellow prom-goers, knowing I'm their new queen, though I can't see many of their faces because of how bright the lights are onstage. Kelsey sits at Caleb's jock table, looking as miserable as she does beautiful. She knows that whether I win or not, after what happened in the hall-way, she won't own me again. Kelsey may have loved me, but her love was twisted and controlling. What's it like to have people loathe you because you refuse to let go? How can you be so deeply insecure that you must pretend to be perfect around even your deepest admirers?

Even at my most publicly perfect, I am flawed. I can be cruel, I can mean, I can be bad.

I'm okay with that, though I'm trying to fix some of my problems. One thing I have never been afraid of is being Abby Wallace. That's why when my friends left me (after I pushed them away, but still), I was ultimately okay. I'm as secure in myself as a teenage girl can be. Meanwhile, Kelsey has so many issues that she could fill up a political candidate's website.

Her biggest flaw is hiding them. She thinks that makes her perfect. In reality, it's what makes her untouchable and villainous.

"Good luck," Marci Jones says to me.

"You too," I lie.

"Harlow High's new prom king is...Caleb Walsh!" Dr. Adams yells.

What the *fuck*. Caleb? Cheating Caleb Walsh is the prom king? My ex-boyfriend, the epitome of thinking with your dick rather than your brain?

Seriously, Carter could've warned me about this.

Caleb whoops and steps forward to accept his plastic crown and polyester sash. I look on, fuming. The one downside of being prom queen will be wearing an ugly, mass-produced, overhyped comb hat. Oh, and standing next to this asshole.

"Congratulations, young man," Dr. Adams says. He waves toward us ladies. I stretch even taller. "And now, your prom queen. Please give a round of applause for... Abby Wallace!"

I smile upon my adoring public, placing a hand on my hip. I did it. I earned this, fair and square. No longer hidden behind Kelsey's diminishing shadow, I'm finally recognized as the queen I was meant to be.

"And now, in a Harlow High tradition, our prom king and queen will dance together," Dr. Adams says. He glares at us. "Please, no grinding or freaking it up."

My classmates burst into laughter. It takes every bit

of my self-control not to do the same. "Too bad," says Caleb. His eyes rove over my semi-skimpy dress like he still has the privilege of admiring my body.

"You literally cheated on me because I didn't want to have sex with you, you horse-looking troll," I say. I step off the stage and into the crowd.

Slater waits for me. I want to share this moment with her more than I've wanted a lot of things lately. I do. But when I reach her, I whisper an alternate plan: the person I have to share this dance with, to end things with, for real this time.

Slater looks confused. Once she gets the gist of what I'm saying, she nods. "Go for it." She hesitates before whispering, "I love you."

My heart swells. Could this night get any better? This is the first time Slater's said that to me, and I know she doesn't mean as a friend anymore. I don't need to hesitate before answering. "I love you, too," I whisper before drifting off into the crowd...

...and extending my hand to Kelsey.

Kelsey, the girl who forged who I am today.

Kelsey, the girl who is adrift and lost, with little support.

Kelsey, the girl I was when I was more vulnerable.

Kelsey looks at my hand like it's crawling with poisonous snakes. "You already won. No need to rub it in."

I dismiss her snark with a wave of my hand. "I'm not. Come onstage with me."

"So you can humiliate me again? No thanks."

I sigh. "No. I'm giving you my first dance. Our first dance. Screw Caleb." Kelsey still looks skeptical. "I'm giving you one last time to pretend you're the queen."

Kelsey gulps and looks at the paper tablecloth. Her eyes snap to mine. "Why not," she says in a deadpan voice. She stands and glides to the front of the room without me. An attempt to steal my spotlight. She can go ahead and try. I won prom queen. I am who the people want. I'll lead this school without her, the way Kelsey assumes I can't.

And I'll finish the legacy of cruelty we created.

I pass Carter and Mei. They look at me like I've lost my mind. Maybe I have. But I haven't lost my heart.

"Miss Wallace, you must dance with Mr. Owens," Dr. Adams says.

"I'm breaking tradition," I say.

"I must say, this is highly irregular—"

"Let them," Caleb says. He flicks his head like he understands. "It'll be hot to watch."

Kelsey and I scowl at each other in disgust. For the first time in forever, we agree.

"Come on, Dr. Adams," I say. "What would the ACLU say?"

Dr. Adams huffs and speaks into the microphone. "Apparently, the dance will be done between Queen

Abby Wallace and, I suppose, her consort, Kelsey Maxwell. My request to not freak it up remains."

Can he explain what the hell freaking it up is?

The DJ begins to play a love song. Kelsey and I clasp our hands together like talons, daring the other to let go. Her hands are slick with sweat, not the smoothness I've grown used to. It's awkward, to say the least. The eyes of my public are on us as we move in a circle. I stare at the arched, peach stucco ceiling. Why did I do this, again?

"You might be right, you know," Kelsey murmurs to me. "I ruined so much that I deserved to fall."

I tip my head to the side and my crown tumbles to the floor.

Kelsey bends down to pick it up. I expect her to take it for herself, but she hands it back. "Take it. You earned it."

I shake my head. I still put the crown back on. "I only earned it by carrying through your legacy. That's not a good thing. I still deserve it, but it's not entirely mine."

"No. Your legacy is something different. You fixed what you did wrong. So...just keep doing that, okay? Because I'm not having the best time lately." Kelsey looks down, fighting tears. I pull her tiny body into mine and hug her as we still shuffle in our tight circle.

"You'll be fine," I whisper. "You can survive this. You

can do anything you set your mind to, including stopping being a megalomaniac."

Kelsey only nods, quietly sobbing. She knows what she lost. Slater and me, and even Carter, could've helped her sort out her issues. She could've leaned on us if she hadn't sabotaged and duped her best friends until we all hated her.

I know what it's like to have your world shattered. But if anybody can make herself whole again, it's Kelsey. She's that headstrong, that determined, that brilliant.

Even when a fast-paced frantic number begins, we stand in our tight circle. We slowly shuffle our feet back and forth until the moment comes where I let go of her forever.

I dance with her because there's something magnetic about a girl who keeps trying and trying and trying though she's been defeated.

EPILOGUE: CARTER

Five Months Later

I WEAR FAKE GLASSES, a black crepe skirt, and a black tank as I wait for Abby to finish her appointment with Dr. Locke. A textbook rests on my lap as I stretch my legs over three reception area chairs. I'm trying to study for my Computer Organization and Architecture class, and it's not as easy as I expected it to be. For the third time in my life, the first being at the Princeton lecture, I'm challenged academically. It's both unsettling and refreshing.

The second time I felt challenged was at the Future Leaders Essay Contest summit in Washington, D.C. Though I avoided the White House excursion, the rest of the trip was a blur of (ugh) team building workshops, in-depth English classes, and trekking around the National Mall. The kids were nice enough, though decently cutthroat. Aside from my roommate, Scarlett, they didn't come to the summit to make friends. Scarlett, meanwhile, welcomed me with open arms. You know, since I'm open to having friends now. We video chat sometimes, complaining about the struggles of dual-enrollment senior year.

At least the other kids in the early college program are as lost as I am. We study together, and I think I'm making friends. Abby pushes me to ask people to hang out after class, but that's a step too far. The best I'll do is go to Strawberry Square with maybe-friends for lunch sometimes. I prefer to eat alone, though. Less social pressure.

Dr. Locke's helping me with my social anxiety and the depression that makes it difficult to even want to make friends. And she's helping Abby with what she diagnosed as rape trauma syndrome. Abby might get on anti-anxiety medication too, which will help with her panic attacks and her tendency to run into bathrooms when distressed. I hope it works. Antidepressants and therapy played a big part in saving my life. My family and friends were also huge factors, along with finding the strength within myself to want to fix my issues rather than hide from them.

I check the folder stashed in my textbook for the umpteenth time.

It contains my acceptance to Howard University.

I started submitting applications to the schools that

sent me free applications thanks to my near-perfect SAT scores.

Abby, Slater, and I promised to apply to at least two mutual schools, but we won't hold each other back. Especially since I'm shooting for computing programs, Abby suddenly wants to be a social worker (Slater and I are taking bets on how long that's going to last), and Slater's going for photography.

"I had a breakthrough!" Abby runs to me, then eyes the folder. "Hey, what's this?" She plucks it out of the textbook and screams when she realizes what it means. "CARTER!" She pulls me up, textbook and folder be damned, and forces me to jump up and down with her.

"Wait, wait, wait!" Abby shouts when I try to sit down again. "Let me take a pic of us for my profile."

I sigh dramatically yet acquiesce. Part of being friends with Abby is dealing when she wants to show snapshots of our lives on her social media. She'll probably caption this selfie like "my side hoe (sorry, Slater *kissy face emoji*) got accepted to college!!!!!! Genius *graduation cap emoji*)."

By now, Dr. Locke's heard the commotion and comes out to investigate. "Carter! We're still on for tomorrow, right?"

"Yep!" I thrust the folder in her hands. "And I have a surprise."

Dr. Locke knows what it's about, too, and hugs me.

"Girl, congrats!" She opens the folder. Abby peeks over her shoulder.

"Howard? I wish I'd put that in my caption." Abby bites her lip, like she's seriously considering deleting and re-uploading the photo so she can brag about me.

"Have I told you girls lately how proud I am of you?" Dr. Locke beams at us, the girls she's molded into strong women by unlocking our trauma and helping us overcome our pasts. "Because I am."

"Thanks, Maryn," Abby says. I will never get used to calling adults by their first names, even when they give me the okay. That's some white people shit.

I sling my arm across Abby's shoulders. "Come on. Mom's going to be pissed that I didn't tell her first. Let's go visit her office. See you tomorrow, Dr. Locke!"

"Bye, girls," Dr. Locke says.

Abby and I strut out of the office building and back into the weekday fervor of downtown Harrisburg. "Speaking of moms, Veronica closed another deal," Abby says proudly. She and Ms. Veronica grew closer during Abby's summer in New York City, far from the trauma our neighborhood holds. She broke the news to her dad that it's possible she'll live with her mom postgraduation, depending on where she goes to college. Though he wasn't exactly happy about the news, he understood Abby's decision.

"She's on fire," I say. "Tell her I said congrats." I stayed with Abby for a week this summer and got to know her mother. We'll never be best friends like Abby and my mom apparently are (gross, I know), but Ms. Veronica is fine when she's away from her husband. She has a huge stick up her butt, though. Hey, Abby's words, not mine.

"Shall do," Abby says. "Now, let's go get your own congrats from your mom." We walk, a bounce in our step, buoyed by our friendship and my good news.

On the way to Mom's office, we pass Harrisburg Hospital. I wince every time we pass it. I don't think I'll ever stop. But in a way, that hospital stay is how I got where I am. Accepted at Howard and arm-in-arm with my best friend—formerly my enemy. Would I try to kill myself again to learn what I have this year? No. I've simply learned to turn a negative into a positive.

Life doesn't have to occur in a straight, beautiful line to have meaning. I'll take my zigzags any day. After all, the challenges are what make me grow. They're what make me thrive.

Challenges have kept me alive thus far, and they will continue to. I'm ready to keep playing the game of life. It gets better by the day.

RESOURCES

IF YOU'RE FEELING DEPRESSED, HOPELESS, OR SUICIDAL...

- HelpGuide.org – Articles on depression, suicide, PTSD and trauma, stress, and health and wellness.
- TherapyForBlackGirls.com – A therapist directory, podcast, and community dedicated to the mental health needs of the Black community.
- CrisisTextLine.org – A free text line for US residents facing any kind of crisis. Text HOME to 741741 at any time to connect to a trained crisis counselor.

IF YOU ARE A VICTIM OF RAPE, INCEST, OR CHILD SEXUAL ABUSE OR KNOW A VICTIM...

- rainn.org – Advocacy organization and hotline for victims of rape, abuse, and incest.
- 1in6.org– For male victims of sexual assault and abuse.
- wscadv.org/resources/supporting-someone-experiencing-abuse/ – Information on how to show up for somebody experiencing abuse.

IF YOU ARE A VICTIM OF OR PARTICIPANT IN BULLYING...

- Cybersmile.org – Resources on cyberbullying, doxxing, reputation management, sextortion, and more.
- BeStrong.global – Resources and support for bullying, depression, and emotional health.
- https://icrace.files.wordpress.com/2017/09/icrace-toolkit-for-poc.pdf – Surviving & Resisting Hate: A Toolkit for People of Color

LOVE THIS BOOK? LEAVE A REVIEW!

Reviews are the lifeblood of indie authors like me, and I would really appreciate it if you left a review on Amazon, Goodreads, Barnes & Noble, your blog, or your favorite retailer. Word of mouth is the best way to sell books, so tell your friends if you really enjoyed this book! Thank you so much in advance for helping me succeed.

WANT MORE? SIGN UP FOR MY AUTHOR NEWSLETTER!

Get the latest information on new releases, events, writing advice, exclusive sneak peeks of new books, and more!

Sign up at sierraelmore.com/newsletter

ACKNOWLEDGMENTS

Death by Society started out as a short story called "Hero", written when I was in eighth grade.

While that story will never see the light of day (thank God), it lives on through *Death by Society*. Thank you to the teachers and librarians who saw me through some of the darkest years of my life and nurtured my love for writing.

I first want to thank you for reading this story. Whether you liked it or want to burn it, you read it! You read my dream, my book baby, the book of my heart. Thank you for helping me realize a dream I've had for so many years.

To Peter Lopez: what can I say? You've been my rock, my entertainer, my inspiration. You're a king, and I cannot wait for the world to devour your books. Thank you for being the stand-up person who publishing deserves.

To Hannah Capin: YOU ARE THE BEST. THANK YOU SO MUCH for editing this book for me, I truly appreciate it!!!! Your improvements and encouragements always make things better. Thank you for reading all the TERRIBLE versions of my books, and for loving them anyway! Also for the endless boat jokes. ALSO thank you for *Foul is Fair*, which I read before I needed then read again when I needed it.

To Sophia Chunn, for the AMAZING cover! It depicts the book so well. It has been a dream working with you. Here's to many more projects together!

To Fadwa, for showing me what it's like to be your best self and helping me be a better person all these years. Oh, and for all of the amazing book recommendations and cat photos. Your blogging and hard work have made the book community a better place.

To the badasses of book Twitter: Vika, Shenwei, Cam, Jia, and Jessi. I love you. May your skin be clear and your reads be good.

There are so many publishing people who I have been simply BLESSED to be in the presence of. I'm going to try to name some here. You've all had a measurable impact on me, and I care for you deeply. In no particular order so people don't yell at me, thank you to Racquel Marie, Jessica "Bibi" Cooper, Cam Montgomery, Dhonielle Clayton, Kelsey Rodkey, Carlyn Greenwald, Christine Lynn Herman, Amanda Foody, Laurie Elizabeth Flynn, Courtney Summers, Ryan Douglass, Briana Morgan, Samantha Eaton, Sonia Hartl, Maggie Horne, Ava Reid, Victoria Lee, Karen M. McManus, Aiden Thomas, Jonny Garza Villa, Shelly Romero, Zakiya Jamal, Michael Waters, Camryn

Garrett, Becky Albertalli, Alexis Henderson, Leanne Schwartz, Julian Winters, Xiran Jay Zhao, Zoraida Cordova, Ashlynn James, Chelsea Cameron, Rae Castor, Tess Sharpe, Hanna Phifer, Patrice Caldwell, and Trinica Sampson.

To Cassidy and Demi, for your friendship that started over a long-haired man who likes to sing about church. Thank you for putting up with my fanfic.

To my best bitch Eddie. Keep hoeing. (I can't believe you made me put this in here.)

To Becca - burritos forever. Love you so much.

To my cousins who are basically sisters at this point, Anna, Val, and Vanessa: thank you for all the laughter over the years, and for being there when I most needed it. I'll see y'all over the holidays.

And finally, to my parents for always getting me the support that I needed, and for *being* the support that I needed. I love you two beyond words and am grateful for everything you have done for me.

ABOUT THE AUTHOR

Sierra Elmore writes YA contemporary and thriller novels about girls wreaking havoc while fighting trauma. Her work has won the YoungArts merit award and was selected for the Author Mentor Match program.

Elmore earned a BA in Sociology from Arcadia University. She's conducted research on the representation of mentally ill women in media as well as relational aggression amongst adolescent girls.

Elmore lives in New York City, where she explores independent bookstores, volunteers for the Crisis Text Line, and goes to as many concerts as possible.

twitter.com/SierraWritesYA

instagram.com/SierraWritesYA